Strong Hearts Are Mandatory

Heart of Glass

Written by

Teelia Pelletier

DEDICATION

To my family, friends, and the supporters who helped me in making this story possible! ♥

ACKNOWLEDGMENTS

I would like to thank Daniel and Dr. Muscavitch, my editors, Yvonne for motivating me to finish the novel in the most unique way no one else could, and my writer's group for being with me since the beginning of writing this tale. I couldn't have done it without the help my mother, father, and sister gave when I needed it the most, as well as every friend, follower, and beta reader who was a part of my social media that made this story possible again with their support!

Thank you!

- PROLOGUE -

Once, in the land now known as Media, there was a population of animals and species in all varieties, many blessed with incredible powers. They were ruled under a queen, a powerful mage by the name of Satisfaction, who reigned over the entire region with a pure heart. The Queen was known for her shimmering violet magic which extended power beyond the scope of any of her exemplars, and was renowned for the blanket of protection cast over the sky to protect her subjects. The coat of magic guarded the land from any danger that came from the neighboring lands across seas, and brought comfort to all of those under it. Even with the vast boundary, the barrier lasted through the day and night without ever wavering in strength, proving the Queen's devotion to her land.

The powerful ruler loved each and every one of her subjects. It was said her wings could stretch across the entire length of the land, and in the darkness of night she could promise a safe night of rest from the dangers that threatened beyond her magic barrier. The embers from her wing tips cast safe dreams for those who slept, bringing harmony and peace to those of the land.

However, the Queen had been unaware of a growing threat within her borders. She had been unprepared when her subjects, those without the same power as her exemplars, turned on her. The mundane subjects claimed the right for equality for both those without and those blessed with the gift of magic, and demanded the Queen make her exemplars and masters of magic build them technology of an equal, or even greater, power to their own.

The Queen and her advisors were hesitant, but over time the ruler agreed and obliged to their demands. Structures of protection, as well as a large city, were built exclusively as shelters for non-mages to escape from the overwhelming energies of the exemplars, and the protests ceased. Unfortunately, this separation unknowingly caused the Queen to remain ignorant of the upgrades to the technology she helped create.

These subjects, led by a cheetah named Control, used the power the mages created for them against the Queen, starting a war between technology and magic that carried on for generations. After years of battle between the Queen and the new technology leader, the two sides reached an impasse. Control decided to propose a battle between he and the Queen alone to determine who would continue ruling the land, and sent the proposition to the mage's boundaries to be delivered to the Queen.

The Queen's subjects refused to carry this proposal to the Queen, believing the technology leader to have malicious intent orchestrated against their Queen; however, a single traitorous mage infiltrated the territory, and delivered the challenge to the Queen under the technology leader's direction. With this mage's assurance and encouragement, the Queen agreed to the battle, and set out with her advisor to face the technology leader for a final battle. The two rulers met in the heart of the land, only their two advisors and the courier of the challenge allowed to witness the battle.

Neither hesitated to start. The fight between the two rulers was said to have lasted for twenty-seven hours. In some of the legends it has been furthered the Queen claimed the other leader was cheating after the battle began, using a form of magic to absorb her own as they fought. It was said to have angered her for the first time documented in history, as well as the last. Both leaders died during the battle, and rumors of mythical artifacts being created out of their essence spread through the region.

It was rumored the mages retrieved the Queen's artifact, a crystal cube that could generate magic on its own and give power to its holder beyond any limitation. This one object was said to represent the row of multi-colored cubes that had circled around the Queen when she flew through the skies at night, casting good thoughts to her subjects so they would rest well for the work of the next day.

The technology leader's artifact was thought to derive from anti-magic, but was never known to be retrieved nor carried openly by his successors, making the subjects who heard the story doubt if the artifact ever existed.

Whether the artifacts exist or not, most, if not all the legends concur the Queen did not die without cursing the land for the leader's actions before her demise. It's claimed that she had doomed them to repeat the unfairness and murder caused by the mage courier who had brought the message to her for several generations, knowing the battle had been engineered against her unfairly.

Control's sister carried on his rulership after he passed until her son, and then grandson, became the Kings of the new land now known as Media.

Mages never attempted to overthrow Media's leader, at least, never successfully...

Smash!

The tape recorder was shattered, mangled to bits while the dark silhouette of a slender, tall primate loomed over it. His eyes narrowed as he walked past the body who had guarded him from the tape in the first place. He then held up the cassette tape containing the speech he was listening to.

With a whip of his hand, he surrounded the tape with a spherical aura of cyan, and a mist infiltrated the tape, circling the reel until it began playing again. The monkey took threads of the magic out from the orb and brought it to his ears, allowing him to listen to the contents, and then walked out of the room.

The dark monkey moved through the castle halls, his long tail swinging back and forth. He walked carefully in the shadows that seemed to cling to the corners of the wide-windowed expanse. Upon the first sign of another approaching, the primate backed into the shadows, his body dematerializing into the dark walls untouched by the moonlight.

A lithe tabby cat padded along, her eyes alert as she turned her gaze to the windows where the dark intruder hid. The primate stilled his breath, closing his eyes to keep the light from reflecting towards the small feline, and remained still. The cat stared a moment longer, and then blinked, her features softening as she continued, unaware of the dangers lurking. The shadow strengthened his form of darkness and kept himself from chuckling at his easy success in remaining hidden.

Once she was out of earshot, the being formed his appearance back into that of a spider monkey and scoffed, continuing down the long hall. Each step was silent and deliberate, the animal's eyes scanning every inch of his surroundings until finally turning the corner. Gradually easing closer to his goal, his long tail coiled with anticipation.

After a few more steps, he passed an open door and halted upon hearing a small voice. The voice was not speaking, it was simply humming. Curiosity getting the better of him, the spider monkey gazed into the dark room, and let a smile ease onto his face upon seeing the sight of another primate.

It was a small gray monkey, fluffy and quite tiny. *A marmoset?* When he recognized the type of monkey it was, his jaw clenched. *It must have been shipped here for entertainment.* The spider monkey scowled as he watched the tiny creature pull on the golden cuffs of a clown outfit. The shadowy figure narrowed his eyes with disdain as he stepped into the room slowly.

The tiny creature turned at the noise, but by the time he squeaked for help, the larger primate yanked him down, throwing him to the floor with his jaw clamped shut by the dark monkey's long tail.

"Are you an entertainer for the King?" the dark primate growled, tilting his head.

He released his tail's grip around the marmoset's muzzle, which let out a small gasp before tremulously looking up at him. "Y-yes...I'm the jester, sir. W-who might you be?"

The dark primate ignored the question, arched his brow, and stared down at the smaller monkey as he pulled out one of the magic threads by his ear and asked, "Would you happen to be jesting for the King tonight?"

He watched as the marmoset swallowed nervously and answered, "Yes, sir."

"Ah. Well, that's good." He grinned before he let the shadows of his magic spread across his features. "Unfortunately, your jesting is no longer needed," he sneered as he eased closer to the smaller monkey, and drove his fangs down directly against the marmoset's skull.

The dark monkey peered down the hall before he exited the room. He licked the blood from his lips with satisfaction. Anyone who might have seen him could only have guessed why. He slowly changed from his natural self, with each bold step down the center of the hall, into a clothed animal. Step by step, cuff by cuff, by collar by headpiece, he became covered with a jester outfit. First the outfit was almost a replica of the clown's uniform in style, but his shadows made the costume shift in shape, changing at each pace, until it was a dark, spindly, and sharpened form of brown and umber.

The somber outfit fitted itself over the shadowy primate with grace.

Next, he formed the metal chimes to the tips of his hat as the final touch to his new outfit. The bright bells turned black as they burst from his cyan magic, dropping with their new size and weight after forming into their solid shape. The monkey grinned with delight at his perfect ensemble.

The shadowy jester walked down the hall boldly, letting a mist of cyan color flood from his eyes before it evaporated as he drew closer to his objective. He let out a laugh as he finally approached the double doors leading to the throne room of the castle. "Here we are!" he exclaimed to himself. Looking at the towering structure before him, he knew it would be easier to fit through the cat door installed within them than try to open the giant double doors themselves, but where was the challenge in that? He let a noise of delight hiss through his teeth, and bound up to the doors.

He rose up on his back legs, lifting up gusts of magic in his hands as he did so until a bursting flash came from between them. The brightness subsided, revealing a floating cube artifact held at the very tips of his fingers, before he propelled it forward at his obstacle. The doors blasted open with a discharge of blue plasma. The primate straightened his posture as he gazed inside the throne room, his eyes bursting with cyan waves that radiated from his irides as he strode into the clearing.

Nighthawks and owls flew in the surrounding hall on high alert because of the hostile noise of the explosion. Ground animals rushed out from the castle's rooms to look at the chaotic avian night dwellers. They could see there was a wall of cyan static holding the avians from entering the throne room.

The monkey gave a smug look to the chaos behind him, the bells now jingling from his jester hat as he deliberately whipped his head back to the resplendent form in front of him.

It was a giant, crowned feline, the form and color of the majestic creature distorted in the darkness. He straightened as the monkey looked at him, realizing this was no act of play, and snarled warningly at the smaller being.

The primate raised his chin, the cyan flashing a brighter hue upon the giant cat's challenge. "Greetings, Your Majesty! I'm replacing your entertainer for tonight," he called out to the giant feline. The tomcat pressed down his paw in further caution, making the primate continue softly, "I don't want to trouble you with an introduction to myself. It's not really necessary." The monkey smiled as the tom's eyes narrowed.

The primate sighed and blinked up at the cat, gesturing out his hand. "You see, I won't really be here long. The act I'm to perform will surely only take a few moments, and seeing as how they'll be your last," his smile broadened as he hissed through his teeth. "I'll get straight to the point." The spider monkey lifted the small crystal cube above his head, glowing with a corresponding hue to the waves emitting from the primate's eyes.

The feline growled and cried out for the guards as the dressed primate took another step without fear. The monkey covered his ears at the King's shout. He shook the ringing from his ears, scowling as the bells made their own sound when he pulled back. The mist and waves strengthened into a current surrounding the two. The monkey stamped his hands onto the floor. "I suppose we don't have to pretend." He laughed.

The cat lunged in attack. The cube slammed down upon him, bursting with the same plasma which had slammed open the doors, precisely directed against the crowned cat's skull. The explosion from the impact shattered the windows behind the two.

Yowls and screeches were heard from outside the throne room, making the primate laugh vehemently as he looked at the scene before him. The cube stayed attached to the cat's head, and the cyan blended and alternated into a red hue, lighting the room with its glow.

The monkey smiled down at the limp form of the giant feline, watching the dark liquid of the giant cat's blood pour from beneath the crown, and pressed his hand down on the tom's muzzle.

"Hey! Stop where you are, Jester!"

"*Jester?*" The monkey narrowed his eyes. His hands whipped upward and around. The colored cube jerked out from the King's skull to follow suit with the primate's movement as he turned to face the guard shouting. The monkey growled. The cube began glowing with power, in tune with the monkey's noise.

That was the only warning to the animals outside as the barrier that held them away from the primate evaporated. Without a moment's hesitation, they were blasted away from the doors by the cube. Windows shattered as the red and cyan plasma exploded throughout the room, catching the attention of animals far beyond the surrounding halls.

Within the royal throne room, the primate glared with loathing at the scene before him. An ornate crystal heart glowed red, much as the cube had, and emerged from the mist. The primate convulsed at the sight. He went to touch it but pulled back as his hands split into shadows upon contact. He brought his shadowed hand to the artifact again, but the shadows splintered, ripped up his arm, and shot up to his face.

"Oh!" He flinched and, wincing, pulled the shadows away from his face and arm to solidify into his primate form once more.

He stretched out his fingertips in front of him, making sure his appearance was whole, and looked back at the heart, realizing it was the object that caused the damage to his person. He choked out a sound of confusion, then growled, the cyan once again casting out from his eyes. "This is ridiculous!" He lifted his hand and flung down the glass heart in anger, shattering the artifact into pieces and causing an aftershock effect.

Animals screeched and panicked as the shards of the heart pierced through the air in another red explosion, shattering walls and other structures as they blasted across the region. It was at that moment the alarm was released outside the castle walls, alerting everyone within earshot of the Capital's distress.

The bird who announced the call flew across the land, announcing the alarm to the villages, cities, and outskirts with known populations. The small avian flew through the central part of the region until he was certain the message had reached the entire radius of Media.

One individual, however, remained unaware. At a window of the home of one of the nobility rested a snowshoe cat. The black, white, and taupe feline lay in her windowsill bed, snoring away the sounds of panic and warning.

- CHAPTER 1 -

COMMUNICATION

Radio slowly woke to the sound of commotion outside her window. She blinked open her blue eyes and turned her gaze past the window's shelf where she slept. It would be another few days before her parents were to arrive, so she knew the noise wasn't them. Her three servants were outside speaking to a tall feline driver of a cat carriage. Whatever the situation was, it looked urgent; the expressions on the two weasels gave away their concern about the news they were hearing even while the lead servant, the only stoat, Stella, kept her features composed. This was even stranger than if her parents had come home early. Radio rose, deciding to investigate what the driver was telling them.

The small, soft-furred feline jumped down from the wide windowsill and stretched her white paws. She extended her limbs to rid them of their stiffness from the solid night of sleep, and arched her spine before she rose again. Her attention was caught by the vanity table across her room, the polished surface holding her collar in its stand, ready for her to start the day. She blinked once and took in a breath before she walked over to it.

Radio knew that she was going to have to put it on before she went downstairs. It was a part of her role as one of the nobility to present herself wearing the sapphire choker at all times. She found herself entranced with it, staring at the silver surface of the necklace, gazing at the bright gems decorating the collar in rows. Radio lowered her nose to touch the core gem, a beautiful center heart piece, and took in a deep breath. Her tail flicked back and forth as she contemplated the role she was about to play, sensing from both her parents' absence and the commotion outside it would somehow be different today. Radio closed her eyes and slowly let out the air she held. That very thought made her take the moment to enjoy the peace of her room before going down to see what was happening.

The drumming of tiny paws belonging to her servants suddenly overtook the silence. Radio quickly jumped back as they whipped open her door, bringing the chaos to her instead.

"Miss Radio! There is dire news from the castle!" Stella pressed, bursting inside Radio's room with the two weasels closely following behind. Radio blinked away the cloudiness from her waking eyes to tell them apart, one sister being darker than the other when given a closer look.

"It's terrible, ma'am! The king, our lordship, has vanished! Taken away by something dreadful, unspeakable!" Hana, the lighter sister, whimpered, her eyes widening with every squeak of her voice.

Radio backed away, shocked as the other sister, Leil, continued with even more news, "Taken away by a *mage*, My Lady! No one knows where it came from, but it succeeded in infiltrating the castle!"

"It's so awful, ma'am!" Hana's paws looked like they were vibrating from her shaking.

The lean cat took in another breath, holding it and breathing out through her gritted teeth. This wasn't anything like Radio thought the disturbance outside was about. She had assumed it was an accident with her sister or parents, at the least, with how the two burst in. *What was going on?* Radio didn't know how to ask, nor knew why they would tell her, either. "A-and what does this h-have to do with me?"

"We contacted your sister, the Frequency Star, My Lady." The darker weasel walked to the other side of her. Radio blinked as Leil gave the Star title to her sister, although she never referred to her with it. Radio was one of the nobility, too, whether or not her parents decided to treat her like one. However, before she could address that, the lighter weasel pushed the offended thoughts out of Radio's mind, saying, "It's very worrisome, ma'am. Madam had no interest in the Capital's request for her to investigate the wishes of the—"

"Of the mage, Miss Radio." Now it was Stella who approached Radio, further explaining, "The driver said the duty would pass to the next of kin of the house. That would be you, while your parents are away."

"But how...can I do that?" Radio asked, blinking to try and compose her shock. She had not once left the house without her parents. How were her servants so willing to foist her into a carriage to embark on a trip to the castle by herself to answer to the Council of Media? "W-why can't we wait until my parents get home?"

"The rickshaw outside is waiting for you now, Miss." Radio felt Stella rise up on her back paws to clip the collar around her young mistress' neck. The cat held up her chin as the smaller mammal did so. "You know if we could, we'd have them wait, but it's too urgent. We need you to go now!" Stella hopped down and running out of the room.

Radio watched as the two weasels followed Stella. When she still hesitated, they called out, "Come! There's no time to delay!"

The feline blinked, then took in one more breath, and exhaled as she followed the three servants.

As she ran downstairs, she heard a noise from the parlor, and skidded in her tracks to see what the source was. Was Frequency here? Radio assumed her sister turned down the offer in her own home. What brought her here this early, knowing their parents were gone on their tour? Obviously, she had no intent of visiting her younger sister, sending the sheltered cat off like a…

"Radio, please!" Stella pressed, interrupting Radio's thoughts. The feline nodded, and ran outside with the three instead of pursuing the noise in the parlor.

The weasels and stoat led her to the carriage, driven by a tall, lean serval mix. Radio blinked at his dark arms and tail. It didn't match the spots on his body, as though one of his parents had been a seal point or something. Just then, his piercing gold eyes narrowed into slits. Radio clamped her jaw shut and chose not to ask anyone about his markings when

Faith said, "Oscillation will bring you to the castle, Miss Radio, and from that point workers will escort you through the halls to make sure you're safe." The small mammal gestured to the carriage. Radio climbed in, looking back at Stella and the weasel sisters with wide eyes. It was similar to her looking down at them from the top of the stairs on any other day, but this time she was staring down at them from a carriage, and it was going to take her away. That very idea made a question come to Radio's mind. When would she see them again?

"She'll be safe with us, small one," the tomcat promised once the darker weasel approached the carriage cautiously. Leil nodded, and backed away towards her sister again.

Radio turned to watch as the two rose up on their back legs. "We believe in you, Radio!" they called out, making her smile. She kept her eyes on them as they ran back to Stella and waved to her.

"Come back to us safely." Stella lifted up her paws in apprehension.

Radio shook her head, mustering a big grin for them. She hoped it wouldn't be too overwhelming. As long as there was always someone with her, she would have that, at least. "I will!" she called back before she closed the door to the carriage. The three would have each other while she was gone, so they would be fine, too.

She nearly fell against the floor when the giant cat started the carriage moving. With a sigh she adjusted her collar from its bumping against the bench, and climbed up to sit for a while. Already, this wasn't a pleasant ride.

Her gaze drifted towards the window, and Radio watched as her house and the servants became smaller as more distance was put between them.

She sighed, wondering when she would go back home, then looked back into the carriage. There was a pile of documents and files on the bench next to where she was sitting. She stared at them for a while, and then turned her gaze back out the window to look at her servants again. She kept her eyes fixed on the three to watch them go back inside, then waited until the door was closed. She folded one paw under her chest as she crouched down on the bench, and opened the files with her free paw. Perhaps a bit of knowledge about the situation would clear up the rest of her worry.

Upon beginning to read it, however, she could only come to one conclusion. All the information was kind of *boring*. Radio flipped through the pages one by one. The first few files were interesting enough; they explained that a mage impersonating the hired court jester had infiltrated the castle, holding a glowing, cyan cube. It was speculated to be a replica of the mythical artifact created by the former leader of the land, before the overthrow and takeover of Media's current government. The information made Radio think of the story that her aunt, the Studio Star, told her when she was young about the overthrow of the mages. The former magic Queen had a collection of artifacts floating around her in different colors, but Radio had forgotten they were cubes. The next file was a historical report of the last attempt of a mage to promote sorcery and infiltrate Media with treacherous propaganda. Radio was surprised the last sighting of a mage with one of the artifacts was a feline.

Radio sighed. All the excess detail and reports were dry and dull, but there were just a few bits and pieces hidden within the repetitive words that made the information worthwhile to know, so she continued reading to learn about the feline magician in hopes she could learn something interesting about the magic user.

The mage was a long-haired calico with almost completely white fur. Radio read through the sighting with interest when she saw the photo of the feline. Apparently the cat had started attacking patrols with white and cyan magic along with a "spider monkey" of sorts. Last seen in the Unending Labyrinth across from the Crater Valleys, the feline would lure the patrols and guards of Media inside the jungle maze and use the strange twists of the plant life and pitch black magic to ensure they never returned outside to Media unless delivering a message from "The Shadow Advisor," as the mage called itself, or the title given by Media's Council, "Phantascope," in an attempt to bring less fear to the followers of Media. The fur on Radio's shoulders started to rise just from hearing the name, and she turned to the next file.

The rest consistently called the cat Phantascope, so she knew at least she wouldn't have to read a continuous confusion of names, although she believed she had heard the title of the Shadow Advisor before, and whatever it had been, it was not a good or happy story.

The mages sighted with a cube before Phantascope were actually a pair of two owls, and the artifact's color would fluctuate between amber and magenta. The two resided in the Rich Top Mountains beyond the altitude the patrols could reach, and once again it was mentioned feline clowders and spider monkey troops were sighted near the area of the Unending Labyrinth as well as the areas between it and the mountains.

Radio's ears flicked and her eyes narrowed. It seemed as though the Council may have had warnings or hints that these events concerning the King might indeed happen. She flipped back to the pages of the most recent attack, and read that the jester mage *was* in the form of a spider monkey when it entered the throne hall where it assailed the King. Why hadn't anyone been there to stop a suspicious spider monkey from wandering about the castle? This all made it clear to watch out for strange primates.

Radio took a deep breath and exhaled. Maybe this was why she was coming to the castle, to investigate and find the answers of why the mages inhabited the labyrinth jungle, and to find why they continued to press this message with the cubes floating around with them. Perhaps the sorcerers were trying to spread the news to other mages to reunite for the Queen's return, which would explain why the Council would have never shared this information to Social Media prior to this: they could be afraid of retaliation from the hidden mages of Media once they learned a rebellion truly existed against the current government.

Radio's feathery tail waved in excitement and anticipation of the thought of all of this potential activity. She had already learned so much just by skimming over the details concerning the four mages. The idea she got to be a part of this! Why would Frequency decide to pass this up and give it to her? Perhaps this responsibility being handed to her was a deliberate decision of her older sister making up to her neglected younger sister. Radio knew she would have to thank the busy feline once this whole trip was over. This was a turn in the right direction. She continued reading, only to find the previous file was the last exciting part in the stack of files.

The owls had been the last sighted mages in Media seven generations ago, if not longer, according to known records. Apparently, as Radio made herself continue to read, a terrible storm had struck lightning in the Capital several generations ago and set ablaze the former Capital's structure, burning most of the archives and libraries that contained all the information prior to the Capital upgrading to higher levels of technology. That was the last exciting thing she read, as exciting as the destruction of buildings could be, anyway.

The rest of the files contained information that was supposed to be for Frequency. Travel costs, scheduling, limitations, reports, and other documents on things Radio would see in the castle and on her mission. The more Radio tried to read, the more the words blurred and seemed to repeat themselves. She tried one more sentence, and then huffed, shaking her head. It was too much. "I'll find all this out when I meet them. This is a servant's job," Radio found herself murmuring out loud. She pushed the files onto the floor of the carriage and sprawled out lazily on the bench.

She sighed as she stared ahead. It was impossible to be comfortable in a small carriage, with the cat pulling it as quickly as possible and not as comfortably as possible, across the bumpy road. She shifted her shoulders and kneaded her claws into the bench for a while, closing her eyes. Perhaps she could catch up on the sleep she missed when the carriage first pulled up to the house. Things were already moving so quickly, she thought it possible she should enjoy the slight discomfort of the road while that was the only issue with which to find fault at the moment.

She assumed so, at least, until she saw the hovering bot flying past her carriage. The highly pitched noise from the propellers of the surveillance device made her ears flatten against her skull, and she stared at the object indignantly as it recorded the carriage for a while before flying away. It didn't look like any device she knew from the Capital; the black outer shell wasn't traditional to Media's technology at all. Radio pondered about the red light emitting from it, as well. The device barely looked to be connected to its propellers. Perhaps the Capital had modified its technology for once.

The device left her thoughts when she began thinking about the Capital. The only thing worse than being watched was actually being in contact face to face without any social cues. Her parents always had accomplished both visiting and conducting appointments at home; it seemed Frequency socially maneuvered this way, too. Radio was just to sit and listen in the back, which had worked well for her, since they usually never talked about subjects she found interesting.

That was all about to change, though. Radio's claws flexed with the trepidation of meeting people by herself, but she was determined to persevere. Her servants had implied she would be with someone at all times, which meant *they* would be handling any issues, whether they be discomforts or challenges. The small feline stretched out her limbs one more time along the bench and drifted off to sleep.

Radio's eyes fluttered open at the movement of the carriage slowing down. While she imagined she had only fallen asleep for a few heartbeats, she looked out the window and saw they were already approaching the Capital gates. Her eyes rounded; she hadn't been to the castle since she was a kitten. It looked even bigger than she remembered it to be, which was unusual for memories of being young. The excitement began to pound in her ears as she tried to take in the sights, the citizens, and the buildings. Here she was, as a grown cat, by herself. It was beyond just excitement. Her tail waved and rose as she leaned up against the window, pressing her paws against the strong glass as they drove past the residential district.

She sat back on the bench, kneading the fabric of the cushion as her driver padded through the city. Now she was stuck thinking about the castle, it was already in sight. She would have to meet new people, and introduce herself to them. The small feline had never had to introduce herself, as it was either her parents or an announcer, but perhaps there would be an announcer at the castle. Of *course* there would be an announcer at the castle. Radio would only have to inspect the scene and begin her mission. That would be just fine. She really was worrying too much now.

She took her paws off of the cushion and looked out while she passed the market district. The high quality fashion accessories and clothing on the shoppers were phenomenal. Radio gushed at the sight of them, loving the glamour, and hoped she'd have time for exploring the districts, too.

The carriage went past the surveillance district, a territory that defined the rest of Media's government. Radio peeked out the window to see the cameras were watching her as much as she was them, except at many more angles. It brought back the thought of the device that recorded her carriage on the way, making her turn away completely. She stayed out of sight from the windows until the carriage pulled up to the castle after that. She hadn't realized she had been holding her breath until they reached the large arched double doors, where a ferret was waiting outside.

The small animal looked at Radio's arrival with so much seriousness and concern; it put a knot in Radio's stomach. She hesitated to leave the carriage. The serval driver had other ideas and pulled the carriage to a complete stop and put on the brakes, making the door automatically open. Radio clenched her jaw before she let out the breath she had again been holding, and slowly climbed out of the carriage. She stretched her paws onto the steps, leading her to the ferret and the double doors, and made sure she was holding a firm expression. The ferret bowed at her approach, addressing her, "The Radio Star, it is my honor." The ferret's accent in speaking feline was quite cute, causing Radio to lose the severity of the situation. She smiled as the ferret led her towards the castle, their tails waving in sync. The two passed through a small flap within the double doors and made their way down the giant ornate hall of the castle's magnificent grand foyer.

Radio's eyes rounded as she took in the intricate details and beauty of the anteroom, but her attention was brought back to the ferret upon hearing the animal speak again, "Enterprise is waiting for you. I believe you're the first to arrive here. The other two are on their way." The ferret nodded.

Radio blinked. Maybe she should have read more than just the papers on the mages and magic. The reports probably contained all the information she needed to know about these other two, and this ferret probably assumed she had read the entire packet. *Rightfully so...* Radio chuckled lightly, hoping the ferret wouldn't notice her hesitance before she answered, "Oh, good! I can't wait. I am looking forward to meeting them both." Radio gave a nod to further the sentiment and swallowed.

Radio carefully glanced behind her, her gaze drawn through the window to see if the carriage still might be there in order for her to retrieve the papers, but the driver had already departed. There was no hope for that now. Radio sighed and followed the small mammal down the foyer, her tail slumped.

The ferret took Radio to an office, where a warm-colored falcon was walking along an archive wall, stacked to the ceiling with files and documents. "Sir Enterprise, the Radio Star is here," the ferret spoke softly, dipping her head to the tall avian.

He seemed surprised, but nodded to her. Radio raised her chin, wondering if he was judging her for coming instead of her sister. She then focused her attention on looking around the room. She saw a few of his feathers scattered across the floor. She tilted her head, narrowing her eyes, and stared back at him, starting to ask, "Hello, Sir Enterprise...are you...?"

The falcon chuckled, watching her gaze. He pushed the feathers behind his desk with his talon. "Oh, with the stress of this ordeal concerning the King, I believe I've begun to molt early." The bird dismissed the ferret with a slight flutter of his wing, and turned to face Radio. "You must have so many questions...or perhaps none at all. I don't believe we've ever had the opportunity to meet each other, my log says I was to be meeting the Frequency—"

"Frequency, yes." Radio clamped her jaws shut when her words came out more snappily than she intended, and continued in a more polite tone, "My older sister was unable to come, not feeling too well herself. Likely over all of this as well, I imagine. I came instead. My name is Radio, titled under nobility as a star with one sapphire row, the youngest in my family." She tried her best not to pause to breathe as apprehension twitched in her paws. "I'm here to achieve the mission for her, and to do anything I can to help, sir." She bowed her head, closing her eyes to keep them from showing the panic she felt as the bird's stare burned into her skull.

"Yes, well, I suppose any help would be appreciated. It is incredibly unfortunate your sister was unable to accept an assignment concerning such

27

a dire calamity." The falcon's tail feathers flicked after he spoke. Radio rose back up to look at him with wide eyes and burning cheeks. He didn't seem to have much respect for her or her sister, so openly expressing his attitude. She didn't even realize how strongly she felt about it, either, until she had snapped out her sister's name. She took in a deep breath, and released it as he walked around his desk and clipped a chip to the band around his neck. Radio understood his attitude was likely from the stress of the situation. However...the chip...it looked like he had picked up the computer chip from the ground, making her tilt her head again as the raptor led her outside the room.

The large bird walked with her down the hall, leading them further into the castle. Radio took in the sight of the beautiful architectural elements put into the structure. The ceiling was high enough that birds could likely fly and speak to each other without the ground animals being able to hear from below. There were also bars and handles along the stone walls for arboreal animals to walk through the halls undisturbed by any commotion below or in the sky. Radio was amazed at her burgeoning concept of the diversity amongst the staff. Her family only considered being tolerant enough as to have weasels and stoats in the house as their servants.

"Pictures is here!" Radio jumped at the shout echoing through the entire corridor, looking behind her to see the ferret making the announcement on the other side of the hall. Radio sighed, wondering if the announcement was for one of the two she was supposed to meet. Radio flushed at her earlier disregard for the importance of the documentation. She regretted not reading the files particular to the other people she was to see and possibly even accompany. Her ears flicked, and she looked at

Enterprise. "By any chance, do you have a copy of the documents I was given on my way here?" Radio swallowed, and then furthered, "I might peruse them further before I have to introduce myself to everyone...unless...there's no need for us to introduce ourselves. It isn't as though I didn't read the biographies in the files..." She dipped her head in shame when the tall falcon looked down at her, his eyebrow arched severely in judgment.

"Allow me to do so, Miss. It is of no consequence," a smooth voice sounded from behind her. She turned around to see a lean, silver tabby tomcat only a few whiskers from her face. The fur on her spine rose as she eased back, her eyes rounding as she looked up into his mix-colored eyes, one blue, and the other a burnt gold. She could only widen her own eyes at the sight of them.

They were both beautiful eyes, crisp and sharp as they reflected the wisdom that came with his distinguished age. He was mature without appearing at all elderly. Radio held her breath as she admired the ice of his blue, and the beautiful warmth of autumn in his gold, only then realizing she hadn't answered him. "H-hi, hello!" She blinked, trying to remember the ferret's words, realizing the ferret must have told him who she was already and so quickly smiled at him. "You must be Pictures!"

"Pictures of Clowder City, Miss, yes. I consult with the Capital and city's surveillance departments and bring back my findings to the Council or their Monitor Director. It's a pleasure to meet you." He bowed his head. Radio stared down at him, shocked, but she quickly adjusted her naive thinking. Of course she'd have to work with someone from Surveillance. He'd be a fine protector for both her and the other individual. Yet the idea that his occupation was to monitor subjects of land made her paws weak. She never liked the idea of being watched, nor of others being watched, for that matter, but it seemed to be getting more evident that surveillance was a constant in Media's reality as she continued running into all these monitor workers and devices.

Of course, it had to be a handsome tom, too. Radio looked down when he rose back up to see her expression, and hoped he hadn't seen her fluster. She decided to instead focus on his one black paw and one white paw, then at his back paws to see the colors were reversed. The pattern was so unique, both blending into dark stripes up his legs, and all the way up his neck until Radio found herself staring into his eyes again. She startled at the sudden huff of indignation from the red raptor behind her.

"The same to you, sir," she managed to mewl before introducing herself, "I am the Radio Star, the youngest of my family. Unfortunately, my sister was unable to make the journey and accept the assignment. I was chosen as next of kin." She looked between him and Enterprise, unsure of what else to say. Was she leading the group? Should she be silent? What was she supposed to do? She swallowed, and looked back at Pictures. "Perhaps you know more about this than I do, considering the work you do. I don't desire to waste your time and tell you what you already know." She gave a timid smile up at the tom.

Pictures chuckled, while Enterprise stared at Radio with more judgment and this time, almost outright disapproval. His expression only made her extra appreciative that Pictures could laugh when he responded, "Well, quite funny about that, really. I had been off on an assignment when I was called into this mess, so I only received the same folder of information you did. I imagine we both have the same amount of knowledge of what's happening, Miss Radio. Don't fret about that." His tail flicked. "I'm looking forward to meeting Video, as well." He then smiled at Radio. "Perhaps we can go over what we read and examine it all again before she arrives?"

Another girl! Maybe it wouldn't be so bad. Radio had worried about being the dead-weight when it came to travelling with two tomcats, but she could easily connect with another lady like herself. She blinked in gratitude at his offer, knowing he probably figured out she hadn't looked over everything. "That sounds quite reasonable, thank you. The more we can gather from the facts and each other's knowledge, the easier this mission will be."

She saw out of the corner of her eye Enterprise was scowling at her. Pictures turned his attention to the bird. He stepped closer to the avian, making Radio blink with surprise as the silver tabby spoke, "You know, you seem familiar, *Enterprise*."

The bird's eyes hooded as he responded, "Well, Pictures, my name's quite well known around these parts. I'm not surprised." The falcon's crest began to rise in the slightest.

Radio looked at the two, taking a step back as Pictures retorted, "No, I think I've seen something about you, a photo, or something, maybe a recording." The silver tom's voice seemed threatening. Radio might have believed it, if his features hadn't been so schooled and calm.

Radio gaped at the sudden change in atmosphere and mood. Had she missed something? Was there some exchange between them that totally flew over her head? She stifled a giggle at the idea that perhaps indeed something *had* flown over her head as she looked at the avian.

Now was not a time to break the tension with a joke, though. Their annoyance might then be directed at her. Enterprise inhaled and clicked his beak, but as Radio eased back to listen to his response, she felt the ferret's paw rest on her front leg. The feline looked down at the mix-colored mammal. The woman nodded up at her, smiling, and asked, "Perhaps you'd like to wait for Pictures to discuss your assignment in the drawing room while he finishes speaking with the honorable Enterprise?" She stepped past Radio, moving down the end of the hall and then began to turn.

Radio didn't wait a moment to let the ferret move out of her sight, knowing she would get lost, and be stuck with the two arguing. "Yes, please!" she murmured as she hurried after the smaller mammal, hoping the men weren't bothered by her paws padding against the marble flooring.

"What's your name, miss?" she now asked the servant, catching her breath as they walked down the next hall. Thankfully, it was shorter and smaller than the last one, and the two turned onto a staircase to climb it.

"Mabel, My Lady," the ferret answered as they padded up to the next floor of the castle. Radio smiled at the simple name. She had expected everyone would have their verification from Media's Council to work in the castle. It was assuring to know there were those without the titles even here, much like Radio's own servants. "That's a lovely name." The feline nodded, to further her opinion. Mabel gave her a small smile, with a touch of surprise at the compliment, and led her into a regal, warm-colored drawing room as Radio thanked her.

Radio climbed up on one of the large, dark red divans, and perched there. She let out a small sigh, and then looked around the room after

Mabel left. The walls were filled with beautiful books on ornately carved, dark wooden shelves, and the floor was scattered with rugs atop the glossy wooden flooring. It was all very beautiful, and nothing like any place Radio had been before. Her gaze drifted to the fireplace, which seemed to be the main piece and focus of the room. It had a giant stone border that looked decades old, with a large chain attached. Radio at first thought the chain would have started the fireplace, but then saw the lever that fed it and the switch that ignited it, making her wonder about all the contraptions. "How curious…" she mused out loud.

Pictures came into the room, and started grooming his ruffled fur. "My apologies, Miss Radio." He flicked his ears, and came up to her. "I have the digital files on my person about the mission. If you'd like me to transfer them to you, we can review them," he offered with a nod of his head. Radio realized he had no physical copies of what she needed. Most monitors worked completely in digital format with simulated screens. Radio blinked, realizing Frequency and her parents likely all had these gadgets, but she didn't have them, nor was she ever exposed to them.

She blinked, and shook her head. "That's fine, Pictures, thank you, anyway. I usually prefer discussing it verbally, as it's much easier for me to comprehend that way." She smiled.

The tom blinked at her, flicking his left ear. It was the first time Radio noticed the nick in the side of it, staring at it before she focused on his response, "Oh, I see. No, that's fine, Miss Radio, I find it quite a bit easier that way, too, actually." He smiled up at her in assurance, and then leapt up onto the other side of the divan to rest against the single armrest. "Miss Video is coming here on foot. She is said to be in the area, so I'm not sure what the wait will be for her arrival."

Radio frowned, not wanting to imagine the stress on the poor dear's pads, and listened carefully as Pictures continued, "As for the mission, it seems we're waiting on Video to find out the main objective. The Council was very secretive with the information given out in the files, as all of what we read was nothing we couldn't have looked up in the database."

"Oh, that is strange," Radio pondered, tapping her dark paw pads against her chin. "From what I read, I thought it was a bit odd that no one found it suspicious a spider monkey was wandering the castle, seeing as all the previous ties their species seem to have with the mages."

Pictures' brow furrowed at her words, making her regret them immediately. He didn't hesitate to explain, "Well, I'll try not to find fault with that so much since the reports stated there were no alerts of the mage on any of the monitors or surveillance until after the first explosion of magic happened. All the images and recordings taken were performed manually when security ran to see the cause of such destruction." Pictures blinked again in shock of her previous ponderings, frowning. "They really didn't get an opportunity to detect what species it was prior to the incident, you know."

Radio clenched her jaw, knowing it was likely in one of the files she hadn't read. "I guess I overlooked that, there was so much else I needed to comprehend," she chuckled, shaking her head and putting her paw up against her head to try and hide the shame on her face from him. She really was going to blow this, and they hadn't even begun their mission yet. She took in a breath, and released it. As long as they learned everything else that was going on, together, she'd be up to speed enough to carry on with the assignment without feeling as though she was out of the loop with Pictures and this upcoming second companion, Video.

As if on cue from her thoughts, Mabel stepped back in. "Miss Video from the Rich Top Mountain Region is here!" The ferret bowed, backing up to allow the woman to enter. Radio's jaw dropped at the sight of Video.

She was another feline, a long-haired umber tabby with white paws and underbody patches all the way up to her chin as well as below her nose. It wasn't the contrasting white and brown that caught Radio's attention, though. Her size was unbelievable, as well as the striking black marble stripes that stretched across her face and long-furred pelt, darker than Radio's own black leggings and back. Even the fur around the cat's neck fell against her shoulders like a mantle, having nearly every shade of brown, cream and white in layers around her neck and two black blotches up each side of her throat, which stood out from the white of her neck stunningly. Radio was sure that the cat was only a domestic feline, but Video was still about twice the height of her. She'd be surprised if even the tom, Pictures, reached the other young woman's shoulders.

The giant tabby cat prowled into the room, her giant thick tail matching the cat in length. Radio's eyes rounded into blue spheres when Video turned her dark sienna eyes onto her. "The Radio Star," the words were a declaration. "It's an honor." The feline's voice echoed through the room as she bowed down and flattened her ears in respect to Radio, making Radio's jaw drop even more.

Pictures let out a chuckle and turned away as though he hadn't noticed, making Radio quickly compose herself so she could address the majestic feline. "Miss Video, a pleasure," she squeaked, removing any dignity she still had left.

Video didn't seem to focus on the lack of poise, though. Radio could almost convince herself the giant cat hadn't noticed. "The situation we're dealing with is very dire, but I could not have asked to be a part of a better team to complete this objective we face. It's an honor to meet you both, truly." Video dipped her head to Pictures, too, who nodded to her before she turned back to Radio. "I am sure by having both fresh and experienced minds we'll be able to tackle this mission wholeheartedly."

Radio had assumed Video was going to be another tech savvy feline who hid behind monitors and was going to enjoy Pictures' company and protection as much as herself. Now she believed that she and Pictures would both be hiding behind Video against any danger as they started this mission. "Well, thank you, Video. I can say the same to you." she dipped her head, and Pictures did the same. It seemed neither of them wanted to hop down from the divan, knowing the giant cat would tower over them as soon as they were at her level. Radio couldn't take her eyes off of the majestic brown feline once she brought her head back up, and hoped that the cat wouldn't be disturbed by the staring.

Radio to looked over at Pictures as he rose up on his paws and spoke, "I'm looking forward to working with you, Video, it's a pleasure to work with someone of your training and knowledge of this situation."

Radio sank. More information she should have read in the reports. However, Video seemed surprised by his words. "May I ask you to elaborate, sir?" the giant tabby asked.

Pictures hopped down now. Both Video and Radio's gaze intently fixed on him as he approached Video. "Well, your father was solely responsible for directing the mission and takedown against the last sighted mage, Phantascope. I would only imagine you were well trained by him to face this, since you still reside with your parents, yes?"

Video paused, and then lifted up her chin. "You are correct, I am residing in the mountain region with them since I have yet to be transferred to the Capital." Video's brow then furrowed. "But it does not necessarily mean I was trained to face threats against magic. Such training is not a mandated assessment."

Pictures' ear flicked, and Radio blinked at him as his brow arched. "That's true. You have a fair point, and for that I apologize, Miss Video. I suppose it was wrong for me to assume you were educated in the subject, after all." Pictures sat, his tail wrapping around his paws.

Radio let out a sigh at the possible insult. It seemed like Enterprise hadn't been the only one looking for a fight. The more Radio thought about it, Pictures had been the one to instigate the argument between him and the raptor in the first place. Radio was relieved Video seemed so level-headed. Perhaps she could mediate any communication the two might have in the future.

"Quite," Video only answered, and now began taking in the room's appearance just as Radio had.

The smaller feline blinked at the similar action, and it made her wonder what she might find out about these two on their journey. They were already so interesting! Radio respected Video for her strength and professionalism already, as the giant cat looked quite young, but already had incredible determination in her eyes. Then there was Pictures, who seemed to be very bold and headstrong, knowing what he wanted and how to get it. Radio sighed, wondering how they might be describing her in their heads, knowing it was likely much less exciting than what she thought of them.

"Miss Radio, Video, and Pictures?" Another voice sounded from the doorway of the drawing room. It was another cat.

Radio turned to see the bulky, dark brown-and-white tom waiting, kneading his large paws against the wooden flooring with nervousness. He still remained in the doorway while a lighter tan tabby walked in, continuing up to the party with her amber eyes gleaming. "Hi, you three, you must be here for the assignment!" The two cats' matching bright eyes made Radio smile. It looked like they were siblings, both with the same ruff around their neck and orange eyes. Even how they carried themselves looked quite similar. The tan tabby sat with her paws tucked underneath her as she introduced herself and the tom both, her voice clear and loud as she said, "I'm Recorder, and this is Tape! We're here to bring you to the Surveillance Department to set you up before we send you out on your mission."

Their verified titles were impressive, too. These two were ones to talk to and get information from if she couldn't from Pictures or Video. "Oh, it's a pleasure!" Radio purred, smiling. "I am the Radio Star, these are my companions, Pictures from Clowder City, and Video from the Rich Top Mountain Region." Radio turned to gaze at the silver and brown tabbies below her, beaming at how well the introduction went and that she remembered where they were from. She tried not to look too proud at her words, and hopped down from the bench when Tape and Recorder approached the three.

Tape bowed his head in respect, and then brightened as he lifted his face back up. "What an honor! The chosen three!" The dark tom looked from Radio to Video and Pictures. "Everything about what we're facing can be explained in the surveillance room. It shouldn't take long to catch you all up with what your assignment is. It really is a pleasure. We're so glad you could make it here in good time." He stopped to catch his breath, and then gave a nod. "Please, follow us." He turned on the back pad of his paw, walking out of the room. Recorder chuckled and nodded at the group to follow him.

Radio gave a small smile, optimistically anticipating everything would go as well as she hoped, and quickly followed the bulky tom, Tape. She only stopped to smile at her new companions, Video and Pictures, who were also trailing behind her with interest.

- CHAPTER 2 -

UNDERSTANDING

Radio made herself inhale a breath, and exhale it one more time as they entered the dark room. Recorder had introduced it as the surveillance room, which brought Radio no additional comfort. The monitors, screens, images, control panels, buttons, and knobs were overwhelming. Everything Radio never really liked in Media was all compacted into a small room. She couldn't believe how much she was running into everything she found so distasteful. The room barely was lit with the exception of the bright screens that lined the walls, and it made her sight blur. She was surprised to see that Tape and Recorder led them to the back of the room with a group of two other felines. *Why are there so many cats?*

Radio knew that her aunt, the Studio Star, had supported the growth of the domesticated feline species by building her city to the south, but she still found the population of cats surprising, especially after seeing the diverse accommodations of the castle. Studio had made a city exclusively for felines many seasons ago, offering education and shelter, which none of the other species had available freely, making it easier for others to find companions and live in a safe environment away from the harsh elements of Media. The population of felines had boomed since, but not so much that Radio thought an entire division would be filled with cat staff in Media's capital, where all species were accepted.

She almost laughed when a golden-winged bird fluttered into the room and perched on one of the staff's heads. Radio quickly thought it was best to stifle the giggle as she realized she might witness a bird being eaten right in front of her and her new companions.

"Oh, Sensor! You're back!" Recorder came up to the tomcat where the bird perched. It was only a moment before Radio realized the tabby was speaking to the bird and not the cat, as she continued, "Was the flight outside fine? Do you think we can send them out?"

The bird nodded, and Recorder purred, touching her nose to the bird's beak. She turned to look back at Radio, Video and Pictures, who all stared at her with surprise. "This is Sensor. He'll be detecting the weather outside and warning you of any danger. He's never been able to speak cat, but he understands it well. We've learned his tongue, too, to make it fair." Recorder grinned as Pictures chuckled.

Radio was even more surprised as Video only nodded.

"It's a pleasure to meet him," Pictures chirped. Recorder brightened, turning back to the two other cats sitting at the computers. She stared at them both, and then tapped the dark brown tom's shoulder, startling him. He yelped out loud with his earbuds still in, as he seemed not to have noticed her presence, and stared up at her with round, blue eyes.

Recorder huffed and turned back to Radio, Video, and Pictures. "This is Widget, our youngest recruit. He'll be helping us to keep you safe and be an extra pair of eyes to look out for any danger."

"I-it's a pleasure to meet you all...all...oh...! Miss R-Radio!" His piercing wide blue eyes locked onto Radio's. Radio frowned, surprised how much the boy looked like a kitten version of her father. The small cat chuckled nervously, immediately looking to Video and Pictures instead. "It's such an honor to meet you all! I'm so glad you could come here to meet us...it's really surprising...we don't get many visitors..." He took off the earbuds as he laughed again, even more anxiously. Radio tilted her head as he waved his paw at Sensor for the bird to fly away, and then hopped down from his seat.

"You too, Widget." Pictures arched his brow and smiled at the smaller tom, while Radio continued looking at the younger tom curiously. He certainly didn't act like her father, making her push away thoughts of the resemblance. However, he had been the only one to call out her name. There were so many felines nowadays, patterns and pelt colors were bound to repeat themselves. She could barely remember their names, having met so many animals and cats in one day, but figured the tom did so because she was the only noble.

She lifted up her chin and smiled in support of Pictures' assurance to the young cat's apprehension. "Agreed. We want to know everything we can about this, sir!"

Widget nodded, and Radio smiled when he sighed a bit in relief and spoke, "I-I'm sure Cassette will be able to tell you about all the information we have gathered. She knows more about this whole situation from Film than the rest of us do, at least. I wish I could listen in and offer more, but I'm afraid I have to take my break." He backed up, bumping into the seat behind him, which startled him again. He turned for the door after apologizing quietly. "Bye!" he called as he fled from the room. Video glared at the door through which the young tom left with rebuke in her eyes, and flexed her claws as though she contemplated chasing after him. Radio barely noticed, still staring at where the young tom had been sitting before.

"Strange," Radio mumbled, realizing Widget had mentioned another individual named Film. Her eyes narrowed the slightest at that. She knew Film, as the surveillance director had dated her sister until recently. They had broken off their courtship only a few days before, actually...

She blinked away her thoughts as Recorder spoke, assuring them, "He is always nervous around nobles." The tan feline rolled her eyes, smiling as she hopped up on the stool the tom had vacated and started straightening up Widget's desk. "The Frequency Star used to stop in quite a bit."

After pushing the tom's earbuds away with her paw, she gestured for Radio and her two companions to come forward to the surveillance wall with her short, thick tail, smiling as they did so. "So this room is where we'll be tracking you and where you'll be going. It is also where we'll give you updates as the signals to your objective become apparent or alternate.

We're still not sure what this mage planned when it did all of this, nor what tricks could be hiding up its sleeves."

"Sleeves?" Radio frowned, and Recorder pressed a knob that brought an image on screen. It was a video of the mage the files described, dressed in a jester outfit with a blue mist surrounding it. Its eyes gleamed the same cyan blue the cube emitted. It was the beautiful hue which caused Radio's fur to rise, seeing it associated with such a power play against and to incite fear within all of Social Media. What was even more terrifying to Radio, though, was the large grin spread across the primate's face, showing each and every one of its glittering sharp teeth. Those hadn't been described in the files.

"This is the creature that did this." Recorder pressed a toggle, showing the three different recordings of the mage. "Our surveillance was taken by the guards and monitors trying to stop it. Explosions of red and cyan fog seemed to appear most often with the strange jester, but there's more to it than that."

In one of the images, the blurry capture looked to Radio as though it was a red glowing crystal heart. "This is your objective." Recorder's voice grew grim as she zoomed in on the object, making Radio's eyes round at the beautiful detail of light and dark threads flickering within it.

Tape nodded, and continued for Recorder, his tone just as serious as he said, "This was the object created immediately after the king's disappearance. The jester shattered the object, and in some unknown and strange way, some power from it—its power, was released, scattering the broken fragments out to far beyond the castle. From the reaction, based on the recordings, it seems this release of power was against the mage's wishes and intent. After the magical creature fled, a message was discovered during the cleanup. It was written in the cat dialect, which was part of the factor in deciding to contact you three."

Pictures rolled his eyes and sighed, looking to Video. The great feline did not respond in similar fashion, and instead looked intrigued and instantly more focused. Radio, however, was the one to pipe up. "The monkey mage wrote in cat!?" she asked incredulously.

Recorder looked back down at the three, answering, "We would assume so, although there was no evidence it had been the mage who wrote it, from our recordings. The explosion of magic which occurred as the guards entered kept us from getting a good perspective and full account of the events, for both the crystal object shattering, as well as the origin of the final message left for us." The tan tabby frowned, turning off the screen.

The calico from the back of the room then spoke, the second cat who had been inside the room when they entered. She faced Radio directly, making the smaller feline look over at the patched and striped worker with wide eyes as she lifted up her chin. "We didn't find that so unlikely, though. To escape, it shapeshifted into an avian form, which wouldn't put it beyond writing in cat. The message was clear to state it wanted the youngest titled noble, courier, and monitor to fix this, and we immediately sent out the notice to find you three. When going through the files, the Frequency Star was the only one to turn up in our database. We weren't aware of you as your parents' second daughter, Miss Radio." The tri-colored feline narrowed her eyes. "The error seemed strange, but now has been corrected. It worked well your sister had been too busy to accept our summons, as she wasn't notified the request was for the youngest feline noble of Media."

Radio blinked, frowning. "Oh, that is strange." She looked over at Pictures, wondering if he had any knowledge about the error in the system. Monitors also scanned through reports and files on the followers of Media, making her assume he knew something, but he only shrugged, looking as confused as she did before he added, "That isn't surprising with a bit of introspective analysis. I wasn't aware the Resolution Star had a second kit until I received the report this morning, either."

That disturbed Radio even more. Why wasn't she in the files? She was already sheltered enough as it was. Her parents never let her venture out by herself even after she had received her title as the Radio Star, while her older sister was allowed to do so. However, the idea of completely being left out as their child... "How did you get my report if I wasn't listed as the daughter of my parents? Even if I wasn't listed as theirs, how was I still not verified as the youngest noble?" she asked, realizing that Pictures was still able to read a report on her digitally.

"Upon my supervisor searching your name, having known you, Miss Radio." The calico arched her brow at Radio. The feline's feathery ears grew hot, knowing the calico was referring to Film. The tri-colored cat then continued, "He found your name in the Council's database, but it had not been transferred for viewing access to other monitors outside of the Capital. We had no trouble adding you in though, dear. Everything is fine now." The older feline dipped her head. Radio frowned, looking at Video to see what she thought of all of this, but the large tabby looked back down at Radio without offering any expression or opinion on the matter.

"I didn't even think he noticed me. I'd greatly appreciate if you thanked him for that, ma'am," Radio requested. She tried to see what Tape was doing, as he brought over a case of technological chips. Sensor was now perched on Tape's head, making Radio struggle not to smile.

"Of course." The calico's eyes then softened. "My name is Cassette. It'll be a pleasure working with you and keeping an eye out for the three of you." She looked over at the stocky tom and bird, and gestured out her paw. "Tape and Sensor will embed these chips into your ears so we can contact you and track your locations. This will allow us to see the amount of time in which you complete this mission, and talk to you if need be. Our technology has been able to detect the radiating magic from the red shard fragments scattered by studying the fragment already found outside the Capital's walls. We're trying to develop the technology to detect all forms of magic, but so far every imprint of temperature and frequency we take of a citizen or artifact has been different, and we have to redevelop the technique for each individual mage we've come across. The detector has come up with multiple signals, which suggests the shards' source all to one imprint, which we imagine belongs to the aura of our King."

Radio looked around at the others, trying to gauge their reaction to Cassette's casually spoken words: the King had an imprint of magic. No one else seemed to show any surprise, or, as she originally feared, condemnation of learning the King had a trace of the forbidden practice. She was careful to mask her emotions, nonchalantly nodding as though she were comprehending Cassette's statement as being nothing out of the ordinary, as Sensor began attaching the computer chip and an earpiece to her inner ear with his tiny beak and precise talons. Radio tried not to let her ears flick as he did so, and then spoke more confidently and assuredly than she actually felt, saying, "Well, it'll be a start, and much better than going out looking for shards without any leads. You do incredible work here."

The two siblings beamed. "Thank you, Miss Radio. We're honored to hear that from one of your stature." Recorder hopped down, smiling as Video crouched for Tape to be able to reach her ear. "We'll take you as far as the Capital's walls to show you the first shard so you can start your journey. We were very lucky that one of them landed close, we may not have been able to invent the device without it."

"We should take you there immediately, so you can get started on your journey." Tape clicked the chip and earpiece to Pictures' nicked ear, and then quickly looked away when Pictures winced and glared at him. Radio gave Pictures a censuring look for his attitude, but Tape backed up, and then grabbed a large buckle with a bag attached on one side. Recorder hurried over. The two strapped it around Video as the giant tabby rose to her feet. "You'll be able to carry the shards in this, and it should keep them safe from any weather or any trouble you may come across." Recorder smiled up at Video, who nodded at the tan cat's words.

Radio looked concerned at the idea of trouble, but neither Pictures or Video seemed surprised as Recorder and Tape led them out of the surveillance room. Radio instead focused on the feeling of Cassette's piercing green eyes staring into the back of her head. The stare made Radio hope Film hadn't said too much about her. He had never spoken to her when he visited Frequency, and the idea he mentioned her at all made her worry, even if it was probably just protocol. She couldn't shake away her bristled fur upon feeling the older cat's gaze on her way out of the room.

Tape and Recorder led the three outside of the Capital. The two surprised Radio by taking her and the other chosen felines off the road and onto the grass path alongside the city walls. Radio hadn't put her paws on anything but manufactured flooring besides the courtyard behind her house, where the grass was carefully planted and the ground was leveled for easy footing. She looked at her paws, concentrating to make each step carefully, and tried to match pace as best as she could. She hadn't realized they were already at the side of the castle wall until the setting sun began shining in her eyes. She looked out into the distance, her eyes widening at the sight.

It was an amazing view. With the Capital being built upon one of the highest summits of the vast mountains of Media, Radio could see the phenomenal structures in the distance, even Clowder City, her auntie's mark on all of Social Media. Radio saw the small villages surrounding the mountain: the abandoned city, the vast valleys that stretched across most of the central region, and the Sanctified Meadows that the folk of Media always managed to keep the Council from destroying. They were the same meadows her aunt had another name for, too. Radio gasped as she saw the structures even beyond Central Media, which looked even more impressive than what she could see up close.

Radio admired the view of it all, and then turned her eyes back to the valleys below. She hadn't understood why the Council wanted to destroy the meadows until now. The meadow was a beautiful, luscious variation of flowers, all of them in hues of violet, purple, and magenta. Those were the colors associated with the former Queen of the land the Council was responsible for removing from the throne and likely a local reminder of her, for both the Council and the mages. Radio swallowed nervously as she followed Tape and Recorder once more.

The two moved along the unsteady ground even better than Video, which surprised Radio. She had expected the courier to not miss a beat with all of the travelling done across the land, but Tape and Recorder moved so effortlessly, it made Radio wonder how much they may have explored the outskirts of the Capital as kittens, assuming they grew up here. She smiled as they hopped up on a ledge in sync, and hurried forward. Radio took the strongest leap she could. She felt the breeze brush through her fur as she came into contact with the ledge, scrambling up to the surface with them. She let out a breath of exhaustion, not used to the hike, or the adventure, like these four. Even Pictures, the slender, supposedly pampered tom from Clowder City, had an easy time hopping up onto the ledge with Recorder and Tape.

"Here it is," Recorder said, walking up to a glowing crystal fragment. Radio's eyes widened at the sight of the object. It was nearly the size of her forearm. It gleamed even redder than it did in the recordings with the setting sun's beams shining against it. Radio frowned slightly. This really wasn't a game. Here she was with two other cats she had never met before this day, about to venture out to explore all of Media in search of these strange, magical artifacts. Artifacts were what her family, the nobles of Media, were responsible for trying to remove from this land in the first place.

It made Radio wonder all the more about their fate on this journey. What would this jester do upon seeing them? Was this all a part of an elaborate trap against the nobles and royalty? If that was so, why were the courier and monitors involved? A grudge against the messengers who brought the rigged offer to the Queen and the bystanders who stood back and only gave witness to what played out long ago? The idea began to slightly sink in, and she only blinked back into focus when Pictures walked past her, looking curiously at Video, who fearlessly sank her teeth into the fragment and pulled it out from the ground.

"Our guards attempted to take the shard from the ground earlier today, and were struck back with severe burns against any area that came in contact with the object," Recorder explained, looking up at Video with concern.

"I-I guess this means these are the right ones, though...th-the ones chosen by th-the Jester," Tape stammered, shocked to see the giant tabby holding the item without hesitation, and then looked at Radio and Pictures with just as round eyes.

Pictures nodded, coming forward. He took the shard from Video's jaws by gripping the tip of it in his teeth and pulling it from her. He lifted his white paw and rested the artifact on the pads of it, while still keeping the top clamped firmly in his jaws. Radio's eyes rounded even more at the idea of the object doing such terrifying damage, and yet these two cats stood exchanging it with each other without showing the smallest bit of fear. She backed up when Pictures slowly blinked at her, managing to turn his head and still hold the object between his teeth. All of her apprehension flooded up to her head when he nodded to her and let the shard go from the grip of his fangs, expecting her to take the item from his paw.

She looked over at Recorder and Tape, who both smiled at her, and stuck out her paw. Her pads trembled in fear as Pictures dropped the shard onto her outstretched paw, worried what the consequence might be if Frequency was really the one who should have been chosen. She quickly lifted up her arm to take the item once it landed against her paw pad, and tightened her claws against the hard crystal surface. She was surprised at how warm the shard was when she gained a steady hold. The light and power reflected directly against her body and eyes as she stared into it, and she had to blink away the light as it blinded her more effectively than the sun's rays had.

She opened her eyes again once she turned her head away, and looked up at Pictures once she felt his gaze on her. He stared at her with approval and excitement, making her cheeks warmer than the shard's heat. She felt butterflies in her stomach seeing him look at her like that, and without thinking, she automatically gave the shard to Tape when the bulky cat approached her. He reflexively took it from her, then screeched and jumped back, hissing as the item burned his paw pad.

"Oh, I am so sorry!" Radio leapt over, picking up the dropped shard between her teeth as Tape ran his tongue against his burnt pad, making both Recorder and Pictures sigh in relief after realizing it hadn't done anything severe to the stocky tom.

Video glared down at Tape for having accepted it, the tom having been the most nervous about it in the first place, and then turned her piercing stare to Radio. The intensity made Radio shrink down with her ears flattened. She immediately let Video take the shard from her jaws, and watched as she put it in the bag Tape and Recorder had previously attached to her. Recorder gave one assuring pat to Tape, then strode past Pictures and nodded to both Radio and Video.

Recorder smiled then, and enthused, "Congratulations, you three. You were obviously the ones chosen for this, and we wish you luck on your journey." Recorder and Radio both turned their heads to look out into the valleys below the Capital, and admired the sight, being even more beautiful from the ledge than compared to looking out from the city gates. "The path may be rough. We don't know what this mage plans, but we know for sure that we'll be here anytime you need help." Recorder looked to Radio now. "We believe you can do this."

"We hope you'll be careful." Tape limped away from Pictures to stand beside Recorder. "So far we haven't seen the one who caused all of this since the incident last night, but we'll let you know if that changes. Currently, the best route to take is to the south. Safe journeys, you three. We're all rooting for you."

"Thank you, Tape." Pictures gave a smile to the shorter tom as he stepped over to Video's side.

Radio touched her nose to Recorder's cheek, and both dipped their necks to touch their foreheads together in an embrace. "We really appreciate all your help," Radio murmured, and stepped back to be led away by Video.

"Of course, Miss Radio." Recorder smiled as she and Tape trailed behind the three. "Bye, bye! Good luck!" the two called out from the ledge as Video bounded down with Radio and Pictures following. Radio smiled at the siblings' positivity, but thoughts began to spin in her head about the whole scenario. This wasn't the "chosen ones" going back to the castle, this was the three of them starting on their way to find the other shards.

She walked in silence with her companions for a while, but the thoughts flooded her mind. What were the odds this whole situation worked out like it did? Radio swallowed and turned to Pictures, who began to look at her with concern. She blinked at him, staring into his round, multi-colored eyes, and let the words spill out. "My sister decided that I should go instead of her. It worked out that I am the youngest noble to be born so I could hold the shards, but it seems so peculiar it turned out fine. With such short notice, the idea of it sounds even more unlikely, like it was almost as though she knew about it or something, which is what really makes me feel weird." Radio looked away from Pictures, her last words drifting into a mumble as she started to worry about sharing her concern with the surveillance officer. How could one ever doubt the Frequency Star? Her ears flattened, waiting for Pictures' censure at her words.

Pictures seemed unfazed, though. "Some things are just meant to be. Calamities like this always happen with strange luck and chance. I know I'm grateful that you're here, Miss Radio." He smiled at her and then looked ahead. "This venture may be beyond anything we've ever witnessed. It could also be the greatest journey of our lives." The optimism and positivity of his words made Radio chuckle, shaking her head and looking up at the setting sun. His words made her think about the opportunity given to her because of this. She couldn't find fault with his outlook.

"Yes, that I have to agree with you on, Pictures," Radio sighed.

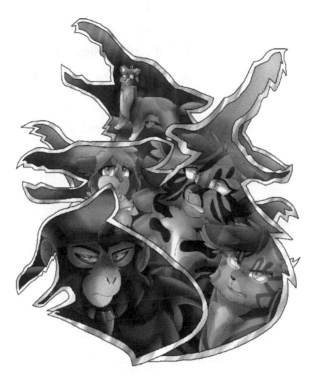

- CHAPTER 3 -

RASHNESS

The night came gradually after the sun set, and the moon rose high into the sky before the travelling three stopped to rest. Once the night breeze set in, Video allowed the team to stop. The three lay down on the flattened earth within the valley. Once she and Pictures were settled, Radio made herself comfortable and stared up at the night sky shining and shimmering above them. The static and energy that surrounded Media's borders wasn't really visible in the day, but at night, Radio was almost able to distinguish every individual thread of energy that flowed and moved in the sky, still protecting Media's followers from the outside dangers.

The barrier's static seemed even clearer when watching from the valley instead of inside the safety of her home at her window. Everything seemed clearer, really. Radio found herself pondering about the next day's events before she cleared the thoughts from her mind. Her head lowered to the ground as the tiredness took over, and she fell into the slumber of the welcoming darkness and warmth of her companions. It hadn't taken long for them to settle into the terrain beside one another, each curled up against the other's fur to keep warm and sheltered from the summer breeze. However, even while they slept, others in Media remained active, including unsavory folk, such as the mages.

Most of the valley was silent, but beyond the territory, into the woodlands, the dark mage roamed. Past the shadows of the forests, deep within a hidden cavern of the woods, a noise of despair and fear echoed through the dark tunnels. The source of the cries came from an unlucky mouse who wailed and struggled in the grip of a tall, lean spider monkey that held him down only with its fingertips. The mouse squeaked and protested, but the monkey kept pressure firm on the rodent's back. Beneath the pillar the two lay upon were snarls and squeals from a shadowy mass of small figures below. The mouse yelped as the primate pulled him up and dangled him over the pillar, where he could now truly see what awaited him below.

Savage rats snapped and hissed at him, their eyes gleaming bright blue as they glared up at the mouse. What was even more terrifying than the group's eyes, were how their tails knotted and wound together with the muck of the earth and filth below their pads. The mouse squealed again once he felt his tail slip in the primate's grasp, but the monkey still kept a hold to bring him back to the safety of the pillar's surface, pushing the rodent down again with one hand.

"P-please...!" the mouse wheezed.

When the monkey raised the hand that had been taking away the air from the small rodent's body, he continued his plea, "Please, d-don't eat me! Please...be m-me-merciful, Gatherer! I have children to raise, a loving companion!"

"That's a bunch of bunk! Stop this!" The primate growled, and rolled the mouse onto his back, pressing the air out of him in a squeak as the monkey's sharp-nailed fingers tapped against the soft rodent belly. "You're wasting what breath you have left with balderdash and rubbish."

"I-I don't mean to, Gatherer! Please, once you let me go, I can show you the—"

The mouse's words cut off with another squeak as the primate prodded him again. The monkey raised the mouse up, level to its hooded eyes. "I'm not interested. You can't carry your own weight here, Mouse." The hooded eyes now narrowed slightly. "Seeing as how that's not a very large expectation, I really have no point to keep you around anymore."

The rodent swallowed nervously, and stammered to find the words to change the collector's mind, yelling, "Pl-please! I understand now, Gatherer. I'll do better! I won't let you down—!" He yelped as he began to sink in the primate's grasp, as though the monkey was considering dropping him. "I won't disappoint you, Gatherer! You can spare me, and I'll bring you offerings...food! Quality food! You won't have to touch another mouse again!"

The small creature blinked in worry when seeing the primate didn't look any more impressed. It was quite possible the monkey appeared even more bored than before "I'm sorry, Mouse, but that's not going to cut it for me. I'm not looking for a reason to lie around, or to have to wait for others anymore." The mouse's eyes widened as the primate sighed and dangled him from the pillar where the rats waited below. "Say hello to your old friends while I go find something better to eat." The monkey chuckled. "I won't be seeing you later so...Toodles!"

"Wait! No!" All that was left to be heard were the cries of the mouse as he fell into the pit of rats, being ripped apart by former companions he had once known to protect his village. The primate rose slowly, giving one more glance down at the rats, and walked away from the scene.

Nothing had been heard beyond the depth of the cavern tunnels. No help was called for the unfortunate rodent. Beyond the forest, past the woodlands, the three travelers slept, remaining in their peaceful slumber until the dawning sun again appeared. The light shining into their eyes brought them back to the waking world which awaited their quest to be completed. They continued on, unaware of the consequence of their stop.

The three traveled together through the valley on the bright sunny day, their steps almost synchronous as they moved through the expansive length of the land. The grass felt luscious and soft against Radio's paws as she listened to the birds chirping brightly in the sky. She looked up to try and see them before they flew past the group. Bunches of very small, puffy clouds were out above their heads today, too, making the vast stretch of the shimmering sky bluer than Radio had ever seen outside her home. She couldn't believe the view that the low valley offered them, especially after considering the view became better the higher one went. It was all such an amazing experience, she had to pause to savor the moment before continuing down the path the two in front of her made.

She smiled at them, the butterflies and excitement bubbling up inside her and making her pounce excitedly forward, taking each step deliberately in a march. "One, two!" Radio counted her paws. "One, two!" Radio counted the two felines in front of her. "One, two!" She bounded forward, prodding both of the cats as she rushed up to them. She kept her paw on Pictures.

The tomcat looked a bit surprised, but then smiled. "Why do you only count two when there are three of us, Miss Radio?" He arched his brow as he removed her paw, then grinned and nudged her as he acknowledged she was the third.

His playfulness made Radio giggle, smiling at him in delight as he continued forward with her. She loved how he looked when he walked, watching his mismatched paws press against the ground, standing out more than any other cat's paws likely did in all of Media. She opened her mouth to respond, but jumped as Video shoved past them. "There might only be two of us by the time we reach our objective!"

Radio looked at her in surprise, wondering how the large feline managed to come to that conclusion from a play of counting. "O...kay?" Radio tilted her head. Pictures only gave a small chuckle from Radio's discomfort.

Video sighed again, her tail lashing as she dug her claws into the ground. "The Capital is in a crisis right now, and you two are playing counting games! The entire *land* is in peril and in danger being without their King, having their Council disrupted, and the both of you, who are to be professional, models for the rest of Social Media, are travelling along like this is a vacation!" The cat stamped her paw against the ground. "It's positively disturbing!"

"Do you know what's *disturbing,* Video?" Radio's brow furrowed, and she lifted up her chin. "That we traveled all night without a single stop for rest besides that small stream we found, had to sleep on the cold ground when you finally *would* let us stop for rest." Radio's tail lashed in nearly a perfect mimic to Video's. "And after only having the morning dew to drink, we still travel nonstop to this place where the monitors only detected a faint signal. Who knows if it's even there!"

Radio blinked then, seeing Video was almost completely out of her sight, and still increasing her pace until Radio called out, "What are you doing? Do you see something ahead!?"

She ran to catch up to Video, worried the tabby had found something, but stopped in her tracks when the large cat spun around and snarled, "No, I don't! But I might if I could get ahead enough and not be held back by you twitty little birds!"

"Fine!" Radio glared up at the striped feline, and growled when Pictures caught up to them, letting Video walk ahead. "I cannot believe her!" Radio scoffed, following the courier with heavy paws and flattened ears. Pictures arched his brow at her, making her lower her head in apology.

She let him walk ahead, and then raised her head with surprise as she watched the tom lift his chin to speak up to their giant, prowling companion. "Miss Video, if you wouldn't mind me objecting—this is a good pace for us. We will tire out less, and can travel longer to meet your demands about the scheduled breaks. We haven't taken a moment to rest since we started this morning. We're not behind schedule with the estimation the Capital set for us, either. There's really nothing to worry about."

Video continued walking, growling through her teeth. She hadn't responded immediately, making Radio hope that perhaps she was put at ease by Pictures' words, but then the giant tabby shook her head and responded, "Nothing to worry about? We need to get this done faster than the estimated time. There is no time for playing around or making excuses when the Kingdom is crumbling around us in chaos! Whether the trouble is there or not by us taking our time, the followers in our land don't know for sure, and neither do we."

That seemed like a bit of a stretch in Radio's view. "Most of Social Media doesn't even know what happened yet, besides hearing the alarms," Radio mumbled out, her ears flat against her head. The tabby's mood had changed as soon as Radio and Pictures requested to stop and rest at sunset. When they insisted, the professional attitude soured quickly. Video had been complaining about their lack of responsibility since.

"Oh, of course. That excuses it all, then, My Lady?" Video's words pierced through Radio. "It's only reasonable that we take our time gathering the only lead the Council has right now while this chaotic creature runs around free, terrorizing Media's followers. Bringing back the King may be a lead in itself to finding this monster if the other couriers and monitors have no luck. We need to get this done so we can bring this savage to justice, and sentence it to death." Video stomped her foot, and then further exclaimed, "Just because we may be the youngest in our classes doesn't excuse us to lie about!" She stormed down the valley.

Radio and Pictures watched her go for a moment, and then glanced at each other to see the shock on the other's face. Their ears both flattened simultaneously, and they hesitantly followed the brown tabby.

For most of the morning, Radio thought the large cat was being sensitive and overtired from the lack of sleep, but the broad tabby brought out good points. Was Video right about all of it, though? Radio didn't think of herself as sluffing off for simply wanting to rest her paws. Tape and Recorder had assured them no other sighting had happened with this primate, and yet, Video was sure the mage was out terrorizing others. They were barely given a deadline, too, which was another reason why her hurry made little sense. All of the tabby's words were concerning, really, but Radio blinked away her thoughts, and caught up to Video, with Pictures following behind. She thought back to the lack of sleep. Video probably hadn't slept at all the night before, and was just venting. Likely, Video was not thinking about the entire situation as a whole.

The three reached the peak of the hill they had climbed, far into the slopes and inclines of the valleys below the Capital City now. They looked down into the woodland territories that awaited them, and continued forward.

Video led them down the path, with the two following close behind. Radio looked around the woods in awe. She had only read about the forests in books, although she had been lucky enough to see the seemingly endless trees as her family's carriage drove past them when her parents would take her to Aureate City as a kitten, but she had never gone inside the woods.

Her paws crunched the twigs and leaves from under her. Her tail snagged on the brush above her. She watched as Pictures and Video moved through the forest silently and effortlessly. Video especially astounded her with the giant cat's size and long fur. Radio quickly bounded forward, trying to imitate their movements of weaving through the branches and growth.

She nearly bumped directly into Pictures when the two suddenly stopped, Video lifting her head. "We should split up and hunt. We can meet back once we've all found something to eat," Video spoke quietly, her ears already tilting back and forth, as though listening for any noise.

This astounded Radio even more than the woodlands itself, as Video just had been throwing a fit about breaks. Radio had not "hunted" once before in her life, let alone roamed around in the forest alone! She looked over at Pictures pleadingly, who quickly chirped, "I'll take Radio with me. We'll hunt better together."

"So be it," Video rumbled. Without any hesitation, she turned from Radio and Pictures, and then leapt away. Radio watched as the giant tabby advanced into the heart of the forest, and disappeared within heartbeats into the thick brush. She frowned, and then blinked up at Pictures.

He smiled at her, and then started forward. "Come on, it won't be that bad," he chuckled, leading Radio to the outskirts of the forest instead. "Hunting is just listening, finding, and pouncing." The tom lifted up his paw, and spoke firmly. "Strike with precision. Make sure your prey doesn't see you. Extend your claws once you pounce to catch your meal, and that'll hold it in place as you dig in." He bounded forward, and looked around, his ears turned up and tilting with attentiveness. "We'll find something over here, as you often will run into bigger things when you go into the deeper parts in the forest."

Radio swallowed nervously, and nodded, following Pictures as silently as possible. After what only seemed a moment, Pictures stopped, lifting up his tail to halt her. Radio followed his gaze when it turned past the trees in front of her. She blinked, her eyes rounding when she saw he had pointed out a small mouse with his nose. Her tail quivered with excitement, and she grinned up at Pictures.

Pictures smiled and nodded to her, and then slowly crouched down. Radio watched as he steadied his paws and readied for the attack. She held back a gasp as he silently leapt forward, pouncing on the mouse and snapping its neck with one bite. The tom tossed it up and then flung it to her with his paw. The mouse landed square between her feet as she stared at Pictures in awe, and she quickly picked it up in her jaws and followed him as he continued on into the forest.

Finally, he spoke again, rumbling quietly, "Once you have a knack for catching prey, you can set your eyes for the bigger ones who fight back." They slunk through the brush. His tail was waving as they drew closer to a noise being heard above their heads. Moments later, Radio realized the source of the sound. She spotted the noisy squirrel munching on the nuts from the tree both cats saw it perched on, completely unaware of the hunters watching below. Radio smiled with delight at the idea of catching something that big someday, and looked back to Pictures.

The silver tom slowly snuck up on the smaller animal, moving silently along on the forest floor. Radio's smile widened when she saw the tom cat's eyes dilate as he drew closer and closer to the squirrel, almost completely taking up his multi-colored eyes. She couldn't help but let out a squeal of excitement through the fur of the mouse she held in her jaws when he leapt up and watched as he grabbed the squirrel right off of the branch. The silver tabby flung the bushy tailed animal against the trunk of the large tree. Radio stared with wide eyes as he then quickly caught it and killed it.

She ran over, purring in excitement at the catch, but put down the mouse to speak to the silver tom. "Pictures, that was amazing! You did just great!" She sniffed the squirrel held in his jaws, and licked her lips. "I can't believe you did that so easily!" She dipped her head in respect for him before she picked up the mouse again.

Pictures smiled at her, chuckling through the squirrel's fur, and mumbled, "Thank you. Let's get back to Video now." His tail brushed along the top of her head affectionately, making her purr louder. He led the young noble back into the forest toward the direction Video had gone, his tail giving a small sway forward to let Radio know she should stay close.

Radio followed along with her tail high in the air, enjoying the delicious smell of the prey in their jaws. She knew it was also the comfortable silence of traveling and being together without the chastisement and judgment of the large courier, Video. Radio respected the strong feline and understood the young female's concern, but learning how to hunt with Pictures was by far more enjoyable. It took all of the worry right off her shoulders about the mission. *This* was a good pace to keep.

She thought the peaceful moment would last, but then they smelled blood. Pictures walked more cautiously until they came across a slain quail in the clearing. The rib cage was ripped open on the bird. The guts of the avian were emptied out and spilled onto the forest floor. Radio looked at the scene and felt a sense of dread. The rest of the meat was eaten, at least. She looked at Pictures, who only blinked at her and continued to follow Video's trail.

It wasn't long before they smelled more blood. Pictures stopped. Radio gazed past him to see Video standing over a flattened bush with another quail. Radio's eyes rounded seeing the split eggs underneath the giant cat's paws, realizing the quail they had come across had probably been guarding the nest. Video stared at them over her shoulder and then dipped down to lap up the eggs. "I see you both found your meals to eat before we continue."

Radio blinked and nodded. Video licked her lips and looked back up as a flying bot hovered though the trees' branches and idled in front of them. "Miss Radio, Video, and Pictures, sir!" Radio recognized the voice of Tape through the flying mechanical apparatus. "We've received an update!" Radio was relieved to hear the excitement in his voice.

"Good. You may give the report," Video responded as she ripped open the hen's chest. Radio sighed and could see the ever efficient feline planned to multi-task, both eating and listening to the report at the same time.

It was Recorder who spoke through the device next. "We just received a report there is a shard in the woods you now travel through. It was located close to a small critter village not far to the east from you. We know one of the leaders there speaks cat, so you might be able to ask her some questions."

Radio was surprised to hear that. She had thought only her servants and castle folk ever learned cat. The idea that a small secluded village had a speaker, leader or not, astounded her once again. She thought how foolish it was of her not to realize the impact her own species really had on the land! Her aunt, Studio Star, leader of Aureate City, was more amazing than she thought. She brightened with excitement to hear more, coming over to the bot she would otherwise have found obtrusive when she heard Tape speak again. "The stoat leader has been making many incident reports as of the last few weeks, though, so be cautious, be it of her, or whatever it is that concerns her!" Tape sounded frightened, but then Recorder elaborated, "We're not sure...perhaps it's a mistranslation of her worries, or perhaps it's all something she's imagining."

Radio rolled her eyes at the very idea of a village leader being delusional, and put down the mouse. "Thank you for letting us know, you two. We'll take it into consideration and see what we can find."

After the two agreed, Pictures put down his squirrel as well so his voice was clearly understood. "Let us know if you find out anything more."

"Will do!" Tape and Recorder mewled in unison through the microphone, and the bot flew away.

Video didn't waste a heartbeat. "We should get moving now that we have a basis for a location. Eat your meals quickly. I've delivered to this village before, and know where it is." She growled as she ripped the organs out from the quail and dug her fangs into the meat. Both Pictures and Radio sighed before starting into their meal, too.

Once the three finished, Video led the two through the forest, moving through it with familiarity, and as always, ease. Radio walked side by side with Pictures, their flanks brushing against each other as they followed the larger feline. Video either hadn't noticed, or decided not to find fault with it, as she said nothing as they trekked through the thick brush.

Video bounded past the clearing that led down into a slope, bringing them to tiny village walls, barely above the giant cat's head. Radio grinned at that, looking over at Pictures, who also cracked a smile. The two monitor assistants had said that it was a critter village, but she hadn't imagined the structure to be an actual miniature village. The idea of it made her excited to venture inside the little place, but the smile disappeared when she heard the squeals of the small animals within the walls after Video entered.

She and Pictures rushed forward. Radio was relieved Video had done nothing more than stand in the middle of the clearing. Radio looked around at the village folk as they all quickly disappeared one by one into their burrows, huts, homes, and dens and asked, "Why are they running away from us? You said you've delivered here before, Video…"

"Well, if I may answer, my dear; they're not fleeing from you," a voice claimed from within the trees. Radio thought it would be another feline, the words spoken so fluently in her tongue, but looked up to see a dark form slowly sink down from the thin limb of a branch end. Every hair on her spine rose when she recognized the magician spider monkey from the recordings she had watched in the surveillance room. Here the creature was, outfit and all, standing before them. "I've simply stopped by for a quick snack," the mage cooed, its tail shooting down and unbalancing one of the fleeing chipmunks. The primate watched with blue rimmed eyes as they squealed and scrambled away, and then turned back to look at Video dead in the eye, who had remained completely still except for her bristling fur.

"I want no trouble from any of…" Radio didn't hear the rest of the monkey's words as Video launched herself forward, claws extended at the primate. Both Radio and the mage screeched at her attack. Video attacked the monkey as though the creature was no more than the squirrel Pictures had hunted earlier. She quickly projected herself off from the tree when the mage leapt to a different one, and went to pounce again.

Radio backed up at the larger cat's fearlessness, becoming even more afraid when she could no longer see where the mage had gone after it had jumped into the higher branches of the trees above their heads. Radio bristled, wondering where the monster might attack Video. Immediately after her thought, the brush directly above her head shook with movement. The spider monkey suddenly hung down just a hair away from her face, wide eyed and grinning. "Hello!"

The scream that came from Radio hurt her own ears and stunned the primate, who barely dodged the swipes of Pictures in time when the tom cat leapt between Radio and the mage. He hissed up at the monkey as it pulled back, and growled when the creature perched back up in the trees to glare down at him and Radio. Its piercing stare struck fear into Radio's core, feeling cold as the primate stared into her blue eyes with anger.

She couldn't move. There was a loathing beyond what she could comprehend in the mage's eyes, hating her for reasons which had existed long before she was even born. She could barely form a noise of fear upon becoming frozen by the Jester's glare and clenched jaw, which had been a smile only a few moments ago. Why did she have to be responsible for the madness, pain, and loss her ancestors had caused? All she could hope was somehow she reflected a plea for mercy and shame in her eyes to the mage before Video once again clawed her way up the tree and went to attack. The monkey broke eye contact and leapt away, jumping past Radio into the low branches which could hold the mage's weight, with Video following behind.

Radio quickly snapped back into reality when she heard Video was travelling out of earshot, realizing the primate was luring the large feline away on purpose. She whipped around, bolting past Pictures. "Video! No! Don't follow it!" She quickly chased after the two, terrified she'd lose Video. "Video! Please, *stop!*" she shouted as she saw the tabby jump from tree to tree, relieved when the majestic feline halted at her plea.

She could only shake her head once Video looked down at her, quickly trying to release the words coherently that had been lodged in the back of her throat as they fumbled and tumbled out now. "This mage is responsible for making our lordship disappear within one evening and throwing the land into chaos, just like you said. If you leave us, you're not coming back! It'll just continue the attack, and you won't win against anything with that much power. We can't take any chances that could risk our safety in such a way," she huffed, dipping her head down. The monkey was doing no more than playing a game with them. Thinking of the sparring the tom had engaged in while at the castle with the avian, she hoped Pictures wouldn't instigate anything because of this, as the tom was already looking irritably up at Video when the feline remained standing on the branch.

Video blinked at them both, and then climbed down from the tree and bounded to them. She didn't even glance at Pictures as she dipped her head to Radio respectfully, her ears flat against her head before she looked back up in the trees where the primate had fled. Radio was grateful that the headstrong feline could even muster a thanks to her, having expected a rebuke instead. She looked to Pictures, and frowned as he turned his head away from the both of them, the only sign of concern being his lashing tail coming to rest against his smaller companion's flank. He was probably just shook up, too, she realized.

Radio sighed, but her ears tilted to the sound of more movement behind them. She turned to see that some of the critters of the village had come out from the city walls, all of their eyes gazing at the small clowder of cats. A stoat was in front of them all, her stature and alertness reminding Radio of her stoat servant, Stella, at home. Yet Radio knew this individual was likely the village leader, and deserved no such comparison.

"You saved us from the Gatherer!" her voice rang out, and the village folk chattered amongst themselves and to her excitedly. Radio smiled, but Video stepped forward, once again serious. The stoat looked up at the giant cat, round-eyed, and only blinked as Video said, "We need answers, Madam Faith. You and your village know this strange being?"

The stoat looked from Video to Radio and Pictures, and then back at her villagers before she turned to Video again. "We do, Miss Video. Please, all three of you." She turned to look at Radio and Pictures. "Come inside. I'll tell you what I've seen, if that's why you're here."

"Actually, madam, we're only…" Pictures started, but Radio and Video both shot him a look, and Radio walked forward. She wasn't going to pass up a chance to learn more, not when the coast was clear now. "We're glad we might be able to take care of this. Please, tell us what you know, Madam Faith."

Radio was relieved Pictures didn't say anything more after the stoat nodded. She and Pictures followed the leader and Video as the two walked inside the village with the rest of the folk. The village was quite adorable,

Radio had to admit to herself, but she couldn't yet muster a smile after seeing the Jester in person. She walked solemnly with her two companions and the stoat leader, Faith, but enjoyed seeing all of the mice, bunnies, and birds flutter and move through the village in peace and without fear of her and her companions with the stoat leader's guidance. Radio looked to the small critter and Video, who walked with each other like they could be longtime friends. This surprised Radio, as it was likely Video had seen no more than two solstices in her lifetime.

Both Video and Radio looked to the leader as she spoke. The stoat's voice was firm and solemn as she explained, "The Gatherer has been terrorizing and tormenting my villagers for over a moon cycle now, picking us off as though it was no better than a common predator, Miss Video. It's been very concerning to us." The stoat led them to a small den, and let Radio and Pictures slip inside first, before she followed. The three looked back behind them to see Video bump her head against the opening of the den, and wrinkle her nose as dirt sprinkled down on her muzzle. The stoat smiled at her, but looked surprised, making Radio wonder if the stoat knew Video since the large feline was a kit, and might have been able to fit inside the abode at one time. Video sighed and sat down outside the den, her ears tilting toward the opening so she could listen as well. Radio looked at the cozy home of the den, wondering how many families possibly had lived in it before now. The very idea brought Radio's thoughts back to the quail family that Video had slain, not giving a thought to the generations that could have carried on if she had only taken the first quail. Radio hesitantly looked back at the stoat as she sat down with Pictures.

Pictures blinked at her and crouched down, folding his paws

underneath himself. She gave a smile, but wouldn't take her eyes off of Faith. Pictures turned to listen to the stoat leader as well, and the smaller animal looked to Video, who gave a nod from outside the den. She dipped her head to the three respectively before she began her story, her voice strong and clear. "It started when we hired a new recruit for our guardians. The boldest of rats guarded and defended us from harm, keeping out any intruders from entering this village, but we were always looking for more help. The recruit was incredibly strong. He seemed to have been well meaning and appeared to have good purpose in coming here, so the guards and I allowed him into our village." Faith then furrowed her brow. "It seemed like everything was going well. The guardians bonded with him quickly, but within a few weeks, the guardians began to have disputes and arguments with each other. Some of the dissension had become so serious, factions within the same unit wouldn't speak to each other, even after returning to the village. Both I and the new recruit tried to reason with them together, since I saw his concern and thought he wanted to help, but it seems the rat had different stories when I wasn't there, and was, in actuality, the one who had been responsible for turning my guards against each other."

Radio's eyes rounded, and she frowned at the very idea. The stoat sighed and continued, "It only got worse from there. The guards started disappearing. It wasn't for days until we all put together the details and realized that we were only losing the unit when they were traveling with the recruit. It was absolutely bizarre. When the remaining guardians approached me, I advised them to work together to stop this strange rat that pitted them against each other, but some of their bitter feelings were still there. I don't know what the Gatherer had convinced them of, but instead of working together, they went separate paths to try and defeat the foe themselves, which led to the downfall of them all."

Video's tail thumped against the ground upon hearing the last words, and the stoat dipped her head before looking back up at Radio and Pictures, who listened, shocked and intent upon hearing the rest of the story as she furthered, "Upon approaching the recruit, the rat transformed into a large black-furred animal with a hairless face, the one you saw earlier. I followed my guards once, seeing their trails all went on separate paths. The magician spoke to me from there, claiming it was my guard's weakness and the bitterness in their hearts that caused this to be their fate. He took them all away, leaving us defenseless against the forest threats since."

Radio tried not to speak or ask questions, knowing the stoat was sharing as much as she could, but her mind was reeling at the idea of the magician taking the form of a rat just to test these tiny villagers. The primate had taken the King away from the entire region, and yet only weeks prior to this, it had chosen to spend its time fooling around with the tiniest of villages? Faith referred to the mage as a "he," but such a thing, a mage, was no person at all if it was capable of this. Her tail tip flicked in anticipation to hear more, and looked over to see the reactions of her companions. Pictures looked just as intrigued as her, from what she could see in the corner of her vision. She was surprised Video managed to keep such a calm expression, listening patiently and scanning the area outside, all after she had so impulsively attacked and then chased after the Jester before.

Radio turned back to Faith as the stoat continued, "After that, what we formerly knew as our recruit continued to return in this new form, slowly picking off my smaller and weaker villagers, gathering them to be taken to the caves inside the forest. It was done with ease, since we were without our guardians to protect us. I've only ever received a laugh upon my questioning, and my attempts at negotiating with the creature." Her voice then grew quieter. "And I've never been able to get a response from the Capital other than to receive simple dismissals of my fear. I wasn't sure where I was going to go from here, until I saw you again, Miss Video."

Video blinked, then turned to the stoat leader and nodded, announcing, "We're here to help you, Madam Faith. My companions and I were here under other business concerning this Gatherer. We'll see what we can do to stop this monster by getting news back to the Capital." The tabby feline rose to her paws. "However, our main objective is currently retrieving some of the work the mage has left behind. Have any of your villagers seen any red fragments of crystal inside the woods?"

Faith looked surprised, immediately blinking and nodding. The instant response made Radio's heartbeat quicken at the idea they might already find another shard, and she perked up even further as Faith answered, "Yes, one of my sparrows found it when scouting for missing villagers. It's not far from the village, actually. Would you like me to assign a scout to take you there now?"

Video shook her head. "We can do so in the morning. For now, any information you have on the Gatherer is more important, Madam Faith, as the Capital is just as lost as we are when it comes to knowledge about this situation." The brown tabby cat's tail tip flicked with irritation at the admitted ignorance as she resumed scanning the trees above the village, and Faith nodded.

Radio blinked, looking away from the two. As far as Radio was concerned, that wasn't the case. The Capital seemed to have had much more warning than she had originally thought, or had been led to believe, about this mage attack, and yet they continued to put aside the pieces of what they knew and had allowed the attack to happen. Radio was able to accept the concept of the primate successfully having snuck into the castle, but Faith could easily have told them about a shapeshifting mage if they allowed her to speak, even in allowing the reports she sent to be accepted. Perhaps this was why the mage decided to attack the smaller villagers, so that it could hone its magic and practice without ever catching the attention of the Capital officials. Maybe this was all deliberate! Did the Capital want the King gone? They surely hadn't done much to prevent it.

"I disagree, we should go tonight, before the mage comes back," Pictures objected to Video's suggestion. It was now his turn to give his tail an irritated flick. He looked at Faith. "Did the sorcerer slay the rest of the guardians that protected you, Madam Faith?" Pictures asked as he stood, the concern tinged in his tone.

Faith shook her head, making Radio blink up hopefully, until she answered, "When my guardians were taken away, they were bound under a curse in the caverns west of our village. The magician told me they were sealed in the heart of the chasm, forever bound to one another to pay for their unit's division." The stoat's voice shook at her own words, and she looked away from the felines.

Video frowned, her eyes shining with sympathy. It was probably the quietest Radio had heard the bold cat speak when she dipped her head. "We can head out now then." Her paw pressed against the earth firmly. "Once we are taken to the shard, could you bring me to the cavern? I'd at least like to see what I can find to report to the Council, if you would be able to take me there."

"We'll come, too," Radio spoke up, getting to her feet as well. She realized Pictures was going to say something, but she still continued when it didn't look like he was going to interrupt her, saying, "This isn't something anyone should face alone. It's also the least we can do after all your attempts to reach Media's officials, Madam. We'll do anything we can to help." Perhaps if she called the surveillance office, they could trail the mage and make sure that it wasn't near the area. It would be logical to help the village leader upon seeing the danger themselves. This wasn't something they could neglect.

The stoat leader looked at Radio with surprise and appreciation, nodding to both her and Video. "Alright," Faith replied. "I will take you to both the shard and the cavern. Thank you all so much."

Radio smiled, nodding for the smaller animal to stand. The stoat led them out of the cozy home. Radio glanced over at Pictures, and saw he was displeased. She realized she had just offered his services and had committed him to come along without even asking him. Her eyes rounded with horror, looking up at him as he scowled at her. "Oh, I...I didn't mean to offer on your behalf, I..." her words faltered, knowing there really wasn't any way she could take it back with the stoat relying on them so much to get the Capital's help. How could he have expected her to offer anything less when the village so obviously needed it?

Pictures only glared down at her before he walked past to catch up with

Video and Faith. Radio sighed, looking down. She just had met these cats and yet she had already irritated Video by her complaining earlier; now she had offered Pictures' help, with him becoming involved with something he didn't want.

Radio remained silent as Faith brought them through the woods. Radio hoped neither Video nor Faith would notice Pictures' change in attitude. She blinked to adjust her eyes to the darkening sky, the plasma threads surrounding Media just starting to materialize, and then focused her sight ahead to see the faint red glow of the shard in the distance.

Just as they sped up to reach it, Radio's ears pricked to the noise of the propellers that carried the gadget Tape and Recorder had used to speak to them before. She slowed her pace, letting herself fall behind the group as the surveillance bot hovered lower. She let them carry on as she listened to the message. Without waiting a single heartbeat, Recorder began to chatter excitedly, exclaiming, "You three are very close to the signal we're getting from our radar!" Her purr was audible through the mic, making Radio grin.

"Yes, we're being brought to it now. Do you have any other news?" Radio asked.

"We do, which is why we're here," Recorder started, but Tape continued, "The next shard's location was detected just outside the Ruined City, near the old residential streets!" He spoke loudly, making Radio's ears ring from the noise of the speaker, but the audio had been just loud enough for Pictures to hear, who backed up and came back over to Radio and the floating device, seeming intrigued.

Recorder explained before Radio could ask about his piqued interest, stating, "Pictures has worked directly inside those areas for his scouting work. He'll be able to get there with no problem. Video may have also had work there."

Pictures shook his head. "Usually it's not advised to enter the city unless being directed to by the Council, so it's very unlikely, taking her age into consideration. We'll head there as soon as we retrieve this second shard, under your direction."

"Yes, please do!" both Recorder and Tape mewled.

Radio smiled, beaming with excitement at the idea they already had the next destination. "We've got this. Good work, team! We appreciate all your help."

"But, of course! Be careful out there!" the two chirped back. Pictures and Radio both watched the bot leave before they turned to catch up with Video and Faith. He didn't seem as bothered now. Radio hoped returning to an old workplace might make it easier for him to handle going into the cavern. She gave the tom a chirp, and looked ahead to Video and Faith as they drew closer to the shard.

The two earth-colored animals approached the object together, with Radio and Pictures coming up beside them. The four all stared down at the miraculous artifact, their eyes round. The red glow was incomparable to any of the technology and gadgets Radio had ever seen, and she could only guess it was the same for her companions. Even its warmth seemed unusual, giving off strength Radio could feel as she stood near it. She watched as Video dipped down to pull it from the ground, carefully fixing her jaws around the sharp edges so as not to cut her mouth. Radio looked to see how surprised Faith was, and wondered if her workers were burnt trying to touch it, too. The fragment pulled out of the ground with a simple jerk from the large feline, and Video pocketed it into her bag.

"Please, if you may now, Madam Faith, take us to the caverns." Video nodded to the smaller mammal, and Faith dipped her head in acquiescence. Radio hurried past Pictures at seeing the two begin to move, and followed beside Video as the stoat brought them through the forest. She kept her eyes fixed on the woods around her, seeing how different the area looked when it was lit by the setting sun rather than a bright afternoon. Even with the light of the sun and barrier still reflecting onto the leaves and brush around the group, Radio wished that she and Pictures had made the time to ask the surveillance group where the mage might be. The further they traveled into the woods, the more it felt like she was being watched. That alone made Radio's paws feel heavier. What if the Jester was among them right now? Be it the form they knew, here in the woods, or...

What if he were to shapeshift into something smaller to follow them without detection? Radio could almost believe it could be one of the three travelling with her, if they had left each other's sides, but ever since the attack, they had stayed together. Who knew what power the Jester had! Radio kept her eyes wide open for any sign of movement.

There was nothing but woodland animals heading towards their dens for sleep, though. The longer they traveled, the more Radio figured she was just imagining it. Pictures didn't look the slightest bit concerned when Radio made sure to glance at him over her shoulder. Video and Faith were too intent on the path to notice anything else. Their lack of concern comforted Radio, so she instead focused her thoughts back on the venture to the mysterious cavern. She was glad that it was still warm enough from the day so the night breeze wasn't overwhelming. Nonetheless, the sun set quickly, much too soon after Recorder and Tape's device left, leaving them in darkness once they arrived at the cavern.

They approached the opening to the giant cave through the mountain, and Faith led them inside. Radio tried to take in the sights of the cavern, amazed at the space and size of the area as they moved further inside, but the unsettling feeling failed to vanquish itself. Her ears strained to hear what Video did, once the giant tabby's ears pricked forward. A moment later, Radio felt a chill run down her spine. She heard the noises of rats, and had to hold back a whimper of fear.

"Their words...they're incomprehensible." Faith spoke up, looking shocked as Video led her closer to the noisy commotion. "I've never heard anything like it."

Radio swallowed nervously, not liking the sound of the stoat leader's words any more than the noise itself. No one knew these former guards better than their leader did, and yet the respected leader walked stiffly and unsure in front of both Radio and Pictures. The stoat might not have moved at all if Video's tail had not guided her along. The very idea made Radio take a deep breath, holding it in for as long as she could before slowly releasing it. Faith's uncertainty couldn't mean anything good, but they needed to assess the situation. If the Jester wasn't there, perhaps Video might even insist there was a chance at rescuing the guardians.

The feathery feline took every pace slowly and deliberately as the sounds and noises grew decidedly louder. She pressed herself against Video in fear as the giant tabby prowled forward without hesitation. Radio instead tried to focus her thoughts on how brave the feline was. It was commendable that although the youngest courier was assigned for this mission, Radio couldn't possibly ask for a better courier to travel with her as a companion. She hoped by the end of this mission, she would have them think the same of her. *If we survive this...* Radio's chest tightened as they reached a stop, like a plateaued landing, in the cavern. Perhaps she was thinking too far ahead.

A ledge came up quickly. The stone surface was shining brightly from the moonlight piercing through an opening above, making it quite hard to miss. Radio was afraid of it at first, pressing even more against Video, but curiosity got the best of her. She walked forward and looked ahead to see the ground dropped down into the dark curvature of a pit below the ledge. What was more horrifying than the drop itself was the mangled, twisted rats, writhing and spitting at the bottom. Radio's eyes rounded at the sight, seeing their tails were tied and bound together, clumped with waste, dirt, and decay. Radio grit her teeth and held her breath as she stepped back again, struggling not to breathe when the terrible smell of the prison made her stomach turn.

She wanted to stop Faith from going forward when the stoat slid past her, but could only try her best not to mewl out loud for the honorable leader to come back as the small animal cried out in pain at seeing her guards. "My guardians! Oh, my protectors, what has happened to you?" she whispered, her horrified and forlorn voice echoing through the pit. Radio and Video both watched as the stoat's head dropped in despair, looking down at her former villagers.

Radio was startled upon feeling another presence, and looked up to hear the dark voice echoing through the cavern. "You knew my intention, and yet you still act surprised when you see the scene before you. It's foolish of you, Faith." From the other side of the pit, the clothed primate stepped out, the bells on his jester outfit twinkling and shining in the moonlight that gleamed down into the pit. His eyes glowed cyan in the darkness of the cavern. Radio watched as he dug his nails into the pillar that was wedged between the two sides of the area.

Radio felt Video tense beside her. The noble looked up at the tabby's glaring sienna eyes, the orange hue appearing more saturated and bright in the moonlight. Almost as though Radio had cued her, Video crouched to attack, and Radio slammed her paw onto the giant cat's own claws. "Just stop for a moment! We can't strike yet, it is waiting for you," Radio growled through her teeth, and looked over at Faith, who hadn't taken her eyes off of the rats below them, and then looked at Pictures, who watched from behind.

Faith spoke quietly to Video and Radio, murmuring, "Look at their eyes. They have the same glow as the Gatherer, but the blue has spread through their entire irides." Her muzzle pointed down into the pit. Radio followed her gaze back to the animals below. With a better look, Radio knew what the stoat was talking about, and saw how the unit's eyes were glazed with a misty cyan. It made Radio's fur rise along the back of her neck. She listened to Faith's stilted words as the stoat choked out, "This spiteful magician has turned them all into a single-minded beast, without any memory of what they once were. These are not—this is not...my village's guardians."

Radio's eyes rounded at the very thought. The idea of no longer being the same as you once were, with just a flicker of magic in the eyes, was terrible to even conceptualize. She couldn't imagine what the stoat leader was feeling, having known these rats individually, before the Jester had cursed them into this strange form. She looked back at Video, who was glaring at the Jester as it perched on the pillar, grinning.

The two locked their stares at each other. Radio screeched and hurried forward to stop Video, anticipating her attack again. It was too late. She wasn't quick enough to stop Video this time. She skidded to a halt as the tabby jumped over her effortlessly, and whipped around to see Video land on the pillar with grace and power. The primate lifted up its chin when the giant cat hissed at the monkey warningly, pressing her paws down on the pillar. "The fact you did this even before taking our King away is horrific! What you plan for Media must be abominable if you find *this* something to smile over, monster! These were individuals who wanted no more than to protect the ones they loved!" *Oh, that's right*...Radio had only realized with the words Video had just spoken these rats had likely been villagers Video had known. Radio's eyes rounded with sadness for her companion.

The mage had a different reaction. It didn't seem pleased by the tabby's words, its teeth baring as the smile disappeared from its face. "As though you have the right to speak about such actions. Like it hadn't been any different for *my* kind—the lines of families and blood you couriers and titled folk destroyed. Don't even *jest.*" The monkey lifted up its chin and glared down at Video. Its blue rimmed eyes shone as bright as its outfit in the moonlight. The primate smashed its hand down on the pillar to crack it, making the part where Video stood crumble.

Radio screamed as she watched Video lose her footing against the crumbling earth and fall. "Video, no!" She ran to the ledge, watching as Video dropped directly into the pit of rats. All she could do was bury her face into her paws, unable to watch as her new companion was torn apart. It was only Pictures' hoot of surprise that made her open them again.

She gasped as she turned to gaze down and see Video fighting back against the snarling and hissing rats attacking her, not a flicker of fear in the giant cat's eyes as she defended herself against the monstrosity that surrounded her.

The tabby's thick fur kept most of the initial attacks from piercing her skin. She was able to take out the first few rats quickly that leapt for her, using paws, claws, and teeth to take them down. Radio couldn't believe the feline was capable of such speed and strength. She drove her fangs down into their necks and sliced her claws across their throats effortlessly, making the rats fall limp one by one. Video fought with all her might as the group above could only stare down in shock, including the mage. The primate closed its gaping mouth, and slowly turned its gaze over to both Radio and Faith, approaching them until Pictures stepped forward in front of them, and glared at the monkey.

Radio backed away until she was comfortably behind Pictures, but glanced back down to see how Video was faring. Only being able to see glimpses of the feline's tail and the whipping of mangled rats against the walls of the pit, Radio turned her gaze back to the dark clothed animal, who seemed to be getting more and more irate. Radio jumped back when she saw black static splice across the Jester's outfit for an instant as the mage narrowed its eyes in anger. She sank down to the ground when the glare fixed upon her again.

The squeals of the rats ceased. The only noise left below was Video's panting and growling. The mage stomped its foot again, barking down at the giant cat, but quickly whipped itself back as Video charged up in another attempt to attack. The monkey leapt amidst Radio, Pictures, and Faith, making Radio grit her teeth to hold back from screaming again. Faith, however, launched herself at the primate and bit into the back of its neck, even as Video stormed toward them. The monkey screeched at Faith's avenging attack, and split apart into black, fractured shadows. The stoat dropped back to the ground as the mage disappeared and reformulated on the other side of the pit. It continued with another screech, this one sounding more offended and upset than panicked.

Video's bloodstained paws skidded against the ledge's ground to stop herself from crashing into the group. She whipped around to face the monkey when she heard its shout.

The mage's eyes pierced directly into Radio and Video's own. "You won't be so easily pardoned for what you've done here tonight. I do not take kindly to my work being destroyed, *pests!*" The primate barked once more before disappearing into the higher tunnels of the cavern.

Radio felt her paws shake from fear, but Pictures' tail pressed against her flank. She looked up into his blue and golden eyes as he nodded to her. "You did well," he whispered, smiling down at her before he turned to leave the cavern.

Video limped forward, collapsing down on her paws before she forced herself to get back up, staggering forward. Radio looked down at her battleworn companion and noticed the bag and strap fastened to her had also taken hits from the rats, and had been damaged, but still held the two shards securely. The stench of blood and death seemed to saturate into and emit out like a visible aura from every hair of the feline's pelt. Radio frowned as she realized the pain seemed to set in for the giant feline now the emotional rush of attacking the Jester was gone.

"We need to continue...and get out of here," Video growled. Radio and Faith both stepped over to either side of her to help guide her out of the dark area.

The four walked together back to the village. Radio closed her eyes, and tried not to think of the stench of her companion's fur that both she and Faith smelled as they pressed themselves against the tabby, knowing the feline had killed the former protectors of the leader's village, individuals who were once sentient and kind and that Video had likely once known. Video would likely have to clean herself for hours to get the smell out of her coat, and the entire village would know the fate of the former guards. Radio knew she couldn't talk to Faith about what happened, because while the stoat went to help Video immediately, the shock and terror of the scene still shone in the small leader's eyes.

When they finally arrived in the village, Video dropped onto her paws and breathed out, the sound harsh and painful. Radio looked over at the stoat leader then, curious as to what was next. That was when Faith got to work. Within one chatter, three other critters came running out of their huts with supplies and aid, beginning to work on Video to bandage her and clean her, their eyes wide at the sight.

Radio smiled at the loyalty and lack of hesitancy the folk showed under their leader's command, and walked over to Pictures. Since he looked at her with no ill expression, she smiled and sat down beside him, looking at the view of the village as they idled against the walls of the small structure.

"Thank you for protecting us, Pictures," Radio murmured,

acknowledging he had stood between her and Faith against the mage when Video could not.

"I just want you safe, Miss Radio. It was a giant risk to go into the cavern like that, you know." The tom looked down at her. "We can't have any harm come to us on this mission; you can't get hurt, Radio."

Radio nodded, resting her head on his shoulder. "I know. I'm sorry." Her murmur was barely above a whisper as she relaxed from the warmth of his side, and was grateful he only nodded and turned his gaze back to the village.

Pictures was only silent for a moment, however. "We're going to have to be more careful for the rest of this journey," he furthered.

Radio managed a small smile, and nodded again. "Alright, Pictures." She hoped her soft purr was not detected from her hearing the caring concern in his voice.

They sat together in silence for a while, but Radio's thoughts seemed loud and unfocused. They kept being brought back to the cavern, seeing the monster that had once been many individuals. She thought of the King, and whatever the monkey might have done to him, then the quest they were on together. She still wasn't sure what everything was about, all because she never finished reading the files.

She looked up at Pictures, and asked, "Why are we doing this, Pictures? Why us?"

Pictures stared down at her knowingly, and Radio saw he was aware she hadn't read the reports. He sighed and answered, "The message said that three individuals, the youngest courier, noble, and monitor, are to unite together in order to recover and deliver the broken shards to the Council, at which time the youngest member of their governing body will restore the heart. The action will bring back the King by doing so, proving even the most incompetent of the verified can succeed in gaining favor from the mages."

Radio scoffed, but held her tongue as Pictures continued, "The three must stay together to keep their hearts strong on their journey. If the heart of one breaks like the glass heart they've been sent to collect, and they fail to prioritize the mission, everything may be lost. This would cause Satisfaction's curse to continue for another generation, unless the Queen herself takes mercy upon Media." His brow furrowed at the last sentence, and he looked down at Radio with an intense expression on his face.

"O-oh," Radio stammered and swallowed, and then nodded in thanks. She was glad he said nothing more and turned his gaze back to the village, as every hair on her pelt was already on end again. That sounded terrifying! Yet Pictures managed to recite it without fear. She felt her heart pound, but knew she needed to keep calm as not to put Video back on high alert. The large tabby was unaware of Radio's irresponsibility when starting the mission. The details were just bizarre, though. Cassette only brought up that the three were chosen because they were the youngest in their respective classes, but hadn't given the reason as to why.

"It said that in the reports?" Radio asked.

Pictures blinked. "In the digital ones, yes. I'm not sure if Video received the same copy, but by her attitude, it's likely."

Radio nodded at that, and settled. They sat together until the care workers backed away from Video, who now rose up to her feet. Radio looked over at the glittering night sky beyond the trees, and then back at

Video. "Will we be looking for a place to sleep so you can heal?"

"No. There's no time for that," Video scowled, and began limping out of the village.

Radio blinked, and gawked at the tabby. They had just faced off with the mage itself. She had directly combated the cursed individuals. The giant cat had faced the fused beast alone, received another shard, helped an entire village, and she still didn't want to sleep!? The more Radio thought about it, the less it made sense! At least it hadn't, until the curse of Satisfaction rushed back to Radio's thoughts. She looked to Pictures, who only shrugged and followed after Video. Radio was left to stare wide-eyed in disbelief. She scrambled to follow them once realizing they had no intention of waiting for her, but ran over to Faith first.

The stoat blinked up at Radio and gave a weak smile. "Thank you, Miss Radio. We appreciate and are honored by your presence here as the Radio Star." Faith bowed, her round ears flat against her head. "On this day, your people still help us end the terror of these cruelly powered creatures. I'm very grateful for that." The stoat looked up at Radio, her eyes glittering with tears from the loss of her guardians.

From the stoat's words, Radio realized this was not the first time the village had suffered from the ill intent of a mage. She held back a shudder after having witnessed the capability of malice from just one mage, and quickly replied, "I'm glad we could be of service to you." *And put their suffering to an end.* Radio nuzzled Faith in farewell, resting her head on the smaller mammal's own before she stepped back, and bolted away.

"Take care!" Radio called out before catching up with the other felines. She quickly ran out past the walls that defended the folk, letting the village close their gates as she and her companions moved on through the woodlands to their next objective.

Two shards down. Radio wasn't sure how many more were to go, but they were formidably sized fragments. Her gaze turned to the limping form of Video ahead, who pressed on even though she had been thrown into battle and faced off directly with the Jester, twice in one day, all without sleep during the day, too. Radio felt her eyelids weighing heavily against her eyes as the three of them trekked forward without rest. She could only hope the next find would go better in the Ruined City, and that less blood would have to be shed to accomplish what was needed.

Drums sounded through the city, the crowd slapping their paws excitedly as they all looked above to the Clowder Office where their leader stood.

The Studio Star bounded up excitedly to the edge of the balcony, and leapt onto the railing to exclaim, "We have been blessed! The skies are without a cloud and the sun is rich with the promise of a beautiful day!" She purred in her excitement. "Are you all ready for the Fourth Annual Aureate Festival, my citizens?" Her voice rang out across the crowd as she looked down at the residents of her city.

The felines cheered in joy at her words, purrs heard all the way down the street of the vast, golden city, and Studio laughed with joy.

"This will be the biggest festival yet, my fellow felines! Four days of rejoicing the anniversary of our city, and we won't be letting anything stop us from overcoming this tragedy and showing that traitor we're stronger than ever!"

The crowd cheered again, and Studio grinned, waving her paw out in a flourish. "May the evening begin!" She cheered with the crowd as the clock struck nine, causing confetti and fireworks to scatter across the sky, and waved goodbye as she stepped out of their view.

Studio hopped down from the railing, and sat in the balcony towards the walls. She sorted through papers on her writing table, humming a small tune to herself before she stopped everything. Hearing a noise in the wind, she put the papers down, and walked to the edges of her balcony, blinking as a breeze ruffled her fur. Why did it feel as though...?

She startled at the sudden voice above her. "They say any official even being seen with me will be questioned and can be charged with treason, which is punishable by death."

Studio gasped, and looked up to see the Jester before her very eyes. Both the clothed monkey and Studio looked past the balcony at the dark orb drone that belonged to the monitor, Signal, the only monitor that would report Studio without question. The very idea made Studio's fur stand on end, and she yelled out, "No!"

The lean feline whipped around and snarled at the monkey, but the primate already slipped from sight and sound. Her nose wrinkled as she tried to smell for any scent, but it seemed faint, even though the mage had just been there. Studio shook her pelt and looked down from her balcony at her city, her eyes round as she feared for her people. She swallowed nervously, and then reluctantly went back into the building.

Studio closed the door on the surveillance bot outside, and turned to her silver assistant, a swirled, dappled tabby tomcat with cloth wrapped across his head and around his tail to hide the scars of an attack on his former home. Studio was well aware he knew the dangers of a mage being seen within the walls of the city, and would take the matter to heart. "Screen, write a message. I was just approached by the shapeshifter. I think the monkey has plans against our future festivities. The Council may think we're not going to have to do anything until those shards are found, but we're going up against a villain who's always moving, always planning, and there's no time to be sitting around. I need to get a hold of someone who can help me with this."

"What would you like me to write, My Lady?" The cat turned his wrapped head towards the lean tabby.

"Hmm," Studio hummed. She paused, narrowing her eyes as she thought of someone she could trust with such a task. "I need to get in contact with Film. He'll be able to look through all of the surveillance to prove the innocence of the wrongfully accused." Studio looked out the window, watching the monitor's drone fly out of the city. "I have a feeling there will be a lot of it."

Screen nodded, and flexed his claws in anticipation to write. Studio watched him find the parchment, and went to the other window to look outside the city. "I only can hope my niece finds those shards quickly."

Dear Film,

These unfortunate occurrences involving this "Jester" are becoming dangerous for us. Tonight the mage approached me under the watch of Signal from the Rich Top Mountain Region, and recited the statement sent out by the Council that established being seen in the traitor's presence is considered treason in the eyes of the monitors. I need you to send out more surveillance and make sure no other officials in the Kingdom are being wrongfully accused by this primate's actions under Signal's, or anyone else's, reports and recordings. Please find out everything you can about the confidential words from the Council being leaked, or if someone's working with the Jester inside the Department of Communications or with the ones to whom they sent the messages.

We cannot afford to make mistakes with this, and need to be as watchful as possible, Film. Write back as soon as you immediately can.

Sincerely, the Studio Star, Representative of the Domesticated Species of Felines and Mayor of Clowder City.

- CHAPTER 4 -

INTEGRITY

"Strike with precision, and make sure your prey doesn't see you," Radio whispered quietly to herself.

Pictures' brow arched slowly upon overhearing, and he stared down at Radio. "I see you've taken my words to heart about hunting, Miss Radio, but—"

"Size the prey out, and pinpoint exactly where they are, to range how far you should leap," Radio added, ignoring Pictures and looking at her newly found target. She took a deep breath, and slowly crouched down. "Extend your claws once you pounce to catch your meal, and that'll hold it in place as you dig into it."

Radio wobbled down lower, still trying to walk as best as she could as she stalked Video, who prowled in front of her. She leapt up on her back paws to pounce and bat at the giant tabby's fluffy tail, her delicate white paws making audible thumps as she tried to catch the tips of the feline's long fur.

Video rolled her eyes, but waved her tail a little as she might have for a kitten playing with her. Radio flicked her ears, but didn't let Video's gesture cause her to waver from her mission to catch the tail.

The three had stopped right before dawn to rest. As Video slept with the exhaustion of battle, each one of the party had been able to obtain a decent amount of sleep, and carried on well into the afternoon because of it. Video had been upset at first, but with the newly found energy from all three of them, even she couldn't find much reason to complain. She walked with barely a limp as they continued.

"Size the prey out?" Pictures questioned, and then sighed, his eyes hooding. "Yes, you see your objective is twice your own size, so what will you do when you catch it?" he asked, now beginning to stalk down with her.

"That is a future consequence of which I do not have to worry about at this moment," Radio mumbled. She grinned when she heard the smile in Pictures' voice as he chuckled, and repeatedly thumped against the ground during her landings of bouncing up to bat at Video's tail, really no better than a kitten with a new toy. She couldn't grip the tabby's fur with her paw pads no matter how hard she tried, though, and began leaping up at the giant tail with her claws extended.

"Hmm, Miss Radio, I don't think that's a good idea..." Pictures frowned, and then winced in sympathy for the marbled tabby as all three heard the sound of skin breaking under Radio's claws. Video screeched out loud as Radio pulled back, and then whipped around and hissed at the feathery, collared feline.

Radio jumped back, her tail poofed out and her fur standing on end as she exclaimed, "Oh no! Oh, Video! I am so sorry, I'm really sorry!" She backed up from the giant cat, who only took one more step forward to glare down at her. The stare piercing through her was too much. Radio crouched down to leap, and then burst into a running bolt past Video.

"R-Radio, wait!" Pictures called out, but Radio kept running. She fled down the incline, worried Video would chase after her, but skidded to a halt at the blast of heat and warmth coming from the growth of the forest she approached. The three had been travelling around it all early morning, and had nearly passed its boundary completely, but Radio realized they had reached the corner of the overgrown territory. The sudden change was too substantial for her not to stop. She already needed to, so the two could catch up to her, but the underlying curiosity that had built up was too much to not explore it now, especially since they were at the very end of it.

She was amazed at the humidity and heat from the area inside the thick forest, and how well the vines, moss, and plant life grew within its domain. It looked more like the jungle she had read about in the books in her parents' library than something found in Media. She didn't even notice the two had caught up to her until Pictures spoke.

"You seem quite interested. Haven't you ever travelled this far before, Miss Radio?" Pictures asked. Radio had jumped at his voice behind her, and looked over her shoulder to see him stepping alongside of her, catching his breath.

She shook her head, looking back into the jungle. "I haven't taken a step anywhere near this close. My parents traveled this far with me before, in an open carriage heading to Clowder City, but it had been on one of the warmest days of the year then, too, so I didn't think much of the extra heat. The outskirts of this mass of foliage didn't stick out as much as they do now...I don't think." Radio realized it had been seasons since that trip. She had been so young, she might not have been remembering it correctly.

"No, you're right. It was especially these last two solstices the area expanded." Pictures lifted up his paw to touch one of the hanging vines growing off of the towering trees. "The Council's been trying to take it down, but it only grows back thicker when it's disrupted. They've stopped trying to inhibit its growth all this summer." He released the vine and then looked past her, almost looking as though he were about to full out grin.

Video's tail brushed along her flank. When Radio gazed up at her with rounded eyes, the large feline dipped her head to Radio, turned around, and started back onto the path. Radio's shoulders sank in relief, knowing the powerful feline wasn't upset for what she had done to her tail before.

"You should see it in winter. It's truly magical, dear." Pictures gave Radio a smile before following after Video.

Radio had to stay under the vines for another moment, though. *Magical.* This was Calotype's forest, the Unending Labyrinth she learned about when she was younger. "Because the plants and trees never go to sleep, still carrying the Shadow Advisor's, or, uh, Phantascope's curse," Radio murmured. She remembered the story about the strong refuge leader, Calotype, who sheltered non-titled individuals, or the unverified of Social Media, against the harsh elements, offering services which had only previously been for the verified, ones who found favor with the Council. Calotype protected her refugees for years and provided for them so they could earn their verification and become a part of Social Media, but her services had been offered during the time the mage Phantascope had been attacking actively. It was so strange to be able to put a story with the name now, after reading the files she received in the carriage on her way to the Capital.

Radio was told that the honorable feline had died during the strong mage's attack against her territory, and the forest had been lost to the sorcerer for ages. Radio always had a strong interest in the story, and was glad her Aunt Studio and her servants fed her interest and spoke to her about the magic of the forest. Even with the mage gone, because of the efforts and skill of Video's father, the Council still never could take back the forest Calotype had created. The enchantments upon the growth to make them grow and live through the summers and winters had been far too powerful. Anyone who went inside the thick forest with the intention of destroying it never came out of it. The mage had been presumed dead for the past two solstices, but Pictures inferred that was when the forest expanded even more. Did that mean something else was making this forest grow?

Radio realized she was halfway inside the forest only when Video grabbed her by the scruff and pulled her out. "What are you doing!?"

Video's eyes were lit with concern and anger. She growled at Radio as she popped the smaller cat on her paws "Why are you going in there, when our objective is *away* from this place? Come on!" Her tail swatted Radio's flank, nearly shoving her down, as Video prowled past Radio towards Pictures.

Radio huffed after catching her balance, and then followed after the tabby cat. "Hear me out! If the plant life is growing more than when the mage who enchanted it is dead, doesn't that mean another mage is probably maintaining the curse? This could be the Jester's hide out, Video!" Radio brightened, realizing how much this might mean to the Council. "We could learn something about how to restore the King and not have to go through all this work! We should report this immediately and see what we can find!" She started to go back towards it, but Video's growl stopped her.

"That's not our objective, Radio Star. Our job is to retrieve the shards we can and deliver them to one of the Council. Nothing else." Video pressed her paw in front of Radio, and glared down at her. "You're the one that didn't allow me to chase after that mage when we were in the village of rodents. Why would I let you go right into its apparent domain? The beast will see us as trespassing and have a justified reason to kill us." Video tilted up her chin when Radio looked as though she would object. "Drop it, Radio Star."

Radio blinked, her rounded eyes complete with a pout, but then deflated and nodded. After the mage seemed so keen on removing them from inside the cavern, it wouldn't be pleased to see them lurking in its hideout. Above that, though, this labyrinth growing lusciously despite the former mage's death would have been, once again, another hint to the

Council about something going on here. Why didn't they see the connections? This was the territory where the old monkey troops had been spotted! Why hadn't they been attacking the forest with full force even before the King was taken away? They probably knew this was all coming!

The whole situation seemed to be getting more and more preposterous. Radio walked with Pictures and Video back up the valley, on their way to the Ruined City, trying not to think about the situation any further. She imagined the two were older than she was, and knew they had more knowledge about the land than she did by far. They would have been concerned about the situation and drawn the conclusion themselves if it had been a fact, but perhaps they only needed an outsider's perspective to realize this was all wrong. *The idea that the* noble *is the outsider is ridiculous.* Radio sighed as she continued on the path with them, not looking back at the overgrown forest, and in not doing so, missed the pair of eyes staring at her.

The three travelled silently along the grassy hills, slowly watching as the darkening clouds drew closer to them. Radio was trying her best not to complain of the aches in her paws after the continuous travel, but the sharp throbbing kept increasing. She had been doing well for most of the morning, but the pain began to set in after they passed Calotype's Forest. She clamped her jaw shut, and pushed forward. There was no way she was going to speak when the other two seemed to be enjoying the silence and walking in contentment for once. Radio would only jeopardize the mood by voicing her troubles. It didn't seem like a peaceful silence happened enough.

She thought the rest would have made much of the stress of the journey go away, but the longer they carried on, the more the pain from the previous day of travel came back, too. It was a wonder the other two weren't faced with the same dilemma. She gazed at Pictures' shoulders, watching as they rocked with each step smoothly, then quickly averted her gaze once he felt her stare and turned to look at her. He looked as though he was going to ask her a question, maybe seeing her slowed pace, but instead, both Pictures and Radio gasped as a screeching static hit their ears, dropping them to the ground in pain.

"What's going on!?" Radio cried out, cocking her head to try and ease the ringing from her ear. The sudden loud noise was unbearable, but didn't last long. Her head pounded once the static ended, and she slowly got back up to open her eyes. She sighed, looking to Pictures and Video for answers after they composed themselves, too, and swallowed nervously when she saw how they were just as dazed as she was.

Video shook her head, rising back up. "There must be an error in communication, these were only to be used if the drone couldn't reach us." She flicked her ear in irritation of the chip and audio piece embedded in the cartilage of it and then started back for the path, slowly padding down another incline.

Pictures had only shrugged. "I don't know either; reception has been bad for me ever since we left the Capital." He gave Radio only a small glance before following after Video. She was disappointed she had only received a look, as he had turned his head in her direction before. She had been hopeful the gaze from before was out of concern or because he wanted to know more about her, but the static had ruined all that. Her shoulders slumped and she continued.

Radio looked around curiously as she followed them, now wondering if the castle was safe and secure. She didn't remember the surveillance crew telling her what Video had stated, but it was probably another "general knowledge" thing. Even so, Radio pondered, "The idea of an error in communication or any of the technology offered from the Capital is absurd..." But anything was possible with a mage actively attacking the land once more.

And here I am, walking about, chosen to stop it. That was a wonder in itself. The three of them were travelling in a vast open stretch of land, and there was no reason why the crew back at the Capital City shouldn't be able to reach them. Radio's apprehension went away when she had to fight from purring at the idea of her adventuring out like this, fighting cursed rats and meeting people from all over the land. It seemed so out of the ordinary, out of reality. It was wild!

As though all those things weren't exciting enough, there was more to it. She was about to enter the *Ruined City,* the very city which had been constructed to protect non-mages from their all-powerful counterparts. Her tail waved, the pain in her paws almost subsiding as she thought about the venture and mission she faced. She wondered what animals now resided in the formerly glamorous city of destroyed structures, built by the mages for the followers without magic once it was demanded of them by the revolutionary leader, Control. The idea made Radio think about what the former city might have been like before the overthrow when it was destroyed, taken down by the mages as their last act of anger when their Queen was killed. She was sure she'd be able to conceptualize what the city looked like once they drew closer, and decided she could be patient.

The Ruined City right now was only a blurred silhouette far out against the backdrop of the shimmering sky. She'd have to wait to see it.

She looked to see if Pictures and Video were still bothered by the static since it had ended for her a while ago, but the two were walking silently. They seemed more alert, but not troubled. That was enough to take the last of her concerns away. Things were looking up, and she was excited to see what this part of the mission would bring for them. She pounced forward and paced with her tail high in the air, walking with them while the excitement of the Ruined City was fresh in her mind. This was going to be the best stop so far! All the more so, if they succeeded in finding a crystal shard.

Radio kept up her excitement for most of their travel toward the city, but over time, Radio's bright bounding eased into prowling, and her pacing turned into trudging, trailing behind the two ahead of her for as long as she could without one of them snapping at her to keep up. All the walking was just too much. No matter how excited she was, the thrill could not overpower the lack of her physical energy when she had to look ahead and see that they were about to travel up another incline.

She almost let out a groan, but held her breath and tongue when she realized the two would hear it. She exhaled her held air quietly, and tensed her paws as she started up the incline, trying not to wince as she felt the strain of them when she made her way up the hill with the two. What was most upsetting about being sore was the fact that the other two *weren't*. Both felines moved comfortably, especially Video, as though she was as light as a feather. They walked with a stride as if they could carry all of the land on their shoulders—Video practically doing so, with the shards of the heart in her bag. Meanwhile, Radio felt like she could barely keep her collar on, knowing it was extra weight.

Every time she thought her bones couldn't ache more, somehow they did. Just when Radio thought her paws would surely give out and she'd have to plead for them to rest, Video stopped. Radio's eyes rounded. She quickly caught up with the large feline to see what was wrong. Both she and Pictures approached the marbled tabby, standing at her sides, and followed her gaze, looking up at the clouds, which had continued to darken even more since morning.

Video narrowed her eyes after giving a closer look, then looked down at the other two and asked, "The clouds are drawing closer, and aren't looking too pleasant, either. Had either of you heard anything from Sensor or the others about the weather while I slept?" When both Radio and Pictures shook their heads, she furthered, "I'm surprised they haven't contacted us. We're passing the Crater Valleys. It might be dangerous to do so if the clouds bring rain."

Radio frowned, not liking the sound of Video's concern, but Pictures only shrugged, starting to walk alongside Video. "It will pass us. Tape would definitely contact us if he was worried," he assured the large cat before he turned his attention on the path ahead, giving a small smirk as though giving thought to the neurotic tomcat as he walked.

Video looked doubtfully at him and hesitantly continued, "That's true, but I haven't heard anything from Recorder or Tape this morning. Do you think anything happened to them since last night?"

Radio spoke up then and said, "That's what I'm worried about, especially with the static from earlier."

She heard the noise of a drone's propellers right then. Both she and Pictures looked up hopefully, but it wasn't a drone controlled by the two monitors they both knew, it was the black surveillance bot. The red light signifying that it was recording didn't help the feeling Radio got from it. The eerie, shiny look of its black exterior shining in the little light the sun was giving them through the clouds only made it worse. Radio watched it closely as it hovered down to them, and she curiously tilted her head. "I saw that particular one on my way to the Capital. It's not an official, is it?"

Video flattened her ears, all of the uncertainty from before vanished. "No, that one is freelance. It's Signal's surveillance from the Rich Top Mountain Region."

"Signal!?" Both Radio and Pictured exclaimed, surprised to hear the titled name of Video's father just after passing Calotype's forest. "Why is he surveying here?" Radio's eyes rounded.

Video shrugged, her eyes narrowing as she walked ahead of them both. "Likely he was hired by the Council as extra monitoring for the hunt against the traitor. The Council may have also hired him with the idea he would be more passionate about the situation while I'm a part of the retrieving patrol."

Radio brightened at the very idea, and quickly turned to the floating bot to wave excitedly. "Hi, Video's dad! Thank you for watching us!" she giggled. Even Pictures lifted up his paw a bit before deciding to move forward, wide-eyed.

Video scoffed at them both, giving them a glare before pulling her head forward again to shake it. "Really? Did you really just *wave* to him!? He's likely going to report you for your incompetent behavior, and hopefully *will,* with how immature the two of you are. The only reason the bot is probably still here is because we decreased the speed of our pace. The complete stop will be marked as an unscheduled break." Video continued on, growling, "We had better make up the time we lost."

Radio and Pictures gaped at her, and then glanced at the bot in shock before quickly hurrying after Video.

Video didn't slow down her accelerated steps, so neither did they. Radio clenched her jaw a bit, but didn't object to Video's demand with how possible it was that Signal *could* report them. After all, he was the father of the cat that wouldn't let them stop even if she was bleeding muzzle to tail tip with injuries, or if her companions were, for that matter. Radio couldn't believe her paws didn't light on fire by how much they were burning. She could only imagine how swollen they were going to be after their next stop. Together the three ventured into the Crater Valleys, and in far too good of time, too. The speed they travelled was unreasonable, and even Pictures' brow furrowed over time. It looked as though Video wanted to venture directly into the vast incline, too, until the three noticed groups of white birds flying into the enormous clearings of the valley's unnatural cavities.

Radio flicked her ears and tried to focus her eyes to see what kind of birds they were, then grinned when she realized what type. "Oh! A flock of seagulls!" Her tail began rising with delight, and gave a little sway with its movement. She heard of the birds that often teased the followers beyond Central Media towards the region's coasts, taking entire picnics' worth of food when it was left unwatched. Radio couldn't help but smile at seeing the strange but skilled thieves.

Video blinked and her eyes rounded. "That's confirmation that the clouds are moving closer. They don't come in this far unless the waters are unsafe." She backed up, then looked over at both Radio and Pictures. "We should rest somewhere on high ground. If those birds being so far onto land doesn't make it certain there *is* a storm coming, I don't know what would."

Pictures' eyebrows rose, and he looked at Video with surprise. "That would be why we received the static from before. If the storm's that bad, it's what could have messed up the communications, and would be what Sensor may have been trying to warn us about when we entered the valley."

Radio's ears flattened, knowing it was she who had stated earlier the static could have meant a message was trying to be sent from the castle, but realized this might be an opportunity for rest, too. "Oh no, we need to get away from here, then!" she gasped. "We need to get to high ground fast!"

She was afraid Video would refuse, and claim they could make the venture across the entire valley in time, but Video nodded, much to Radio's relief. "The whole valley can flood if the storm's bad enough. You're right; we need to get to high elevation immediately. I'm sure the Council knows of the danger, and will excuse our detour." She rushed past both Radio and Pictures, and quickly led the two smaller felines up the clearing.

Radio tried not to squeal as she kept up with the two cats, her paws still burning. The running finished taking the air right out of her. She stumbled and fell down, gasping. She was going to drop completely, panicking as her sight began to blur, but Pictures brushed his muzzle against her flank, and helped her get back up to her paws as Video stopped to wait for them both. Radio dipped her head to Pictures in thanks, and walked with him to catch up to Video until the three could travel together.

They moved quickly as the clouds drew closer, Pictures keeping his side brushed against Radio's for support, until Video found an empty den in a tree trunk at the peak of one of the surrounding hills. She sniffed inside to make sure it was abandoned, and then looked back at Pictures and Radio. "This should be high enough. I don't think the rain will reach this far."

The two nodded, and Pictures hurried inside. Radio thanked Video, smiling up at the large feline, and then went inside, almost collapsing immediately upon entering the hollowed out tree. Video moved into the entrance, pushing Radio further into the hollowed area with her paw, and then wrapped her tail around all three of them. Pictures and Radio both looked at her. She blinked slowly before turning her head to the entrance, watching as the clouds grew darker than the shimmering sky above them.

The three rested together as the rainstorm took place, unleashing its power right before them with bright lightning and thunder that made their ears ring. Radio curled up in Video's tail. She always thought that the static in the sky's barrier would be indistinguishable from the lightning she always hid from in her home, but that wasn't the case at all. Lightning was much more frightening. When Radio kneaded her paws anxiously, she felt the rat bites in the Video's large tail and realized she had struck one of the wounds when she was batting at it before. She sighed, mumbling apologies inside the tabby's long fur, and closed her eyes. Video was so impulsive when it came to battle and what she thought was right, yet had this patient side to her, too. Somehow, she could tolerate the biggest of annoyances. Between Radio's lack of understanding, and Pictures' love for instigation, Video was dealing with quite the pair, yet managed to handle them. Radio admired that from the young feline, and hoped she could find the balance that would keep her in line with her powerful companion.

Pictures stretched out between them, lying on Video's side, and chuckled as he poked the tip of his paw to Radio's nose, making her blink open her eyes. She couldn't help but return the smile he was giving her, and purred. He grinned, looking at her and Video as he asked, "Who's ready for that next shard, ladies?"

It was the most playful thing he had said so far. Radio giggled as Video huffed, picking up her tail away from Radio and covering the silver tom with it, almost completely hiding him under the enormous mass of fur. "Obviously not you, with such uncouth conduct," Video muttered, looking back out into the valley.

Pictures spat out the fur and wrapped his paws around the giant cat's tail, grinning once more. "I apologize for enjoying myself, Miss Video, but now I find that I have even caught myself a blanket, and will immerse myself in the coziness." He purred now, too, as he nuzzled into the fur, but his words cut off into a yelp as Video lifted him up with her tail, and he dangled from the ground. Radio brightened, raising herself up on her back legs to lean on top of the giant tail and pin it down carefully. "Well, then, your blanket is my pillow!" She laughed with Pictures as they both landed back onto the surface of the tree hollow. Radio deemed herself daring enough to stretch her neck out to rest her muzzle on his.

Video growled, her tail tip beginning to flick. She then narrowed her eyes and looked outside again, her gaze intent on watching the pouring rain. Radio and Pictures both laughed once their noses touched, but Radio turned to Video then. Her eyes had stayed narrowed into slits for a while, but softened as she looked out into the valleys. The sienna color almost faded to umber with the storm's reflection. She stared out only for a moment before she quietly mumbled, "It must be nice to be so carefree."

Radio blinked at her, wondering at her words. The quietness of them took away the fun. She slid back from Pictures, falling off of Video's tail, and sighed. She knew when it came down to it, Video had been the only one to try and attack the mage so far, and was the only one to fight the bound rats in the pit where the beast had dropped her, taking all the damage upon herself by doing so. Radio's ears flattened, knowing that was likely what the reserved feline was referring to, and looked up at Pictures. He gave her a nod of understanding the play was over and turned away. Radio rested her head down on the cold ground.

It wasn't fair that Video had faced that alone, nor that Pictures had to slow down his productivity to help Radio. Their whole mission would just go better if she wasn't a factor at all. The idea devastated Radio, but then it left her with a new goal in mind. She had to prove herself to them, and have it be far beyond what was expected of her as a noble. Radio nodded to herself, determined she was going to make that the case. This mission would only be the beginning. Tomorrow they would arrive at the Ruined City, and she was going to show her capability, whether the Jester was there or not. This was a mission for change. Radio closed her eyes with the assuring thought she would succeed in her new plan to make both Video and Pictures proud, and let her light body settle into the dark, cool earth.

After the two days of travel and exhaustion of the hike to high ground, all three slept well through the night and into the morning. The dawning sun was bright through the clouds after the rain, greeting the three with its beams shining down into the cracks of the hollowed tree.

Radio yawned, and got to her paws. Today would mark the day she would prove herself, and was the day she was going to enter the Ruined City. Video and Pictures weren't going to know what hit them! She stretched out her limbs and stepped up to their shelter's opening, looking out into the drowned out valley below the large incline.

It was astonishing to see the amount of water. The craters of the valley were completely filled, like miniature lakes. Radio's eyes rounded, and she only moved away from the entrance when she heard movement from the other two.

"We had better get moving," Video rumbled from behind her, and got up. Radio wouldn't be shocked if the cat could be sleepwalking, with how distorted her words were.

Video saw the amusement on Radio's face, and brushed her tail against the smaller cat's muzzle before she walked outside the tree, giving her tail a thump against the trunk as she went past. Radio wrinkled her nose from the fur brushing her face, and watched the earth-colored cat move down the slope. She blinked, realizing Video wasn't stopping, and how serious she really was, once again not hesitating to leave. Radio looked back over her shoulder to see Pictures stirring, then followed after Video, knowing Pictures would be able to catch up to them.

The two felines walked down the large hill together, and when Video made no move to start a conversation, Radio took in the sights, remembering how the other two seemed to enjoy the silence while traveling the day before. All of the dips and clearings which had surrounded the three had filled with water. It made sense that it'd look larger up close, but actually venturing into it, and seeing only small paths for them to travel through, left Radio speechless. It felt as though they were walking through wetlands.

She knew this valley was also a historical battleground between the mages and the growing government of technology, having heard it from her father when they travelled through on their way to Clowder City. After seeing how the Unending Labyrinth was consistent from the mages' interference, it made Radio wonder if magic affected the plains, as well. The water of the craters reflected the newly cleared sky with crispness and clarity, and it put Radio in complete awe as she walked with Video.

When Pictures caught up with them, he laughed and yawned. Radio looked over, and saw a twinkle in his eye that she knew meant he was up to no good.

It was confirmed immediately as he said, "Well, it seems like that long night of rest was just what we needed. I'm sure we'll be able to trek through these next few days without a blink of sleep!" He grinned mischievously at Radio, his tail waving.

"No!" Radio pushed him with her paw, and shook her head as she giggled, "You're terrible!"

Pictures chuckled, then narrowed one eye and eased up to her ear, whispering, "Just wait until she says…"

"That wouldn't be a bad idea, considering the amount of time we lost because of the storm." Video nodded, and Pictures laughed again, the white tip of his tail flicking the top of Radio's nose while she stared at him in horror. She could not believe he suggested it! He knew Video would take it seriously, too! Radio only got more flustered knowing *that* was the reason why he did so. It took all she had not to muster out a screech and pounce on him.

After two days, her paws finally didn't ache and burn with all of the travel the three had accomplished, and she was not going to risk aggravating anything like that happening again. There was no point to attack, either; he *wanted* the attention. Radio had to keep back a huff when she saw Pictures staring at her, waiting for her response. He was like a kitten himself! She narrowed her eyes, then pouted, and lifted up her chin, following after Video. She heard him sigh behind her, but he didn't further it, continuing on with his eyes to the sky.

The three traveled as the morning eased into the burning afternoon. If it wasn't one thing, it was another. Radio panted as she looked up at the shimmering sky, trying not to look too long at the sun. Even with the blanket of clouds still covering the region, the sun cast beams to beat down against her fur. The further they walked, the surer Radio was that the rays were roasting her. There was not a tree anywhere near to offer the slightest bit of shade, and the sun was right above their heads. She couldn't even hide behind Video or Pictures to use them as shade unless she climbed right under them. *It wouldn't be so bad if I was napping in it.* Radio sighed, knowing if she was at home she would have curled up on her window sill and happily baked in the sun without worry.

But that wasn't the right mindset. She was no longer that lazy cat. This journey marked a new noble, an honored individual ready to give back to her land just as her aunt did when she built the Clowder City. Radio was going to retrieve the shards with her companions, and she was going to change Media for the better once her name was known for helping to save the King, even if her fur had to melt off to do it.

Two days of travel away, the dark-furred primate stood on the antenna of the tallest landmark of Clowder City, and waved up his hand to draw his artifact to himself. The object whipped up to him, barely brushing against his fingertips to give him the power he needed for his next attack. He smiled down upon the foolish felines below, and drew the energy from the cube with a twist of his hand. He felt his body jerk as the power shot down his arm, and cast down a powerful blast at one of the busier streets. The beam stuck directly in the middle of the street, and the monkey watched as cats scattered and scrambled for safety in a panic, but a few looked up and met his cyan eyes.

"What did you do that for?" one called out haughtily, making his eyes round.

Another flabbergasted him with their fearless agreement, yowling, "Yeah!" He was practically left speechless when yet *another* feline shouted out, "Why in the name of our Stars and City would you think that's okay!?"

The monkey leaned back in confusion at the cats. They weren't even intimidated! Didn't they know who he was? What a bunch of blasphemy! The entitlement astounded him, and he knew they were due for some correction. He narrowed his eyes, drawing more energy for another blast until it suddenly clicked.

They didn't know him as a mage of mystic beams or energy, not a controller of one of the most powerful of magical forms. No, the technology the Council stole could practically do that by now with lasers. They had no reason to fear it when it was something familiar to them. It was that these cats knew him and feared him for wearing that stupid jester outfit that *one* time.

Really, now.

The idea was far-fetched, but the primate still slapped his fingers against his palm and the hat appeared. He felt the tension of the felines below immediately, and watched as they gasped as he put the hat on. His mouth nearly dropped in disbelief realizing they really had no idea who he was before the clothing materialized. *That was a joke! Are you kidding—*

"It's the Jester!"

"That's the one who cast our King away!"

"He's going to blow up the city!"

"Oh, by your Stars and City," he mumbled as the cats began to smash into and claw each other in the panic, all crying out in fear and worry. The monkey almost forgot what he had been there for, in shock upon realizing how stupid these creatures were. He shook the dismay from his head and readied his cube for another blast.

"Don't you dare."

He looked over to see the Studio Star staring up at him from her balcony, and gave her a pout before narrowing his eyes, letting the rest of his outfit appear on his form while their gazes met.

"Hmmm...Are you going to stop me? I'd like to see you try. You're already going to be dealt with for speaking to me as it is." He glared at her, never taking his eyes away from her as he positioned the artifact.

Studio lifted up her chin. "I would hope I don't have to, if you're half as intelligent as your apparent enemies. These cats have done nothing to warrant your cruelty, Jester."

He scoffed, and narrowed his eyes. "Oh, nope, you lost me. Silly kitty, almost had me there." The monkey grinned as Studio's ears flattened, making him spin his cube between his hands. Without breaking their stare, he shot down a giant energy blast upon the civilians, his eyes gleaming as they both listened to the city folk's screams. Studio startled when he immediately vanished into shadows, leaving her at the balcony.

Once the sun had mellowed and eased back down into the sky again, the three arrived at a rundown rural area. There was a large road cutting across the decaying homes and broken buildings, making a runway straight for the main city. Radio stared in shock at the rough dark stone, and for how long it stretched. The whole thing looked like it might extend across the whole city. It was astonishing! The former dwellings were bigger than her home near the Capital, too. Everything seemed super-sized. Radio looked at the structures in awe as Video and Pictures moved forward, her tail swaying as she imagined the powerful folk that once roamed along these streets and lived in these abodes, filling the streets with their freshly built mechanics. She saw that Video and Pictures were scanning the area. She followed their gazes to see a fox family sleeping and a raccoon family rummaging through waste, very different from the powerful beings Radio had been imagining.

Surely after all these generations, there would be no more food left for these individuals, yet the raccoons found edible meat left by larger animals, and dragged it out of the waste pile for their kits. She looked at them in shock, having never seen anything like it in all her days. What kind of life was that? Not even wanting to imagine having to scrounge for food for a family of their size, she turned her gaze away.

They continued silently down the large road, twice the size of the streets of the Capital. Radio startled at the booming noise of a large animal, and whipped around. Video turned her head to Radio as the small feline watched a coyote barking wildly as it chased a cat, which hissed and yowled as the feline fled from the giant canine. Radio whimpered, and pressed up against Video.

How could such behavior be allowed in Media? Was this why the Capital advised their followers not to enter the city? Radio felt Video's tail touch her flank to assure her as she continued staring where the two had run. All she could choke out was the question, "What if they attack us!?" Radio wanted to ask if the cat would be okay, but she was too afraid of the answer she might get from the blunt tabby cat.

Her eyes rounded when Video merely scoffed, "Nonsense, Radio Star, one paw upon that collar of yours and they would receive a punishment worse than death. You have nothing to worry about, and *we* can handle ourselves." Video's tail now pulled forward to brush along Radio's neck where the silver collar hung before looking back at Pictures. Her words didn't comfort Radio at all, and what the giant cat said to the silver tom next was no more assuring. "Let's split up and try and find anything we can about the shard so we can move onto the next location."

Radio squealed when Pictures nodded, completely dumbfounded. Her ears flattened to the back of her skull as she exclaimed, "We just saw a giant dog chase a harmless little cat down the road, no larger than me, and you want us to separate!?"

Video sighed, and clenched her jaw. "Look, we have no pointers from the surveillance besides the knowledge the shard is somewhere near the outskirts of this place, so we're going to need to cover ground fast. I can defend myself if I run into anything, Pictures has been here before, and you are the Radio Star. No one will touch a hair on your head unless they're looking for an early demise." Video turned away to prowl down the dark road, announcing, "We'll regroup when the sun is setting if we haven't found anything. Get back and regroup as soon as you find something worth telling us."

"Yes, *ma'am*." Pictures' brow arched. He glanced at Radio, giving her a long stare and a bit of a sheepish smile before he took off in the opposite direction of Video. Radio watched them both leave, completely speechless, and let out a small noise of dismay. She bounced her paws against the earth anxiously before she felt the city folk's eyes resting on her. She quickly decided not to wait around in the center of the street, and she bolted toward one of the buildings.

- CHAPTER 5 -

OBSERVANCE

The small feathery feline looked around, passing by each structure slowly. She scanned the entire area, every step, looking down the alleys as she drew closer to the towering skyscrapers within the abandoned city. She slowed her pace once she heard commotion deep within one of the alleys. In the corner of her sight as she passed the dark area, she saw two enormous black birds tearing apart an old corpse. She stared at their hairless heads and dark bodies, every detail of their long pale beaks, ragged feathers, and ugly pink faces. All she could think of was the spider monkey, and its piercing stare when she faced it in the caverns with Video and Pictures.

Neither Pictures nor Video were here right now, though. Radio's paws tightened as she backed away from the enormous vultures, and quickly fled further towards the city. Every pounding step she took against the hard pavement was cold, so she knew the shard wasn't anywhere near this area. She sighed and slowed her pace, hoping that Video and Pictures were nearby.

What was she going to do if she actually did find something that suggested the location of the shard? Radio's paws slowly drew her to the city. She shook her head and hoped one of her companions would find her soon. How did Video expect them to regroup when Pictures was the only one who knew the area? Radio quickened her pace again, hoping to see something familiar, and trying not to fume at the situation. Why was she suddenly this master navigator that was going to find her way back?

Radio stopped when the air around her grew colder. That's when she saw the looming figure only a building's distance away from her. She narrowed her eyes to focus on the form, and realized it was a canine, a wolf, of sorts. What was something like that doing alone in the middle of the city? Radio blinked her eyes and rounded them when the wolf moved. Her spine chilled when the enormous canine's eyes glittered cyan as it stared directly at her. She took a step back, watching its lips curl into a snarl.

Radio could only muster a whimper at the sight, realizing it was the same look that the rats had in the pit near Faith's village. The wolf had been altered by the Jester. She heard the slight chime of something, and her gaze shot up to the building between her and the wolf. She locked eyes with the dressed primate itself.

Its eyes gleamed the same bright blue color as the wolf's as it looked down upon her as it controlled the wolf's actions. Radio could imagine it no other way, as the canine moved forward only when the mage's eyes glowed brighter. She shook her head at the mage, pleading with rounded eyes it wouldn't sic the animal upon her. What did the beast have to lose, though? The mage was far out of reach, and likely had no connection to the wolf. Radio and the mage seemed to ponder the question at the same time, and she watched as the dressed monkey slammed its hand down, making the wolf charge directly at Radio.

She screamed, scrambling to catch herself from falling and whipped around. Her paws drummed against the street as she ran as quickly as she could away from the animal, closing her eyes in fear as she heard it coming closer. The heat of the canine's breath blew against her fur as it drew close, and then she heard a yelp of pain. She skidded to a halt once she saw Video slice her claws against the canine's wet nose, the blood splattering across the solid ground. Radio stared in awe at the large cat, who barely reached the wolf's chest as she hissed and spat at it, until Video turned to face her.

"Get out of here! Find Pictures!" Video yelled sharply, leaping away from the wolf's snapping jaws just in time to slice her claws against the creature's muzzle. Radio glanced at the battle only for a moment longer before she bolted away, running towards where she had seen Pictures head when they had gone their separate ways.

It wasn't until after the two were out of sight that Radio regretted leaving, hearing their barks and screams in battle. *I should have fought!*

How could I have left Video there? Tears streamed down Radio's face as she passed the decrepit buildings and ran faster than she ever had before, hoping to find Pictures. She kept her eyes and ears alert, turning her head to listen to any noise or see anything she might miss, but then finally heard Pictures' voice speaking just off the street.

"Pictures! Pictures!" she called out and skidded to a halt, trying not to yell when her paws scraped against the cement as she did so.

Pictures came out from an alley, his tail bristled when seeing her. "Radio! What's wrong? What happened?"

Radio shook her head. "The Jester's here! It sent an animal to attack Video! We have to help her, please!"

Pictures looked bewildered and more suspicious than concerned, but quickly stammered, "Oh...of course! Let's go now!"

Radio frowned at him, then quickly turned back around, leading the silver tom to the scene as quickly as she could. She nearly bumped straight into Video, who was puffed out to be twice her size with eyes rounder than Radio had ever seen them. *She hadn't realized Pictures came this way!* Radio saw it on the feline's face. She had probably meant to lure the wolf away from the group, but it was too late for that. Radio heard the canine approaching rapidly, the smell of blood flaring Radio's nostrils. She growled, and leapt past the giant tabby to scratch the wolf across its nose, just as Video had, when it rounded the corner.

She growled in pain as she landed against the pavement with her scraped pads, but she had given enough time for Pictures and Video to recover their shock, and dodge the canine's next attacks. As they recovered from their own leaps, Radio jumped at the wolf again and bit her teeth into the beast's side, ripping her claws against its stomach. She ducked down just in time to avoid the vicious jaws of the animal attempting to clamp its fangs into her scruff.

Pictures leapt at the canine's neck and drove his fangs through the thick fur and into the wolf's throat. Radio was amazed at the size difference of the tomcat and enormous canine towering over even Video. The smell of blood became nearly overwhelming as Pictures was successful with gripping the tender skin, and started pulling down with the flesh firmly gripped. Video ripped her claws against its eyes until blood ran down her fur, keeping the animal from digging its massive paws into Pictures, instead snapping at Video. Pictures yanked his head down, blood dripping down his chest before he released his grip and bounced back, watching with cold eyes as the wolf fell over. The canine groaned and gasped before dropping its head against the cement ground, rocking its paws back and forth as it tried to get back up and failed.

"We've disabled it for now. Let's go!" Video commanded, and turned on the pad of her paw to run down the walkway where Radio had found Pictures.

Radio's heart was pounding heavily against her chest. She wheezed and huffed as she ran with her companions, overjoyed they were all one group again. They made it as far back as the city's outskirts, but Video didn't stop until they heard the noise of a cat yowling. She quickly turned and charged towards the sound.

It was the coyote from before, snapping at the feline that it had finally cornered in one of the residential alleys. After the cursed wolf, the smaller predator seemed like nothing. Video launched herself at the canine, ripping at its pelt and driving her claws into its flesh. Radio listened as it yelped and howled in pain, only trying to attack Video once before she struck it again with her sharp claws. The animal quickly trekked away from the golden cat cowering in the corner of the alley, running for the terrain outside the outskirts.

"Are you alright, ma'am!?" Video asked, dusting the dirt from her own pelt with just a sweep of her long tail. Radio wasn't sure if the loudness of Video's tone was concern for the feline, or if she was still riled up by the wolf's attack. Radio's own fur was still bristled.

The golden colored cat got to her feet, and looked at the three of them with gratitude. "I am, thank you!" She stared wide-eyed at Pictures. "P-Pictures? It's really you!" She purred, coming up to the tom. "What brings you back to the city?"

"Nothing good, Receiver. This time it's about our government." Pictures shook his head, and looked at Video.

The ochre-colored feline turned her eyes up to the giant tabby, who explained, "The Capital sent us down here to reclaim some artifacts which were scattered by the mage that attacked the castle a few days ago." Video then asked, "Do you know anything about any glittering red fragments being sighted in the area?" She looked at the slender feline hopefully.

The cat blinked, her brow furrowing. "Red fragments? Like glass? I think I might actually have something, if that's what you're looking for. My colleague and I are scavengers here, but he is injured right now, attacked after he came across a strange shard outside of the city. I didn't think anything of it, other than having to leave him in such a condition to carry on with my work, but it could be related. Please, come with me, and

I'll take you to him. Maybe he can tell you something more." She nodded to the three, then cautiously prowled out of the alley.

Radio watched the feline for a moment, but Video and Pictures both followed her without question, so she hurried along behind them, guessing they trusted her because of her verification, she had a name given her of technology. Receiver led the three back into the Ruined City through a side entrance, once likely a city gate, and towards the towering skyscrapers. She crossed down the wide, dark alleys that defined the skeleton of the structures fearlessly, leading the three without a moment's hesitation. Radio stared in shock at the rusted beams and decomposing walls that barely held up what had once been beautiful buildings. Gray foxes, opossums, and raccoons littered the city even more than they had in the outskirts. Radio felt a shiver down her spine seeing them, as they didn't seem as healthy as the folk of the outskirts, either, much as the structures didn't, further into the city, compared to the outskirts.

The entire place was as terrifying as it was described in the history books, if not more so. Radio had imagined she'd be able to picture what the buildings looked like prior to the destruction of the city, but looking at it now, this was not the case. Dust and particles clouded the entire city, desaturating whatever color the structures once were, the original colors having faded long ago. Even some of the windows and doors were impossible to be reimagined, nothing but crumbled brick and holes smashed through where they once were. It would be safer to level the whole city, or salvage what could be saved, but the Council never put anyone on assignment to do it.

Now they were deep into the city, and Radio could no longer see the tops of the buildings. The fur on her tail bristled in fear of the Jester still lurking about, possibly cursing another animal upon them in attack. The stoat, Faith, had spoken so well of the rats who protected her city before they were taken by the vengeful mage, making Radio wonder what the life of the wolf might have been like before the attack. It could have been a poor animal having come down from the mountain scouting, or perhaps leaving the group it was a part of, feeling secluded and helpless like Radio imagined the Jester had done with the rats. The canine wasn't even sentient anymore, the individual it had once been was gone.

Those words replayed in Radio's mind, and as they did, she held her breath. Whatever might attack them again had nothing to hold them back. That was all this knowledge meant. An attack could come from anywhere in the city, and while they had another set of paws to help, it was likely the mage would have that in mind, as well. Radio looked around, still not seeing any sign of life in the alleys or along the streets besides small critters. *Then again, the mage can take control of multiple animals.* Radio shuddered, remembering the sight of the group of rats viciously attacking Video as one, and was grateful when Receiver picked up the pace.

Radio stared at the feline, who had run beside Pictures before she sped their progress through the city, and kept her eyes on the road. She found herself biting her lip at the idea of how well they weaved through the city, almost in sync as they led Radio and Video to their objective. She glanced towards Pictures when he slowed enough to lag behind Receiver, and tried to catch his stare. She hoped that maybe he could elaborate on knowing the sandy-colored tabby, but he followed the feline silently and didn't catch Radio's silent plea. It was hard to believe someone as observant as he didn't notice her looking at him. It seemed almost like everything he did was on purpose, and Radio supposed he didn't want to share. She looked over at Video, who was on the other side of her, ahead. The giant tabby gazed at them both over her shoulder, seeing the exchange, or lack thereof, between the both of them.

Radio let out a wheeze before forcing herself to catch up to them. Her paws were already starting to ache and burn from their earlier travels and having scraped them on the pavement didn't make it any easier, either. She bit her lip as her paws pounded over and over against the hard ground so as to stay in line with her companions. Her chest tightened as she held her breath in attempts not to wheeze with every bound and step, and was wondering how long she could keep up this journey at the same pace of this courier and surveillance director. Of course, they expected the flighty little noble be half as capable as the trained travelers. Video made that very clear, earlier. Radio was amazed at how well she already has done so far, but winced and growled as one of her raw paw pads scraped against a small, but far too sharp, rock on the road. She may have done well so far, but she had about reached her limit.

There was no telling what this friend of Receiver's would be like. Radio was grateful when the golden tabby slowed her pace and bounded onto the sidewalk. As soon as she could, Radio hopped off of the road and onto the smoother surface of the sidewalk, too. She let out a sigh of relief, but then inhaled the scent of blood, and backed away as Video and Pictures raced into the alley with the golden tabby. Her stomach turned at the smell, thinking back to the wolf and the rats. Fighting the monsters the Jester had created was the only time she had ever had such a strong memory of the scent, the only exception being when she and Pictures were hunting prey. Simple fighting and playing with her sister and servants when she was a kitten led to nothing more than a scraped forehead or slice of the paw pad, a few drops of blood at most. She managed to make it this far and help as much as she had already. She could take a step back from this situation.

"Oh, Transmitter!" Radio heard Receiver call out, and the young noble's tail flicked with apprehension. Eventually she looked into the alley where they had run, only to see a raccoon lying on its side, bleeding out onto the rags placed under it. Radio stared in amazement as she heard the raccoon speaking to Receiver in cat. She eased closer then, trying not to gag at the smell when she came close enough to hear what he was saying.

"Receiver, I'll be fine..." the raccoon rasped, then lifted up his muzzle. "Tell me why you're here. You need something."

The light tabby nodded. "Yes, these three are seeking objects much like that shard you told me about. We're thinking you may have seen what they're looking for. Where did you see it? We don't need many details— just anything that can lead us to it." She touched her paw to the raccoon's face reassuringly.

The raccoon blinked at her, then shook his head. "It's just a moment east of the shattered tower, right before you reach the incline to the Sanctified Meadows. I'll show you there now..." He broke off in a chatter of pain as he attempted to stand, making Radio startle. Receiver immediately weaved around him and supported him.

"Please! Don't hurt yourself. You've told us the location, and I can take them there myself. Stay here and heal," the ochre feline murmured as the raccoon rested against her flank. Radio stepped back when Receiver groomed between his ears to clean off the dried blood while Video and Pictures asked for more details. They acted as though they hadn't even noticed the interaction. Radio hadn't even heard what their question was until the raccoon started to answer again.

"Tell us about this object, sir," Video demanded.

The raccoon frowned, then offered, "I-It was this glass fragment inside the earth, and it wasn't like anything that could be a part of the shattered tower...it was of a different crystal." The raccoon patted his feline companion reassuringly when she made a nervous noise, and looked up at Video and Pictures. "It burned to touch, as though it had been cooking in the sun for hours, and glowed this deep *red*. I've seen nothing like it before."

"That sounds like our objective." Pictures gave a small arch of his brow at Video.

Radio's ears flattened as Video looked more intently at the raccoon. The giant tabby's tail lashed in excitement after Pictures' words, and she nodded. "That's what we're looking for. Your companion told us you were attacked after finding this fragment. Who did this to you, sir?" she asked.

The raccoon hesitated, giving a wince at Receiver's paw pressing down on his shoulder when he tried getting up again. "It was an immense dark canine. His eyes were blue. I had never seen him in these parts before. He barely seemed responsive before suddenly..."

"We understand, we had a similar encounter," Video spoke up as the raccoon's words tapered off, and looked to Pictures before he gave her a lift of his chin. Video stared at him and sighed, looking at the silver tabby a moment longer, and then turned back to the raccoon. "You're not going to live if you stay like this. We need to get you in a stable condition."

"What? You don't want to get right to it?" Radio piped up, but clamped her jaw shut when Pictures shot her a firm look. Radio blinked at him, but her eyes rounded when seeing Receiver and Transmitter turn to look at each other. *They* are *friends!* Hardly colleagues or business partners, Radio perceived it was beyond friendship...the feline cared for him! Radio's ears flattened as Receiver helped the large animal back down onto the rags, and slid back up to Video and Pictures, who seemed unfazed by the connection. Radio frowned when she came up to the three, figuring it must be more common than she thought for cats to interact, and involve themselves, with others.

Despite Pictures' stare, she still pressed, "Shouldn't we head out right away for the shard? We might be able to get there before the sun's light is gone." Her voice sounded more irritable than she had intended, but it still came out smoothly enough. She didn't continue now that Pictures was on the borderline of glaring at her.

Video blinked, looking slightly surprised at Radio, and then back to Pictures and the raccoon. "There's enough time, Miss Radio. I'll be right back. I think what I need is just outside the city, possibly still in the outskirts." she looked directly at Pictures. "Stay with him and Receiver until I get back. I won't be gone long, but I don't know where those two dogs went."

"I'll keep an eye out if anything comes up." Pictures nodded.

"So be it," Radio mumbled as she watched Video leave. Her gaze followed the giant marbled tabby, and then turned back to Pictures, who was walking over to Receiver. Radio's eyes slightly narrowed, but she looked away with a blank expression when Pictures started to turn back to look at her. She wasn't going to be *overly* blatant about her displeasure toward the situation, but she wasn't going to suggest anything that offered approval of it, either. Her gaze fell down to the raccoon, and she watched his shallow breathing for a moment before turning her head toward the rest of the city.

All she could see was decaying structures, the sky well hidden behind the dust and buildings surrounding the four. Radio sighed, and got as comfortable as she could on the hard ground. She folded her paws under her chest, and laid her head down, hoping Video would be back soon. The time spent for this was ridiculous, especially when they had what they needed to find the next shard. What was the bulky cat looking for, anyway? The question buzzed in Radio's head. She never thought of Video as compassionate or a worrying type, yet the formidable tabby postponed the mission all to help a scavenger and her raccoon friend.

Radio understood stopping to help Faith, the stoat was a village leader Video had delivered to before, and seemed to know well. Above that, the rats had been guardians of the village, and needed their reputation and memory not to be tarnished by the mage. There was something honorable about what they did there, but these two were just unlucky. They were verified, but were assigned here, and as scavengers. Pictures may have known them at one time, Receiver, anyway, but their mission wasn't for making stops to help old friends, it was for saving the masses of Media. If Video had waited a moment longer instead of acting so impulsively, she might have come to the same conclusion.

Radio remained where she was until the large cat was seen in the distance, and then got to her paws. The tabby's jaw was packed with clumps of leaves, and her bag seemed to have moss hanging from it. Pictures and Receiver looked at Video, concerned, but Video strode past them both, and hunched over the raccoon, pulling away the rags with her paws, and dropping a clump of the leaves at his.

"Eat these. They're plantain, and will help you get better. Focus on it while I clean your wounds, if you can," Video instructed.

Pictures cocked his head. "What do you know about first aid, Miss Video?"

Video blinked, and after she ripped up the rest of the leaves and crumpling them, she speculated, "With how you read about Signal's dealings against the mage, Phantascope, I would have expected you to know more about my mother's studies in apothecary and herbology." Video's eyes softened as she continued mixing and crushing the leaves. "I studied with her before I received my title, and learned what I needed to be able to survive by myself as a courier."

"Huh." Pictures stared as Video kneaded and smashed the leaves, then nodded, and looked back to Receiver, who was watching Transmitter as he ate.

Video stopped mixing and applied the finished poultice to the raccoon's wounds with the tips and pads of her paw. "I've had to use the skills for many others than just myself already, but nothing quite this vicious." She was surprisingly careful, despite her large, long-furred paws, and worked cautiously with the raw skin. Radio looked away when Video groomed the fur and blood off of the large gray animal, but looked back when Video started placing the moss around the raccoon's wound, holding the poultice in place and staunching any new blood flow after cleaning out the wounds.

It made Radio wonder if Video had been treating her own wounds after she and Pictures retired for sleep, as she had never noticed the large feline doing so before, but with further thought, Radio realized she had smelled the scent of the leaves on the long-furred feline before. Once the masked mammal finished eating, Video took the extra moss and leaves from her bag, and placed it down beside him. She nodded to the raccoon, and then looked to Receiver. "He may need your assistance to continue applying and cleaning the wound, but otherwise, just continue reapplying as needed. He should make it if it doesn't get infected."

"Understood, ma'am. Thank you so much." Receiver dipped her head gratefully as the raccoon nodded, as well.

Video's ear flicked, and her tail swept along the raccoon's flank as she moved towards the exit of the alley. "Thank you for telling us what you know, Transmitter. We'll leave you be so you may heal."

"I'll take them there, Transmitter, just stay here and rest." Receiver smoothed the raccoon's fur on the top of his head, and rose up to her paws.

Video nodded, and started out back for the road. Receiver didn't waste a breath to give Transmitter the time to refuse as she jumped to Video's side, walking out from the alley quickly with the larger cat. She immediately led the three of them away from the city again, leaving the raccoon sleeping in the comfort of the moss and plantain leaves. Radio winced as her paws hit against the pavement once more when she followed the other women, and if that wasn't enough, she then heard Pictures' chuckle from behind her.

She looked at him with a furrowed brow, wondering if he really found amusement from her pain, and had to make herself relax when he gave her a small sympathetic smile. When she still stared at him, he bounded up and let her rest on him as they walked. "It'll be alright, you know. After we get out from the city, the ground will just be the earth, and it'll be a lot easier on your paws."

Radio blinked. She sighed, and turned to look ahead. "Yeah...probably." She thought perhaps she should use some of the plantain poultice for herself, too.

"As for Receiver..." He surprised Radio with his next words. She quickly looked up at him with rounded eyes, and he shot her a censuring look before continuing, "She, like me, was not raised by feline parents alone. Even with the shelter and security offered now for the cats all around Media, we were born before the city was open to accepting followers. We did not grow up together, as I went from home to home with many different animals for most of the early seasons of my life, but similar aspects are still there. I didn't think moving from place to place was going to end for me, until the Studio Star employed me in Clowder City, but Receiver remained stationed here and stayed closer to her roots."

Radio's head sank. She had offended Pictures because of her reaction to the cat and raccoon's relationship. Without a doubt, now, he saw that she was upset about the two.

And maybe that you were jealous. Radio swallowed, and ignored the taunting voice in her head. She turned her gaze up at the silver tabby, hoping he didn't consider that she was jealous of his relationship with Receiver. "Oh, I..." She blinked, and lowered her head more. "I didn't know." She hadn't thought of the felines born prior to Studio constructing Clowder City as having hardship. There were so many programs and help in Media that made felines a privileged species. Radio was surprised the Council still sent cats to the Ruined City at all. It seemed strange to even conceptualize the idea of cats born before Clowder City's debut might not be offered the same opportunities, as Pictures came and left the Ruined City knowing Receiver, yet he returned today and Receiver was still stationed in the area.

It made Radio wonder about the Council's actions again, but she blinked away the thought and looked up at Pictures as he chuckled again, more lightheartedly, answering, "I know you didn't, Miss Radio." His nose gave a twitch as he went onto explain, "What can I say? I have a bleeding heart for these kinds of things, but nothing in comparison to Receiver. I met Receiver during my first mission in the autumn of last year. While I myself accepted Clowder City's culture, and the expectations the Studio Star set for the rest of Media, Receiver kept the values and respect for the other species that her guardians taught her, and never separated herself from them as her people after she earned her title like I did with mine."

"Ahh…" Radio nodded, and continued on for a while before she blinked and looked back up at him. "You know, when you say it like that, it seems absolutely unfair, Pictures." Radio stared at him questioningly. She hadn't thought of Pictures, a surveillance director, out of all the verified followers of Media would have had such hardship in his youth, let alone feel so strongly about the change brought by the rules and limits of her auntie's city where he resided.

"Oh, by no means, Radio Star." Pictures smiled. "The bloodline of the

Studio Star is what helped successfully colonize this land to become Media. Honoring the species would only be reasonable of Media's followers. I'm surprised it hadn't happened earlier, if I may be honest with you."

"Yeah, I guess..." Radio swallowed, nodding as she leaned further onto him for support, hoping to end the conversation. She really didn't know what to think of what he said. All her life she had been taught about the goodness her aunt brought to the land by making Clowder City and the greatness brought by their family after the overthrow of magic, but this mage's bitterness and loathing towards her, even after all these generations, and Pictures' bringing up the effect the city had on others made her rethink the matter. Radio always thought of the beneficial action Studio accomplished and managed was the best for Media. She never gave a moment to think about the idea of how different it would have been if a bird or a raccoon had helped with the colonization instead.

It all really made her think. Why hadn't she ever thought about these things before? She had always been stuck in her room dreaming about the world outside her courtyard, and within a few days, she'd offered to venture out only because of her sister passing up the opportunity. Just the taste of it in all its grotesque detail made her fear being out and learning more after this mission. It seemed like any new knowledge she found was just going to be negative. Was it really the Council that was responsible, or were the people just not grateful for the help they were given? Radio sighed, and pressed on, clenching her jaw at the pain in her paws.

Then she realized the ground had changed under her and she could breathe easier again. She let out a breath of relief as she inhaled the burst of fresh air once they were back in the outskirts of the city, this time on the other side. They hadn't been attacked again! That didn't promise they wouldn't be attacked in the outskirts, but they had made it through the city! The bubbliness began flooding back into her with each step, more and more assured they actually made it out of the ruins, and were all still speaking to each other. Radio giggled at the idea of them taking on a giant wolf, speaking to a raccoon, and making it through the Ruined City. *What a story, a real story!* Not one she read in her books. Radio saw the clowder in front of her staring at her in confusion, and laughed again, leaping up ahead to exclaim, "We did it!"

Pictures laughed. "We're not there yet, Miss Radio!" He grinned at her while Video rolled her eyes, but may have made the tiniest smile when shaking her head. Radio chuckled when she saw even Receiver smile before turning back onto the path again. She was having so much fun with them, living through adventure and danger in the middle of this calamity. How could she be negative and judgmental when accomplishing something like this was her dream? She ignored the pain in her paws as she ran beside Video and Pictures, growing more excited as they drew closer to the enormous tower looming at the end of the city outskirts.

"But we're getting closer, Pictures! This is so exciting!" she breathed out, her eyes widening as she took in the sight. She could imagine what this building had been, staring in awe of the broken crystal structure, imagining all of the work it took into making the imposing building which was still standing, majestically enduring the ravages of time and neglect. The shard was just past this, before they reached the incline to the meadows. Radio replayed the words from the raccoon freshly in her head, and made the group quicken their pace to match hers as she sprinted excitedly towards it. Another shard, another step closer to their goal, and another step closer to getting off the pavement.

She startled when she felt something rest on her shoulder, and quickly looked over to see it was only Receiver's tail to slow her pace. Receiver smiled at her, and continued to lead, bringing them away from the giant building and towards the grassy terrain off of the abandoned offices leading to the building.

Radio followed on pace with Video and Pictures, and flicked her ears and tail tip once they finally reached actual land once more. The ground was still artificially hard from all of the broken particles and rubble scattered out from the city, but it cleared a little more with every step, becoming easier to walk upon each and every heartbeat.

Radio kneaded her paws into the soft earth once they finally reached unadulterated grass, and remained behind as Video and Pictures rushed after Receiver once the fragment's red gleam was visible in the distance. The twilight sky complemented the item's faded red color. Radio then stared in confusion, however, and came up to the three once she did indeed see that the shard was more faded than the other ones had been. Video held it up to the light. It was still unquestionably magic, from what Radio could feel from the shard's faint warmth, but it didn't seem as bright or as powerful as the other ones.

Once Video put it in with the other shards, which had begun to fade as well, all three gleamed a bit brighter. Radio felt the sudden warmth through the bag, and was relieved that the shard's power was all connected. She looked up at Video, who stared down at her and Pictures to state firmly, "I think we're running out of time."

The giant cat flattened her ears when Pictures and Radio dipped their heads, gazing down at where they had retrieved the shard. It made Radio wonder how much time they had to find the others. She listened to Video sigh before the marbled tabby turned to Receiver. "Thank you for helping us, ma'am."

"Of course, Miss. I wish you luck on your mission, and am glad I could do what I could." The ochre tabby tipped her head to the larger feline, blinked slowly to Radio, brushed her side along Pictures and nuzzled him before she raced away from them towards the giant structures once more. Radio watched her leave in amazement, realizing she had no reason to be jealous of the strong feline, and could whole-heartedly hope she would continue to fare well in the dark city. She blinked her goodbye, and turned to Video.

The long-furred feline stared beyond the slope into the vast meadow that expanded across the entire valley, and lashed her giant tail before tilting her head slightly to look back at both Radio and Pictures. As if on cue, Pictures took a step forward to stand beside the larger cat, and Radio walked to the side of them, staring down into what lay ahead for them if they took this route. She couldn't believe they were really as far as the meadows. Sanctified Meadows was beyond beautiful, seeing it up close. Radio had already been amazed by the valley of flowers when seeing it from the castle, but now only being moments from it, her tail waved in excitement.

Pictures turned his chin up towards the sky. Radio followed his gaze to see the monitor device hovering down to report to them. The two behind the speaker didn't bother to greet them before they quickly chattered and mewled, "You did it! We had trouble finding the next shard's signal but located it just beyond the borders of the Sanctified Meadow! Your best bet would be traveling through it!" Tape exclaimed.

Recorder then continued, "You've all done fantastic work. We've sent devices to fend off the Jester for now, so don't waste a moment! Be safe, and stay strong. We're depending on you!"

"We won't let you down," Video murmured.

Radio had remained silent at first, and then the words clicked. "Do we really get to travel through Conscience's Meadow?" Radio beamed up at Pictures, watching his brow arch. Once she realized it was directed towards her, she frowned, realizing she used the name that Studio taught her as a kitten, and quickly furthered, "My dream was to always see the Sanctified Meadows, always reading about the Council's petitions to remove it. I can't believe we get to go through it! This is just amazing!"

"We're not here for sightseeing," Video growled as she sent the surveillance bot away, and turned to the two smaller felines. "We're already risking this mission enough by the breaks we've been taking to help these folks and because of the storm that passed through. We can't waste any more time. Let's go." She whipped her head back to the incline, and bound up the path without waiting for them.

Radio gaped at the feline, wanting to bring up how much time Video wasted by going to find plantain and moss for Transmitter, but Pictures let out a hearty laugh, silencing her thoughts. "Are you ready, Miss Radio?" he purred, seeing the excitement in her eyes as he crouched down, as though if he were readying to leap. *Like a race.* Radio's heart pounded with excitement, and she giggled as she crouched down only for an instant before projecting her back paws off from the ground and leaping into the air. She and Pictures both laughed as they ran down the slope, and Radio only laughed harder when Pictures lost his footing and rolled down the hill before pulling back up onto his paws.

Radio expected him to stop to catch his breath, but he raced past her when she sprinted ahead. She squealed and chased after him, having to giggle again as this time they passed Video, who looked at them both with concern and confusion in regard to their fun and games. Radio hoped she wouldn't mind, as it helped them make progress and made it fun, too. She would likely never get the chance to venture out this far again, proving herself or not, as the three were at least a day's travel from the nearest road now.

The ground was plush once they reached the meadow. Radio actually enjoyed when her paws pressed down against the soft leaves and smooth petals of the flowers, and watched them scatter across the valley for almost the entire stretch. She purred as she and Pictures led the way through the various hues of purple, magenta, pink, periwinkle, powder blue, and couldn't believe that there was really every color in between, too. All of it was even more beautiful in the setting twilight, and Radio couldn't be happier being able to travel through it now. She grinned as she caught up to Pictures, and pounded her hind legs into the ground as powerfully as she could to leap right into him, and send them both rolling into the plush bed of flowers.

Petals and leaves soared through the air as they both landed in a dip of the meadow. Radio laughed with delight, purring as she pinned Pictures down and touched her nose to his temple as he laughed, too. She eased back, staring into his multi-colored eyes, the beautiful blue ice of his right, and the crisp golden autumn of his left, making Radio smile as she flopped down on top of him, her paws wrapped around his shoulders.

Video caught up to them simply by walking, and with a whip of her tail, she knocked Radio off of Pictures to tumble into another patch of flowers. Radio closed her eyes shut as she rolled back into the meadow, but then bounded back onto her feet and hurried after Video. "You have to be excited, Video! I know you're a courier and you've gone all over the place, but this is unbelievable! We're making progress meeting our objective! We know where the next shard is, and we've already gathered the first three!" Radio beamed and purred, but her smile fell into a frown when Video only continued to push forward, not responding to Radio's words with so much as a tilt of her head.

"There's not enough *time* to celebrate what we've succeeded in doing when we still haven't finished our mission. We can have fun and feel accomplished once the crystal fragments are brought back and the mage is put to death." The giant cat's jaw clenched as she continued, "Stop playing around like a kitten and focus on what we have ahead of us!" Video said the last words through gritted teeth, and prowled forward.

Radio's ears slowly flattened against her head. She frowned as Pictures came up to her and brushed his tail along her flank in comfort. He gave her a smile, and nudged his nose up after Video, and led her forward. She was so amazed by the tom. He had such a strange balance and intent of things. He didn't even give Video's words and chastisement a thought or concern, just simply took them to heart, even bothering to get them as far as he had, and moved forward. He handled everything as well as he wanted. She sighed with a touch of contentment, her tail whipping upwards in delight, and kept pace with him.

The sky was slowly darkening into night, but enough of the light still gleamed from the vast shimmering space to enrich the meadow's colors. Radio stared at it, trying to take it in with every sense she could so she would remember it forever. She blinked and focused her eyes into taking in every crisp detail of the leaves that were the cushion under the flowers, and inhaled deeply to take in the scent of the flowers and taste the cooling air. She relaxed every bone she could as she leaned against Pictures, feeling his soft, thick fur against every one of the thin feathery hairs on her shoulder. This was something she would always be able to appreciate, and would take the time to remember for ages to come.

Pictures didn't seem to mind their closeness, making Radio relax even more. She walked step by step with him, letting their paws slowly synchronize in movement, and began to purr again. He looked at her over his shoulder, smiling, and touched his nose to her head. She blinked up at him, and brightened before she rested her head on his shoulder and continued walking side by side. This was something she could especially get used to, and something she never really had before. Radio inhaled, and let her exhaled breath out through the tom's fur, watching it move without ever ceasing their trek through the field of flowers.

She hoped with all her heart that they could still stay in contact after this mission. Even Video spoke about celebrating their accomplishments. Maybe after they reach their objective, the Council might see how well they worked together, complementing each other's strengths as a unit.

Radio watched as another surveillance bot hovered across the area, the same one she saw on the way to the castle, the one they saw before the storm, the one that belonged to Video's father, Signal. Radio's eyes rounded as the camera turned on them, wondering what Signal might think of the situation lying before them, as well as her closeness to the silver tom beside herself. She didn't bother pulling away from Pictures, knowing the surveillance consultant had already seen her actions, and turned her gaze towards the path ahead that was set by Video, knowing everything was fine at this moment.

- CHAPTER 6 -

SOVEREIGNTY

The three travelled far into the night. Radio did all she could not to fall asleep on Pictures' shoulder as they walked, as he remained silent as though he was encouraging her to rest. She purred as she looked up at him, and touched her nose to his jawline while they continued to move through the seemingly endless meadow. Her paws and legs ached from the walk, burning from the continuous strain into muscles Radio hadn't been aware she had to worry about, but the leaves and petals beneath them were a tremendous comfort, letting her continue beside Pictures. "It feels like I'm walking on clouds." She sighed into the silver tabby tom's fur, smiling.

Pictures chuckled, letting out a bit of his own purr as he looked down at her, and rested his head on hers as they walked. Her purr only grew louder as she opened her mouth in a giant smile, and brushed her shoulder against his. Video prowled forward, and rushed ahead when the faintest of red gleams was seen in the distance. Radio was amazed. It had been a painful night of travel, but had they really found another shard that quickly? No interruptions, no attacks from the Jester? Radio looked around cautiously, as though waiting for the clothed monkey to leap out and attack. Surely even with the surveillance monitoring the sorcerer, they wouldn't be able to detain the magician, would they?

She already heard the regular surveillance bot hovering down as they approached the shard. It made Radio grin all the more, imagining the group having a much easier time tracking them with the clear skies and widespread area. It dropped down further as Video picked up the shard and put it into her bag. "That's one more down, guys," Recorder cheered through the speaker. "The next one's faint, but we know it's past Clowder City. Head towards there, and we should be able to give you an update the closer you get."

"Yeah!" Tape chimed in. "From what we've found so far, the signals get stronger the closer you come to each individual shard, so as long as you get near the area, we should be able to pinpoint the location and give you an idea on where it is. Keep going, you three!"

"We will, but first we need to rest," Video said, making both Radio and Pictures stare at the volatile tabby in shock as she furthered, "We'll head out at dawn, if it is acceptable."

There was a pause on the other end of the device, but then Recorder answered, "Of course, Miss Video. Have a good night!"

Video nodded, and let the device float away from the three. "You too," she called out, and then continued on the path towards a thicker clump of flowers.

Once the device was out of earshot to record, Radio quickly raced up to the marbled tabby. "Hey, Video," she yelled to the feline, feeling her throat tighten in apprehension. She felt comfortable around Pictures, and thought as though she could call him her friend, but she didn't feel Video felt the same of her.

"What do you request, Radio Star?" Video responded formally as they drew closer to the flower bed.

Radio swallowed, the tone wasn't helping her concerns. She contemplated not even asking, knowing she could waste an opportunity of rest, but Video didn't stop to rest unless Pictures or she were falling on their paws. "Are you alright? You don't generally make the decision to sleep for the night and...I'm sure the battle with that dog thing was hard, but it didn't hurt you badly, did it?" Radio bit her lip, knowing that she would likely be dead if Video hadn't been there to save her, and hadn't been there for most of the fight, either.

"I am, but we've found two shards, with no rest in between, and we need to rest sometime. While we're at the border, I'll go out to see what I can hunt, but you two can rest for the next day's travel. We need to be energized to make good time."

"Are you sure you don't want me to hunt, Miss Video?" Pictures asked, stepping forward beside Radio.

There was only a long enough pause for Video to sigh before she replied, "Yes, you two will need it. This is my job, I'll be fine." The large cat shook her head as she had her tail sweep along the blanket of flowers to mark their resting spot. Radio stepped into the area and looked up at the long-furred tabby, but she already turned away, on her way out of the meadow.

Radio considered possibly going after her, but Pictures spoke first. "I think she just needs a moment alone. You know couriers aren't used to being around others."

"Neither are nobles, but I'm still more happy to be around you two than be anywhere else." Radio looked up at him, knowing her eyes were reflecting her sadness as she stared into his.

"Being a part of a bloodline isn't a choice, Miss Radio. Video chose her seclusion as a courier, so I'm not sure if it's quite the same on her end. Let's rest." He then smiled, and looked at her mischievously. "Unless you have something else in mind."

Radio gasped, and pushed her paw into his chest. "Stop that! You shouldn't even jest!" She laughed, surprised she somehow still was able to use that word in a positive manner after the Jester, and pounced on Pictures again, wrapping her paws around his neck. She squealed when he didn't even stagger with her weight, then pulled up her back legs from the ground, and screeched as he suddenly dropped to the ground with her.

She wheezed and mewled under his weight. It felt like a rock was pressed against her lungs and rib cage. She squirmed and pressed her back paws against him as he lifted himself off of her, and only then was able to laugh. He composed himself and leaned upward, arching his brow and grinning down at her. She kept her grip around him and ran her rough tongue against his jawline, beginning to purr.

It was such a wonder and amazement, to be resting and travelling with a director of everything she had feared as a kit. Terrified of all surveillance and the very idea of being watched, here she was with one of the composers of the secretive and mysterious orchestra of monitors, and not the slightest bit afraid to share herself with him. She rubbed her head up against his, her tail beginning to twine under his own. There would never be another moment like this, either. *Unless, maybe...*

"Pictures, do you think we'll stay in contact after this?" She swallowed nervously. "You still want to know each other when we're done with our mission, right?"

The silver tabby turned his face down at her, and blinked his golden eye at her while he kept his blue eye closed. "Hmmm...Do *you* want to stay in contact, Miss Radio?" The corners of his muzzle turned upwards into a mischievous smile. He looked down at her with that twinkle in his golden eye that was simply the definition of mayhem. Radio scoffed, knowing she shouldn't even be surprised that he'd make her answer that.

When she didn't respond right away, he lowered his head closer to hers. "I only wish to clarify before I answer, dear," he teased, and touched his pink and black nose to her shiny dark one.

"Well, yes, Pictures, otherwise I wouldn't ask!" Radio answered as sharply as she could muster. She went to nip his nose, but he pulled back in time, and laughed.

"Oh, good, I just had to be sure. Forever and longer, Miss Radio, I would be with you. I will answer only to you, if you wish, every command

and request, I am your eyes and ears," he purred smoothly, so dramatically spoken Radio couldn't even tell if he meant it.

She felt her fur puff out as she huffed defensively, "I mean it! I want a serious answer, Pictures!"

"Then yes!" he laughed, and brushed his tongue along her forehead. "I'd love to get to know you more and be with you, Miss Radio. It's been an honor traveling with you, and such an eye opening experience. I'd be delighted if our relationship wouldn't have to end after this mission."

Radio purred, "Then it's just Radio to you. That's exactly how I feel." She leaned her head under his chin, and curled up with him in harmony. So much could come from this mission, more than Radio had ever dreamed of, back in her sheltered home, staring out her window in wonder of the world without ever venturing beyond her courtyard.

Video returned not long after the two fell asleep, and placed the fresh kill out on the flattened turf she had made, then curled up to sleep away from the two.

The smell of the fresh meat flared in Radio's nostrils. The feathery feline stirred and knew that Video had come back, but was too exhausted to say anything. She was just grateful she had made it back safe. After another spell of rest, she felt Pictures had left during the night, but didn't wake until she realized both of her feline companions were gone from their beds.

Radio looked around, but neither was in sight. She frowned, and adjusted her collar before getting up. Where had they gone? Even as she stood, she saw neither Pictures, nor Video, and just barely caught the smell

151

of their fur in the night breeze. The food Video had brought back was still untouched, so they hadn't gone hunting, either. She had to look for them, and probably should quickly, too.

The two feline's scents were faint, and Radio's pelt twitched when she realized they must have been gone for a while now. She followed where the breeze took her, and continued walking until she heard their voices not too far away. There was irritability, if not anger in their tones, perhaps urgency. Radio flattened herself against the flowers to not allow the wind to betray her, and prowled towards sound of their voices.

She held her breath as she drew closer, not wanting any noise to give her away. She scanned the leaves and petals every step for the safest path, travelling silently through the meadow as she listened to their words.

Or tried to. Radio couldn't hear anything they said from the low growling and hissing. She slowly peeked her head out from the incline they slunk along and through the flowers down the slope where they were. Her eyes rounded as they adjusted to the moonlight's beams casting down upon the two cats ahead of her.

Video towered over Pictures, and both looked battered with ruffled fur as though they had been tussling through the meadow. She loomed over the tom and stared into his eyes, so intensely there seemed to be no need for expression from either feline. Their only movement besides moving lips and throats in their quiet communication was their tails, both lashing and flicking.

Radio stared at the scene, speechless. She had been shocked and surprised enough that she didn't even realize she was standing again, her claws digging into the earth as she tried to fight back the tears that threatened and burned in the corner of her eyes. Out of all the times they could have done something like this, it had to be tonight. *What are they doing?*

Video saw her first. She was pressing her paw against Pictures' throat when she looked up at the collared feline. "R-Radio Star." Video's eyes rounded, seeing Radio's tears. "Wait, Radio Star, don't!" She hurried to Radio, but the smaller cat's hiss and snarl kept her back. "It's not...It's not whatever you're assuming." Video frowned, leaning back from the feathery feline.

"It doesn't matter what I assume. No matter what, it's not right." The tears made her eyes burn but she refused to stop to clean them when she whipped away from the giant cat. Either way, whether or not Radio thought Video was attacking Pictures for some reason, or that Video actually loved him, too, it wasn't right. The idea of Video being in love with Pictures was probably a lot less likely. Radio knew she was projecting her own thoughts onto the other feline. No matter what, it wasn't right, and there was no justifying it, not when they were so close to completing their mission. "You're the one that wants this mission done more than anyone! The mission the three of us must complete, according to that mage's prophecy!" Radio huffed her indignation, but then her voice grew quiet. "You should sleep so we can get ahead as early as we can," she said through her constricted throat, and padded away from the both of them.

The more she imagined what she had just witnessed between Video and Pictures, the less she could understand it. It was very unlikely that Video loved Pictures, which made Radio frustrated and angry the idea even came back into her head. That was just an impulsive thought because of what *she* had shared with him. Nevertheless, it didn't make much more sense that Video would attack him. Whether it was his personality or his carelessness, it was Video who had suggested they rested, so it wasn't that time had been wasted, either. Radio had respected Video for not letting Pictures antagonize her initially. There wasn't much reason for that to change. Yet it seemed it had.

This all could have been avoided by one thing. *Why hadn't they both gone to sleep?* What had happened while she slept? Radio allowed more tears to stream down her face once she knew she was far enough away from them, and sat at the peak of the meadow, able to stare past the end of it into the lower valleys below, and the rising land above to Clowder City. They were so close to the next objective, possibly the last, seeing how large the fragments were. Why would they do something like this?

Radio clenched her jaw as she let the last of the tears she had held back trickle from her eyes. She heard Pictures' footsteps from behind her, and looked back to gaze at his neck, unable to meet his eyes after seeing how intently Video had stared into them. "What do you want?" she choked out, and looked back out into the distance.

"I want to apologize," he murmured quietly. "I don't want to hurt you, Radio."

She almost wanted to correct him and have him address her as the Radio Star after what had happened, but she only grit her teeth and kept her eyes away from his. "Of course not, Pictures. You'd be put down for that." Radio's chin lifted in a regal posture, in imitation of the Frequency Star's demeanor. Pictures eyebrow did the same, rising up to the stripes on his forehead as Radio continued, her speech pattern also mimicking her sister's. "However, I won't demand you apologize. I don't even know the situation well enough to accept it."

Pictures scoffed at her attitude, but explained, "You know how serious Video is about the objective, Radio. We reached a disagreement about priority, and Video decided to take the argument away from you, which led to…" Pictures paused, giving Radio a chance to look at him as he continued, "Video deciding she could win the argument by simply making me agree to hers." He sighed when Radio stifled a chuckle. She could actually imagine Video deciding to beat someone up until they agreed to her terms.

"She's like a big kitten," Radio mumbled, lying down and resting her head on her paws.

Pictures managed to smile at that, sitting down with her. "She practically is."

Radio smiled, and then sighed. "Fine, I'll believe you. No matter what, though, we'll just wait until after all of this, we're almost done. After it's finished, we can get to know each other and maybe develop something then. I don't think Video is this wound up when she's not on a mission. I want to give her a chance to not be a robot around us."

"I'm really not too sure about her…" Pictures started, but then smiled when Radio turned her gaze up to look at him, and said, "But I'm sure I can give her another chance when this is done."

Radio watched him sigh and look away from her doubtfully when he thought she was no longer looking at him, and turned her attention back onto the view of the dark glimmering sky. "I'm looking forward to tomorrow."

Pictures lay down beside her, staring out into the open land. "Me too, Radio."

The two only watched for a moment longer before they curled up to sleep, waiting for the coming dawn.

Within a day of travel away from the three companions, the Aureate City continued another day of celebration. The Studio Star was now among her people, proud they had recovered more strong-willed than ever after the Jester's attack. She stood on a stage, where a line of beautiful felines stood proudly as the mayor announced, "Today, before we start another evening of festivities, I believe it's time we announce the winner of our Callisteia Contest!" The lithe leader purred. Her feathery tail made an audible swish as it whipped up in excitement. "While every citizen and guest have hearts as gold as my city, only once a festival can I choose who may join me at my side for the grand parade. The Callisteia Contest's winner will be that individual, and we will embark on our celebration immediately upon the announcement, so be ready, my friends!"

The felines below the stage purred and cried out their excitement, and Studio laughed, even hearing the finalists mewl to each other on who might be the winner.

Studio took in a deep breath, wanting to enjoy the moment before her announcement, then yelled out, "The winner of the Callisteia Contest is…"

"No need to announce it!" The sudden shout made Studio jump. She looked up with wide eyes at the interruption, almost immediately narrowing her eyes when she saw what the source of the voice was.

"I'm here now, I can do it myself." the clothed monkey mage began walking down from one the golden threads that streamed through the city for easy travel access for the citizens. Studio's ears flattened against her head as the primate approached the stage.

"What?" she growled under her breath, knowing the Jester could hear her.

However, she was ignored. "Wow, what an honor!" The monkey walked past her and her assistant, Screen, and shoved the contestants aside from the pillar that held the golden flower crown made for the winner of the contest. "I'm surprised. I really only have to thank myself for this lovely form. Giving it further thought, I don't really know why I was shocked at all, the winner should have been clear when it came down to evident beauty. You've all seen me before." The Jester smiled over its shoulder at Studio with hooded eyes, and dissolved the jester hat on its head into shadows to toss the golden crown in its stead.

Studio gasped as the beautiful and rich gold color of the crown was tainted into a black metal that matched the centerpiece of the Jester's collar, and had to hold back a hiss, trying not to panic her citizens, who stared up at the monkey in complete fear.

She went to speak, but the primate continued, "Yes, to the dear Clowder Callithump, I can only condescend to the conception of such a contest to show, despite all curbs to your comprehension: I will conquer, and you will cower, Clowder City." The mage's eyes hooded again, and it shot Studio a grin before turning towards the crowd once more. "Your King has been vanquished, your technology has failed, your camaraderie inadequate…"

Studio stared in shock as the mage only continued the spiel after insulting the chosen three, bringing her gaze away from the primate only when Screen shifted the fabric on his head. "Well, it does *look* absolutely lovely—" her blind assistant started.

"Screen." Studio growled the name slowly at the silver tom, who seemed to hold back more amusement than Studio appreciated.

Radio yawned as she woke from the night's rest, happy to see Pictures was still curled up beside her. She looked directly at him, enjoying watching his chest rise and fall as he slept. His striped tail was wrapped around himself protectively, but he seemed relaxed. Radio let out a small sigh, then turned away, knowing he'd feel her stare if she kept on any longer. She stretched out her paws, which were slowly but gradually healing, and rose up to look out at the beautiful rising sun.

She was amazed at how beautiful the view looked, even with the glare of the early sun. She prodded Pictures awake, and went down the peak to find Video, who was curled up in the lowest dip of the valley.

"Video, it's dawn." Radio spoke as strictly as Video had when waking her and Pictures up, but what would have startled the other two felines awake like mice, simply caused Video to lift her head up from the ground and nod to Radio. Radio returned the nod and turned back to walk to the peak. The three stared down at the day's travel that awaited them. Radio moved forward to lead them down the incline. She had been a bit disappointed the large feline wasn't even phased by her tone.

It felt strange to be leading the path at first, Radio always just blindly following the two from the beginning of their travels, but now they were on their way to the central east, the one part of Media where Radio was actually familiar. This was something she could do, especially with them so close now. As the three continued to advance through the meadow, Radio's excitement grew.

All her life she wanted to visit Clowder City again, ever since she went there as a kitten. She knew she would make it her goal to live there as an adult, and to be able to help her Aunt Studio manage the city and continue the work far beyond the structure's borders. Now she was going to be only moments away from it, all for a quest which would enable her to prove her worth to the Council, her parents, and Studio herself. Radio would be able to fulfill her own potential and set her imprint upon the land of Media, one that wasn't only remembered for being the descendant of a courier to the Queen.

Radio beamed at the very idea of it as she led the two out of the meadow and carried forward. For the entire day they would travel east, and it would be just in time to end their night in Clowder City. With enough persistence, Radio might be able to convince the two to go into the city, just long enough so that she might catch a glance of her auntie. Radio's tail waved in delight, and she pushed on forward.

It wasn't just her alone, now, either. Now Radio had Video, she had Pictures, she knew Receiver, Faith, Mabel, and even Enterprise. She could work with Pictures into getting a more secure and private surveillance system, she could have Video spread the message of the growing City and its enriched potential, she could bring Receiver out from the Ruined City to scout for others that might need help, and that wouldn't be all. Radio

159

dreamed of bringing everyone she knew with her to help her accomplish what she wanted to do. Video might not even want a friendship after her disagreement with Pictures, likely about the priorities of relationships, but the idea still tickled Radio, and she had to imagine what she might be able to do at the end of this all.

Mabel was sure to know everyone in Capital City with her announcement work and knowledge of the castle. It was an atrocity that she didn't have her title. Mabel could easily help Radio with finding connections within the Capital's walls. Enterprise was one of the most influential individuals in all of Media, basically carrying the weight of the Council on his shoulders as he helped the followers of the city and beyond. Once Radio finished this and helped save the King, they would all know her potential, and be game for her plans. Even Faith might bring connections with the smaller species and find others who spoke the languages of the most commonly verified species.

What a venture! It made Radio carry on boldly and proud, excited at the possibilities of what Media could be if she expanded Studio's programs beyond just felines, and really helped out everyone in the region. She sighed and pressed forward, glad all of her thoughts kept her from tiring and able to trek on even as the sun continued to rise. It was all a remarkable mission, and she was amazed at the goodness that could be brought out by such a tragic and terrifying incident; all the more if they truly could bring the King back.

Video and Pictures remained silent behind her for as long as she led, so she continued on until they came across somewhere they could hunt and drink. Once there were burrows and a stream in sight, the three split up to gather their food for the afternoon. Radio was proud when she caught herself a small rabbit, and feasted on it with excitement. She had learned how to hunt, she had learned how to fight, and she had learned how to travel. *It was remarkable!* Radio raced back to the others as soon as she was done with her meal.

Pictures shared a portion of his meal with her, having caught a much larger rabbit, and the three set back out after going to the water and drinking their fill. They traveled side by side with Radio between them as they progressed through the land. She was amazed at the lack of attacks from the Jester, happy they weren't getting bad news from surveillance, or suffering tribulation from the followers of Media. Radio beamed at the exciting amount of luck. They would be able to do this!

Radio led them on until the sun was setting. That's when they came upon the remarkable sight, unlike anything else in the land. *The Aureate City.* Studio's private name for the commonly titled Clowder City was firm in her mind. Radio held her breath at the sight of the golden cat-head shaped structure, but had to let it out. It didn't come out silently, rather quite the high-pitched audible squeal. Pictures laughed while Video looked at her with dismay.

"There it is, you two! Clowder City!" Radio purred and kneaded her paws into the earth, grinning ear to ear at seeing the beautiful structure as a grown cat now. Here it was, just as beautiful as she remembered it, and she was astonished. "Oh, please, we must travel through it! We'd save so much time! Can we, please?" She looked pleadingly at Pictures.

"Absolutely not," Video growled, prowling forward. "That is one of the most densely populated cities in all of Media, second only to the Capital, itself, and by winter, I'm sure it may have the potential to surpass it. We would find hundreds of problems, taking up all of our time inside there."

Radio pouted and walked with Video down the slope. "Video, it's *Clowder City,* there *are* no problems there!"

"Absolutely not, everyone would demand your attention, Radio Star, especially since knowledge of your existence is rather new around here. No one would leave us alone, and any confidentiality the mission once had surely would be gone by the time we were through the streets."

"We could just go through the two city gates, front and back, and save so much time! I won't talk to anyone!" It may have been the biggest lie Radio ever told, and Video knew it.

"No."

Radio gasped at the tiny response that crushed her whole world. She wailed, and pleaded, "Please..! I did so well! I led you both all the way here!" Of course, there was no mention that Pictures lived in the City and the path was worn all the way to the beautiful, golden walls that had just recently come into view.

Video rolled her eyes and growled, prowling at a quicker pace. "Fine! We'll go through the city, but not a peep, Radio Star!"

Radio giggled, and brushed her flank along Pictures when he caught up to them, and then raced ahead of them both. Her purr sounded out from her throat audibly. She was leading them to Clowder City! A dream come true! This wasn't a carriage ride paid for by the Council or her parents, no, Radio was storming in by foot, with her true companions beside her. It was much too exciting for her not to purr.

She smiled in delight and love as the two larger cats matched pace with her, knowing they'd likely love the city as much as she did, Pictures, of course doing so, likely have residing in the city for a few years by now. That in itself made Radio so excited to be in such a close relationship with the tomcat, knowing they feel comfortable in the same environment. She bounded down towards the city with her tail high in the air, now thinking of all the possibilities that might happen. They traveled without breaks until they finally reached the gates, determined to make the best time they could to enter the city.

- CHAPTER 7 -

IRRESPONSIBILITY

Even before entering the city, the three felines heard the drums and instruments playing almost the same rhythm of Radio's anticipatory gait to the gates. She felt them as her pounding heart pulsed in time with the thundering music, making her have to slow down just to calm herself when the song quickened its pace. It sounded even more incredible than she remembered. She didn't wait for Pictures or Video as she moved forward. Her ears rang as they entered, but that only made her more excited for the possibilities inside. This wasn't just any normal parade she heard within the city walls. Radio knew by the strength of the parade and cheering of the felines inside, but she couldn't voice her assumption out loud until she knew for sure.

Her eyes squinted as the bright light shone directly onto them, completely blinding her at first after coming from the dark night outside. The entire city was gleaming as though it was day. Only the dark sky gleaming beyond the high gold city walls reminded Radio that the sun had already set. Having looked up, Radio's eyes slowly came back into focus to see the parade was heading straight toward them along the cleared street.

All the city's domesticated cats and assorted felines were a part of it, singing and marching in harmony and joy together. Radio stared in complete amazement of how many mixed species of feline there were as members of the band, and that was just for the music alone. There were dancers, performers, and participants of the parade trailing behind the band, and past that were all the floats.

Radio couldn't believe the detail and beauty of them all. There was one for each population in all of central Media, where Studio gathered most of the folk who frequented the city when making the enormous structure, and developing the programs for which the city was now known. Radio could only smile recognizing floats representing the Capital City, the Ruined City, Crater Valley, and Sanctified Meadows, which looked like its flowers came directly from the meadow, all just by her own personal knowledge of the areas now. She recognized the other areas by the readings in her book, but there was just something so much more special about having been to some of the destinations herself.

Out of all the amazement from the parade itself, Radio looked up to see an even bigger excitement. There was the dark, golden-collared feline above all of the floats. Her bright gold eyes were visible even from the distance she was from the three. Radio stared up at the powerful leader in

165

awe. This was her auntie, no less amazing than she was when Radio met her as a kitten. Radio watched as Studio stopped to look down at the sidewalks, where the crowds gathered below. "Let me hear your enthusiasm, citizens!" The elegant tabby's voice rang out through all the speakers of the city, making Video flatten her ears at the volume.

The mass of felines cheered and meowed in excitement, making Video even more dazed. "I have never seen so many cats before!" she shouted through the voices to Radio and Pictures, who excitedly moved forward into the city.

"You've never been here, Video?" Radio shouted back, laughing as she roamed closer towards the sidewalk. She hoped that they actually could stay to the side and pass through, knowing her aunt would be far too busy to actually entertain her. Besides, this was all she really needed to see to confirm that this was what she wanted to do with her life, and that this was where she wanted to be. The happiness and excitement of the citizens were amazing, as Radio had never seen such genuine delight anywhere else. This truly was the Aureate Festival, the largest festival in all of Media to celebrate the city's anniversary, increasing by a day every year.

She smiled even bigger when Video answered, "I heard that the population boomed for small cats because of this sanctuary, but this is just beyond anything that I could have imagined!" She looked at Radio and Pictures, but neither of them seemed surprised. "How…!?" The large tabby grew irritable, letting the two smaller felines lead her forward into the crowd.

"Video, this is just Clowder City, you can't be surprised." Radio grinned, knowing Video was getting quite the impression, entering the city during the Aureate Festival. Radio had *wondered* if maybe this was the situation they were entering, but hadn't known for sure. She was now more than delighted to be here, though, and looked back up to see the dark tabby above the crowd once more.

The collared cat, the one everyone knew as the Studio Star, let her laugh boom through the city. She swayed to the beat of the music on the pedestal she stood upon, and then began bounding through the floats again, leaping down, and starting her song:

Welcome one and all to the Golden City
Your aura can only shine with the brightness
You smile can only glow with the happiness
Of our beautiful Aureate City!

The felines laughed with joy and sang, and Studio bounced back, focusing her gaze upon Pictures and Radio. Video quickly backed up, her tail and spine fluffing up at the intense feline's stare. She puffed up even more as the other cats along the path looked their way. "This wasn't supposed to happen at all. Why hadn't anyone notified us tit was the Aureate Festival!?" Video hissed at the two of them.

"Because we were supposed to go around it." Radio sighed as she basked in the attention with Pictures, smiling at him as the golden light shone down on the both of them, and looked up at her aunt as the dark tabby lifted her chin. Was she going to announce them? Radio was in disbelief. How did she manage to see the three of them in the hundreds, if not thousands, of cats!?

"Greetings to the Frequency Star and her companions!" Studio announced, and the crowds cheered.

Radio's eyes rounded with horror. She had just been mistaken for her sister. Frequency was always the one to go to these events while Radio was left at home. The gray and black feline flattened herself to the ground, completely embarrassed and ashamed, but Studio was already bounding closer to them, jumping from float to float to see them better. It was too late, she couldn't flee. Radio was pulled up by a swing that sent her through a bounding of floats to her aunt, screeching as she was brought up to the distinguished city leader, and dropped onto the structure with the tall feline. It didn't take a single moment for Studio to gasp, her microphone now off. "Oh!"

Radio's ears flattened. "Ah, yes, Frequency was too busy, so they chose me," the smaller feline said monotonously over the parade drums. What could be more humiliating now? Of course Studio expected her sister, everyone did. How could she not be surprised? Video even warned her on the way that she wasn't known to exist!

She was even more surprised by what Studio said to her, though. "I'm so sorry, Radio. I haven't seen you since you were just a kit." She dipped her head, and blinked back up at the smaller feline. "I hadn't realized it was you when they notified me Resolution's daughter was travelling across the land on assignment. You hold yourself proudly now, much as your sister, yet you are quite yourself now that we're close." Studio touched her tail to Radio's shoulder, making Radio startle. Her aunt smiled. "Come with me, dear. I want to show you the city."

Radio stared at her in shock, waiting for the laugh to tell her that the tabby was joking, but it stayed a genuine and bright smile. Radio brightened as well, realizing this really was her auntie offering, and moved with her side by side as Studio continued her song:

Join us one and all in the Golden City
Your needs will all be met, your wants all fulfilled
Your requisites are more than satisfied, content!
In our beautiful Aureate City!

Radio beamed at the wonderful tune, and joined into the song with the crowd, as she well knew the chorus from all the recordings she had listened to at her home:

Aureate, Beautiful Golden Glow!
Everything you need!
Anything you want to know!

It was surely a dream come true. She was beside her aunt, one of the most powerful felines in Media, during the largest celebration of the summer solstice. Radio purred as she weaved through the floats nimbly with her aunt, all the travel having trained her for the slopes and hills of the structures that made the giant moving things. Radio giggled in her excitement, and carried on with Studio fearlessly, not caring a moment about her paws.

Studio showed her all of the different streets and sectors of the city just by bounding through the floats and marching past the parade itself, before a swing took them back up to where Radio first saw her aunt, allowing the tireless cat to continue on again as they approached a different street. "Isn't it just remarkable, my dear?"

Radio giggled, "Of course. It was made by you."

Both of them laughed, and Studio purred as she pressed her head against Radio's. "I'm so glad you could make it through here, Radio. I'm delighted to see you again."

"As am I. We're almost done with our mission. It's going to be amazing coming back here, Auntie."

"So, I'll see you once you're done?"

Radio nodded, and brightened up even more. Studio seemed just as excited as she was, and laughed out into the cooling air as she bounded down from the float again, dancing with the beat as Radio hopped down to join her. "Oh Radio, that is so exciting!"

"I know! Auntie, it's so good to see you again!" Radio brushed her flank along Studio's and twined their tails, but looked down to see Pictures lurking in an alley, his gaze intent and his ears flattened back. Radio realized she needed to get back to him so he could keep focused on their mission. She smiled at her aunt. "We'll catch up later, okay?"

"Of course! Continue forward, my dear." Studio dipped her head in respect, and then leapt up onto the swing to continue her song, gazing down at the crowd cheering below.

Radio smiled at the happiness her aunt could bring to so many. She bounded down the float to find Pictures again. It was much more difficult to see him once she was on the ground again, and she winced at the roughness of the pavement before she made it to the sidewalk. She took in a breath, and exhaled it, then weaved through the crowd to find the silver-striped tom amidst all of the other cats.

It took a while, but she finally emerged on the other side of the mass of cats, and flopped down on her stomach once she squeezed out from the group, which had barely seemed to notice her after she jumped down from the float. She landed right in front of Pictures, who arched his eyebrow and helped her up to her paws with the tip of his nose. She stared at him for a moment, then asked, "Where's Video?"

"I'm not sure. Either she didn't keep up, or she went ahead. I got distracted by the sights," he answered and then laughed.

Radio grinned, happy he could enjoy it as much as her, but then turned serious as she remembered his flattened ears. "We have to find her. She was already uncomfortable enough. I don't want to imagine what she might be thinking now that she's lost the both of us. Let's go."

Pictures nodded and followed her. The two searched forward and back toward where they had come into the city, with no sight of the giant tabby. "She must have really made progress. Maybe she decided to just meet us at the other side..." Radio shook her head as fear and apprehension set in. She quickly led Pictures through the crowd, not caring who she bumped into as they raced to the other side of the city. She sped up her pace when she realized it was where the parade had already begun wrapping around.

She tried to clear a path, but most of the cats didn't even see her, or her collar because of her height. The city crowd pushed through in better attempts to see the parade, almost knocking her down to get a better view of the upcoming floats. Radio's ears flattened, and she continued making her way forward through the vast party of cats, asking her companion,

"What if we don't see her? There are so many cats, Pictures!" Radio grew more concerned the further they went.

"We have to keep looking, Radio! Just keep going!" he called out, and walked beside her once he caught up to her pace. "She can't be that hard to find! There aren't too many cats like her." He said the last words with a chuckle.

Radio wished she could laugh along with him, but Video took the objective too seriously and urgently for Radio to push it off any longer. Radio knew not finding Video, not continuing the mission, was not by Video's choice. *Something is wrong.* This was all Radio's fault, she was sure of it. She talked them into coming to the city, and now they were separated. Furthermore, the largest one of the mission's party, the only one that could tower over most of the crowd, was the one missing.

"Oh...Video..." Radio fought tears again, thinking about how uncomfortable Video had been when she arrived in the city, and now she was alone.

She heard a wail from the large feline above all the crowd. Thinking back of the dangers the large, battle-ready feline had faced, whether it was a horde of rats or a savage wolf, the sound seemed unnatural and out of place in such a safe haven. Radio stifled a laugh from hearing the yowl, realizing Video could handle facing the mage behind both encounters, but not the crowd of Clowder City.

Nonetheless, she hurried towards the sound. "Come on, Pictures!" she called out to the tom, and dashed toward the noise. The crowd was easier to move through now that they were pulling away from the congested streets and towards the abandoned alleys. Radio hoped Video hadn't become too overwhelmed by it all, and hoped they'd just be able to set out from here.

What she saw wasn't she expected, though. It really *was* distress Video had wailed. Radio rushed to the fallen feline. Video was pressed against the wall of the alley completely dazed with shut eyes as though she couldn't focus. At first Radio thought it had been an anxiety attack, until she saw the blood dripping from Video's head. "Video!" she cried out, coming up to the giant feline and immediately grooming the surrounding area of the wound.

Pictures came up next, his brow furrowed with confusion and concern. "What happened?" he asked.

"He did." Studio bounded into the alley from a side road, and pointed her tail toward the gates, where they saw a nearly black-brown tabby racing through them, his own long fur and size putting Video to shame.

"I received an alert that something was amiss down by the eastern alleys, and raced here as fast as I could once I knew everything was all right with the parade." Studio explained as she walked over to Video, and began to assist her.

Radio swallowed nervously when she saw the giant tom begin to exit the city, and shuddered when he looked back, turning his piercing ice-blue eyes onto her.

It was the mage again! Something wasn't right, though. She looked to both Video and Studio, who both must have fought him, and had to ask to be sure. "Was it another attack by the Jester? He had *such* blue eyes."

"No, those are just his eyes," Video growled through her teeth, trying to stand with Studio's support.

"Who is he, then?" Radio wanted to ask thousands of questions, her tail waving until she realized that was the cat that harmed Video. She went to go help Video upon asking, but Studio was already handling it.

Once Studio helped get Video to her paws successfully, she looked at Radio. "His name is Stereo."

That wasn't much help, and Radio was glad when Video elaborated, "A former rival courier of the Council. He worked with me on many of my assignments, especially when we were both assigned under the private work of Signal." She paused as she lost her balance, but Studio kept her up, allowing her to continue. "He was very efficient, and did work for most of the early summer and spring with me. After it was discovered his travel companion was a spy for mages, she was removed, and he turned rogue."

Radio blinked, amazed at the connection between the two. They both had worked under Video's father and probably had known each other since they were kits. That was when it clicked for Radio, but by the time she could form the words, Pictures was already stating, "He's your brother."

"I've worked alone since his betrayal. I only agreed to this assignment because it was mandatory." Video's voice shook with emotion as her ears flattened.

Radio came forward, and pressed herself against the giant tabby to support her as well. "Thank you for your help, Video. We're going to get through this." She purred to comfort the feline, and sighed as she walked with both Video and Studio as Pictures patrolled behind them.

When Video staggered again, both Radio and Studio helped her back up, setting her back on her paws. Studio's eyes darkened when she spoke low to the tabby, murmuring, "You're not in well enough condition to travel. I'll be taking the three of you to my penthouse, and you can sleep there for the night before you head out in the morning." She spoke more firmly when Video began to protest, and said, "I *insist.*"

Radio pursed her lips to fight back a smile at her auntie being able to speak so firmly to the monster of a cat, and watched as Video scoffed and nodded reluctantly, her tail lashing with anger behind them. She looked over her shoulder to see how Pictures was faring and saw his sharp eyes darting their stare across every alley, street, and rooftop, before they softened upon looking at her.

She smiled at that, and closed her eyes as she turned her head back onto the path ahead. She rested her head on Video's shoulder as her own supported the cat's weight with her auntie. Video had three felines around her willing to help her, and ready to face whatever was going on with her. Radio had no idea the ambitious feline had a sibling, as both she and her older sister, Frequency, were single-birth litters, but the vague details Video gave about the situation explained a lot of her behavior toward the objective. This only assured Radio more that they could be friends by the end of the mission. It made so much sense that she would be so strict and firm with everything when she had to make up for the loss of her brother! Radio couldn't imagine if she had to face Frequency in such a manner.

It then made Radio wonder if Video had only been able to pick up the shard because her brother ceased his courier work, or if perhaps that it meant Stereo could possibly hold the shards, too. The idea made a shudder race down Radio's spine, and she looked to Video's harness. "And you still have the four shards?"

"Of course." Video allowed Radio to peek inside the bags attached to the giant feline, where she counted four faint shards, and let out a sigh of relief. The bag and strap was more damaged, but everything was still intact.

"Oh, good," she mumbled, and kept pressed to Video. The very idea of the shards possibly being taken from them chilled her fur, and she knew they'd have to be careful for the rest of the way back to the Capital.

Studio brought them to the clock tower towards the gate of the city, and led them inside with Video still pressed against her. Urgently and immediately, workers rushed down and helped Studio carry Video up onto a stretcher, and the two felines rushed towards the personal elevator. Radio and Pictures hurried after them, but a buff, fluffy, dark orange, brown, and white feline pressed her paws against both their chests. "Hey, we need some form of identification before you two go any further."

Radio scowled and flattened her ears. "We were *just* traveling with the Studio Star," she growled.

"I don't make the rules. You're going to need to identify yourself before you go up there. We've had a lot of trouble with impersonation as of late, and you're going to have to either understand, or leave. The line's over there." The burnt tortoiseshell cat pointed them toward a line of at least twenty felines.

While Radio understood the trouble with the impersonation and now knew the Jester was attacking far beyond just the village and Capital, the wolf from the Ruined City fresh in her mind, the situation was still preposterous and unbelievable. She growled again, and whipped around to the guard. "Do you have any idea who I am!? I am the Radio Star, the younger daughter of the Resolution Star herself, and I find this unacceptable! I'll give you two breaths to wrap your mind around the importance of the individual you're standing before, and one breath to move aside so I can accompany my aunt to help care for my companion. Otherwise, you'll be hearing about this from my *father*!" Radio stamped her paw and growled at the thick furred feline.

She stared at Radio for a single moment and then chuffed, "Never heard of you."

Radio cursed the day the feline was born as she was led to the line, and placed at the end with Pictures beside her, who just gave a sheepish smile before refusing to make eye contact, as though he was not to laugh even while his look emitted a distinct, *"We told you so."* Radio felt her fur begin to fluff up in frustration, and growled at the tom before she turned back into the line, watching as one by one, they slowly drew closer to the feline at the desk, all the while explaining to everyone Radio was a noble once another small cat pointed out her single-rowed collar.

The moon was high by the time they were through the line that prodded and asked questions about her history as a noble; having never heard of her. Every hair on Radio was bristled as she gave her paw print-covered collar to the receptionist to confirm her identity, glaring at the feline as they looked at her doubtfully until the report came back from the Capital as a perfect match. Radio was handed back her collar, which had now been wiped down from all the paw prints from the line of cats before.

Suddenly, the screen started flashing, and the dark red-and-white tabby looked back at the screen.

"Video, Radio, and Pictures are here!? When did they change their route?" Widget's voice sounded out from the speaker, making Radio and Pictures both startle upon hearing the monitor assistant's voice. The tabby receptionist rolled her eyes, turning the screen to Radio and Pictures. Radio hadn't known the servers were connected, or that they were possibly a high alert in them, either. The trackers in their ears should have notified the surveillance crew when they first entered the city, unless the mage was messing with that, too. She swallowed when waiting for what the monitors had to say.

"We didn't hear that was a part of your path. Are you alright?" Recorder asked, concern tinged in her tone. Before Radio could even respond to tell them about Video's injury, Tape furthered, "I-I don't know if they were supposed…"

"No, they weren't." Widget, Tape, and Recorder turned their heads away from the camera to see Cassette stepping in, and stepped aside as she walked up to the screens. "This is unacceptable."

They were all speaking at once. Radio barely had a chance to interrupt. "Please now, wait, Cassette. If you'd let us explain," Radio started, her ears flattening as a small feline came around the desk to help her place back on the collar.

"Ah, um, they're still making good time, Miss Cassette." Tape cleared his voice, seeing Radio's worried stare, and smiled reassuringly. She smiled back, but Cassette looked no more pleased.

"O-Oh no." Widget came back to the camera. "It looks like they aren't sticking together, either, I don't see Video there," the young assistant said curiously, jumping in surprise as Recorder rounded on him. "She's probably just off screen, Widget!"

"No, she's actually not right with us," Pictures spoke up while Radio was getting her collar fastened. "See, we…"

Pictures' ears flattened immediately as Cassette came up to the screen, and narrowed his eyes as the tall tri-colored feline stated firmly, "I'll repeat myself in saying that this is unacceptable. We gave you a route, made the objective clear, yet here you both are, dallying in Clowder City!"

"Cassette, please," Recorder pleaded as the older woman leaned back, beginning to change the toggles on the control panel.

"The signal is faded enough as it is. We cannot afford this." Cassette scowled.

Tape shook his head. "We know the three of you are the youngest in your field, and that prioritizing and time management can be difficult, but you two really should have known better than to travel within the city walls. Especially you, Pictures." Radio held back a gasp at the challenge in the usually placid tom's voice, but tried to understand why they were concerned.

Cassette lifted her chin in agreement with Tape as Pictures narrowed his eyes into slits. Ignoring him, she said, "Tape couldn't say it better. I'm sending in more monitors. Thank you for notifying us of their location, Register."

"Of course, Miss Cassette." The fluffy red tabby-and-white gave a firm nod and dip of her head in response to the tri-colored cat.

"Now wait, Cassette, there's really no need for..." Pictures started through gritted teeth, but stopped when the lean feline narrowed her eyes at him.

"A-are you sure you want to do that?" Widget's eyes widened with surprise, looking as though he regretted what he said once Cassette glared at him, too. "I just don't know if—"

"No, Cassette, Film's already done that—wait!" Recorder said as

Cassette pressed her paw down on the switch above the control panel, shutting off the camera.

The screen went black. Radio gaped. They never let either her or Pictures speak. She was on the brink of tears, but she held them back when she heard Pictures groan, "Oh, for the sake of our Stars. They never waste a moment." The silver tom's tail lashed, and he pressed his white paw against the side of his face once the receptionist brought her monitor back towards her desk.

"Everything about this is ridiculous. If we never had to confirm our identities in the first place, we would have been with Video and this wouldn't have happened." It took every bit of effort Radio had to make sure she didn't hiss at the red feline before she walked away, letting Pictures confirm himself with his paw print as she approached the elevator and set it to come down from the twenty-seven floors it had already climbed what seemed an age ago.

She should have insisted on it being summoned to come down before all this, as it was barely halfway down to the ground floor by the time Pictures was finished and came up to her. Radio sighed and looked at him, wondering if he had any clever or sassy words to say from the mischievous mind of his, especially with Cassette's outburst, but he only smiled at her and waited with her silently as the elevator came down. She gave him a small scowl, but then rested her tail on his.

"They didn't even let us explain why Video wasn't with us." Radio's tail tip flicked, and her shoulders slumped.

"I know. I think it's just all the panic going on. She was right in pointing out the fading signal, and I'm sure being together for as long as they have has just made things tense."

"We're fine, though." *More than fine, really, with the exception of Video's injury.* Radio sighed. "It's just unprofessional on their part." She lifted up her nose haughtily, but then gave Pictures a sheepish look so he knew she wasn't serious with her attitude before the elevator door opened.

"Quite." He smiled at her.

They entered the elevator together. Their sides brushed along each other's' as they sat, waiting for the elevator to bring them up to the penthouse floor. Radio rubbed her head along Pictures' shoulder and purred as they were able to appreciate the almost completely silent moment together, listening to the mechanics of the elevator and the band playing excitedly outside. She tried to not let the voices of the four surveillance workers drill into her head. It was possible when Pictures was beside her. It wasn't until now, once they were together, alone, when Radio could bring herself to relax. He brought her so much comfort, and gave her the confidence she could do this. She wouldn't have been able to face the surveillance crew without him.

So quickly her attitude changed, just by a few moments alone in an elevator. She was in love with this tom, even if she only knew him for a few days. She felt as though she could almost call Video her closest friend, and now the two of them were with her in her aunt's city, the very place Radio had wanted to live in nearly her whole life. It was going to be a venture in itself to stay connected to all of them, making sure each one reached their goals and knew they could count on each other. She just had to figure out how to tell them what they meant to her, especially what Pictures was to her. She suspected he already knew.

The elevator door opened, and the two of them padded out to greet Video. Radio was surprised to see that Video was asleep with Studio sitting beside her, looking more peaceful than Radio had seen her in a while, if ever. Radio came up to them and brushed her tongue along the sleeping tabby's bandaged head, then nuzzled the giant cat's poofy mane. She was safe here, and actually resting for once and that was what was important. She got back up when the large cat's breathing changed, knowing she needed her sleep, and turned to Studio. "You probably should get back to your parade, Auntie, there are not many festivals like this in a year." She cracked a smile for the older noble.

Studio chuckled and replied, "And there are not many missions like this in a decade. I'm here for you three, and want to help as much as I can. We've had a lot of interesting guests lately, to say the least." When Pictures and Radio looked to her curiously, she furthered, "It took a lot of effort from our workers to repair and set up the parade in time after the storm and visits from a particular unwelcome monkey, but we managed." The dark tabby-and-white smiled, making Radio and Pictures frown.

"The mage has been open with its attacks against you, too, then?" Radio asked. "The Council hadn't even realized how often it had been frequenting the critter forest, uh, Faith's Village, and Ruined City. Do they know of the mage's attacks here?"

Studio smiled at Radio's correction of the village's title. "They do, but there wasn't much they could do besides increase the security and patrols. The festival made it difficult for any additional measures to be taken." She sighed, coming around to sit at Radio's side.

"Whatever the mage plans, it certainly orchestrated it well." Radio sighed. "All the timing and foes were very well planned in what we've come across. We still haven't heard what its plans are." All of the outbursts from the surveillance crew earlier were pushed away from Radio's thoughts when thinking of the mage. "I'm scared, Auntie." Radio frowned.

"I know, Radio, but I'm glad you're here to help." Studio took Radio's head by her paw, and groomed the smaller feline's forehead with her tongue. "You've done very well so far."

Radio purred and grinned up at Studio with pride. All the praise in the world wouldn't be able to match hearing it from her aunt, Studio.

Studio gave the small cat a warm smile, and Radio brushed her head along Studio's chin in an embrace, resting beside the older feline as Pictures settled close to Video.

"There's been a lot of danger around the city: threats, attacks, all from that shapeshifting mage." Studio looked at Video as the giant cat's ears flicked and her brow furrowed. Even as she rested, the long-furred tabby still looked intimidating. The golden-collared feline continued then, facing Radio and Pictures when she said, "I've advised all of my citizens not to travel outside past the evening hours, and that goes for you, as well. The magician *has* gone as far as attacking during the morning hours, but it seems like the creature focuses mostly on the north near the Capital in the day."

"We were never notified how frequent the attacks were during the daylight. That's strange," Pictures mused, looking over at Radio. "We didn't know he was attacking at all with the exception of when it was against us personally, really. There's been a lot of confusion about the entire situation, and we've been left in the dark."

Studio arched her brow at Pictures curiously, as did Radio when she realized that Pictures referred to the mage as though it were a person. Studio merely nodded and turned to Radio to continue her words, saying, "Yes, as we have, too. The Capital's failed to notify of us about anything, except not to have any contact with the mage. It's already too late on my part, though. It's been striking its magic directly into the city, and I've encountered it face to face. So far, there have been no casualties, only unnatural burns from the magic this creature casts."

Radio's fur rose with fear, her eyes rounding. Studio sighed. "I'm afraid it might have been building up for tonight, though. Each attack has become more and more powerful and dangerous toward my followers, always within hours of our festivities. Up until this moment, I've been able to keep my citizen's fears at ease, but my own anxiety has only continued to grow. I don't want any of you travelling in case it decides to attack outside of the city, because so far we've been able to handle whatever's been thrown at us inside the walls."

"Huh. Maybe we can just stay until tomorrow afternoon, then, in case it lurks outside the walls in the morning. That way Video can recover through the morning, too." Radio looked up at Pictures, her ears flattening and eyes rounding hopefully.

Pictures sighed, and nodded. "While that might be for the best, we really need to prioritize finding the shard, Radio, especially with—"

"But Video really needs to heal," Radio interrupted, blinked slowly, and then brightened at the chance of convincing Pictures to stay a bit longer. "We need to think about what's better for our own health if we want to locate those shards to the best of our ability, especially with how much

Video's strained herself in battle."

Pictures arched his brow. Radio couldn't help but give a small grin when her tail gave her away by swaying. She leaned onto Studio, who chuckled and looked at her niece with amusement. The older cat quickly brightened as she offered, "Either way, it'll be a while until she wakes and is ready to travel out of here. Maybe you'd both like to oversee the rest of the parade with me while you wait?"

The two silver felines looked at each other and back at Studio with their eyes wide. "Really?" Radio chirped, her ears pointed all the way forward in her excitement.

Studio nodded, and even Pictures smiled as Studio guided them out to the balcony. Radio giggled and bounded after her, walking beside her. The dark brown tabby stopped at the doorway. Radio followed her gaze to see Studio look down at Video as the giant cat rested. Her aunt left the door open for the injured cat to be able to hear them.

Radio hoped that maybe the tabby would rise and come out to watch the event with them, but she remained in her bed, and so Radio turned her attention to the parade. Video resting and keeping away from the loud noises was probably for the best, anyway. Radio still thought about the apprehension the tabby had expressed when they first entered the city, and hoped she'd be able to give Video the thanks she deserved for agreeing to the change in route and going through what she did so they could enter the city.

While Radio knew it was likely they would have retrieved the shard by tomorrow afternoon if they had walked around the walls of city, outside its golden borders, she was still delighted they got to spend this time with

Studio and learn so much more about the situation they were facing. It was remarkable they could get the older feline's help at all. Radio knew she was going to enjoy the rest tonight. *Actual beds!* Radio purred at the thought.

Radio and Pictures watched the celebration and floats going through the streets of Studio's city with their leader. Video rested with her ears flattened. Once Video expressed no interest towards the parade, Radio closed the door a little more so the feline could sleep, and came back to sit between Pictures and Studio. The three smaller cats watched contently, silently admiring the festivities besides an occasional giggle or laugh, allowing Video to manage sleeping.

What a delight it was, to be able to share such an experience with the two she trusted. Radio grinned and brushed her shoulder along Pictures' side, then giggled when she saw Studio's brow arch. She quickly sat back down, her feathery tail sweeping around herself instead of entwining with Pictures' lean one. She could behave for a moment and sit still for her auntie's sake, even if a part of her wanted to flaunt Pictures as her companion.

She was so glad the three could sit together in peace. She rested her head on Pictures' shoulder, and closed her eyes for a moment, listening to the sound of the parade's music along with the tom's heartbeat. She knew this was another moment she had to stop and enjoy every sense of so she could remember it forever. She loved the smooth gold surface under her paws and the softness of Pictures' fur, her aunt's laugh of delight as it carried in the wind, the smell of the food and treats being offered for enjoyment below the balcony. *Aureate City food.* That was going to be a marvel in itself if Radio could enjoy some of that before they left.

As if on cue, Screen came out with a tray, a long centerpiece with a handle being held perfectly in his jaws as he set the tray down. Radio sniffed, smelling fine cuisine, fish with toasted bread and a cream sauce of sorts, all topped with fresh herbs. She licked her jaws, purring as the tom dipped his head and turned away.

"Thank you so much, Screen!" Studio purred as well, and Radio quickly swiped up one of the breads, dipping it in the sauce before savoring the taste as she ate. Pictures took one, too, and the three all partook in delight. "Whoa! This is amazing, Auntie Studio! Not that it can compare to the parade, but I am in awe!" Radio laughed.

Studio chuckled and grinned. "Can't it, though? These are my favorite. Screen knew it was an occasion." She took one of the filets, and didn't waste a moment to enjoy its taste. Radio tried one, too, when Pictures made a noise of approval at it. Radio looked over her shoulder to see Video had a plate, and all that was left was one piece of bread. She couldn't help but chuckle, and then tried another filet, now with the sauce, wondering how such good food could possibly be made and also stay so warm and fresh. She could probably fill up on the bread alone, and might just do so...

That was until Studio's ears pricked and eyes widened upon an echoing, booming laugh carried through the sky. Radio felt her breath quicken as she recognized the laugh of the primate mage, and immediately scanned the sky and buildings for the hidden creature. She realized quickly that she had no need to search for the hiding Jester; the monkey decided to make itself quite visible. The dressed primate chuckled deeply as it swung through the floats, and cast magic from the crystal artifact with it.

"What is it doing!?" Radio wailed, pressing herself against the balcony to watch the volatile monkey below. "It's destroying the city! It's hurting the citizens!" She yelled when she saw some of the crowd get struck by the blast, and ducked her head down in fear of the Jester seeing her.

Studio was right! It was preparing for its attack tonight! How much worse would it be if the mage knew that she, Video, and Pictures were here? The attacks could become more severe. The monkey could even start to target her aunt. Just then, Studio's eyes narrowed, and she walked up to the balcony as well, but instead of cautiously hiding like her niece, she stood tall with her tail bristled, making the two younger felines step aside. She dipped her head to Radio and Pictures, who stared in shock at the lithe feline. "If you'll excuse me, please," she said firmly, but kept a politeness to her tone as she looked at them.

Radio and Pictures nodded, and took another step back as Studio crouched down and then leapt into the air. Radio gasped and ran back to the balcony, hopping onto her back paws as she pressed her front paws on the golden bars to watch what her aunt was doing. She stared in amazement as Studio landed and bound onto the first float with outstanding elegance. Radio then gawked as her aunt leapt onto the top of the following floats one by one, without a single stagger or hard landing. She was even more shocked seeing the dark feline speed up her pace and catch up to the dark monkey, who didn't seem to be paying attention to the brave noble.

The Jester turned toward Studio when she bounded onto the float behind the one it stood upon. It growled. Radio held her breath as the two locked eyes. The primate arched its brow. "The Studio Star," the mage acknowledged. "Do you think just staring at me is going to accomplish—"

The words cut off into a screech as Studio launched straight for the monkey. The mage quickly maneuvered out of the way, but not fast enough for her next swipe, nearly falling from the float at the force of the blow. Radio squealed in dismay at seeing her aunt fighting with the monster who single-handedly took away the king of Media, afraid it would turn its play into real battle. "What is she doing!?" she cried out. The primate stumbled back as Studio disoriented the primate with another hit, but it quickly aimed the floating artifact, the crystal cube, in the direction of Studio.

The strange object began to glow an intense, cyan aura, and Radio screamed as a blast of energy emitted from its core towards her aunt. She was going to die! Radio was going to be witness to the death of her auntie!

Radio barely kept her eyes open long enough to see Studio gracefully dodge it, and stared in even more amazement as the dark tabby's golden gaze followed the blast to make sure it only went to the sky, and not her city.

"Of course no harm could *ever* come to your City—" the primate's voice broke off into a yelp as it leapt back from Studio as she bounded back down to the spider monkey.

"Silence!" Studio hissed.

"No one ever lets me talk!" the Jester outright whined, and glared at Studio. "It's so rude, really. I expected better from *you,* Studio Star." At that moment, robotics with black mirrors rose at the cat's sides, making the mage startle. Studio turned back to face the spider monkey as it curiously leapt on the float ahead of her, its eyes round, making her eyes narrow.

"You have threatened my city for the last time..!" her voice sang out above the commotion below, and she flattened herself against the float she stood on to pounce.

Radio, Pictures, and even the Jester stared at her in shock, as though they all had to take a moment to ponder if she was really going to sing. "...What?" One of the monkey's eyes squinted at the sing-song tune in the cat's voice in disbelief. It looked as though the Jester was just going to carelessly reply, but instead screeched as Studio leapt for him again.

"What I have done is nothing compared to what is to come!" the Jester shouted back, and leapt up to throw another blast.

Radio's jaw dropped. The mage was going to actually sing back, like this was some show for the people. What happened next even furthered the illusion of showmanship, as the monkey jester dramatically held the cube until it glowed brightly, then projected it, smashing it into the shining surface of the golden road below, between the two floats where the Jester and Studio stood. At immediate contact with the artifact, the golden streets turned black, and the darkened color began stretching past the road to the crowd like the shadows brought of a setting sun.

The felines hissed and jumped back in fear, but the darkness only stained the structures around them. They were left unharmed. The shadows spread all the way to the outer walls, darkening every golden building and structure on its path. Radio stepped back once it reached her, horrified as the balcony around her drained of its rich color. Not even the golden tray that held the food was spared from the dark magic. Radio looked up at the now black ceiling, and then down at what was once a golden floor, seeing her reflection in the black surface. She blinked as she realized it was her own bright blue eyes staring back at her and not some magic of the mage. That made Radio happy that at least the shine of the structure remained intact.

190

Once she caught her breath, she gaped at Pictures, and then looked around. The floor and surrounding walls looked akin to black glass, similar to the shadows surrounding the mage as it absorbed the color from everything around it, and only left the lights and lamps with their bright golden color. Radio sighed, and then looked back out past the balcony to the crowd beneath her. The sudden darkness seemed to drain the color from the panicked clowder who watched from below. Radio had to reassure herself it was only an illusion from losing the reflection of the golden shine before she could bring herself to do anything else.

Radio turned back to the floats and watched with her eyes as round as a full-moon while Studio gasped, but collected her emotions and replied,

"You threaten my people; don't even try when it's all feeble!" Studio jumped back to dodge the next blast from the Jester, which was absorbed by the black mirrors around her, and then progressed towards the monkey as the cube returned to the mage's side.

The primate's eyes narrowed at her words, and its voice rang out in response:

How deceitful! To think I once called you my equal!

You will burn with the rest of your home, down into the ground while I will stand gleeful.

Your legacy will do nothing to heed my warnings; I only wish you had listened.

But alas, I have conquered what is needed and will rise far beyond simply being regal!

The clothed monkey bounded back when Studio continued to advance upon it. Radio watched as it jumped from float to float, but it was too late. Studio leapt down from the taller float she had been on behind him, her jaw closing in on one of the launch tubes of the firework cannons, and she whipped it into the Jester's direction with her paws. She sang all the while, and the firework launched directly towards its chest:

Everything you've done can only be seen as evil.
Nothing you've done here is anything more than a poke from a needle.
If you leave now, I'll make sure my next act won't be lethal!

She growled as the Jester deflected most of the blow with its glowing cube, but was still sent staggering back. It only regained its balance when Studio stepped onto the same float, her launch tube aimed at the monkey with her paw firmly clasped against it.

I've said it once, I'll say it again, leave my people alone.
I've been patient with you; I've given you your chance.
It's time you pack up your box and leave. You're no longer known!

She launched another firework, and the Jester leapt out of the way just in time, then bashed its head against its own cube when the artifact flickered gold for a heartbeat and collided into the mage, leaving it dazed. The firework's blast struck the flower-covered float and erupted, making Studio quickly jump back.

The Jester's eyes rounded at the sight of the fire, and quickly leapt away. Studio chased after the primate, but it didn't fight back any more. Instead, it burst into a shrapnel of shadows and disappeared into the darkness outside the walls. Studio stared at the sky in shock, her ears flat against her skull, and then flagged down the felines below. Studio's staff quickly came to extinguish the fire.

Video, Radio, and Pictures were all watching the scene from the balcony, their eyes all rounded in shock, amazement, and surprise. "By the Stars and King, that was astonishing," Video marveled, her ears tilted up and eyes wide with inspiration from the actions and reactions of the powerful leader.

Radio gasped at Video, not only for the stoic cat's uncharacteristic behavior, but because the dark tabby was actually being *inspired* by something. She wanted to laugh, or be happy for the feline to be inspired by the Studio Star, but instead felt jealous and possessive. That was *her* aunt, and Radio didn't like the idea maybe Video, who was already in the penthouse before she and Pictures arrived, had been able to talk to Studio as much as Radio had, and could possibly develop a partnership with Studio, too. Radio considered the idea of Video receiving Studio's blessing instead, even with how foolish she felt for thinking it. "Well, I'm the one related to her..." She looked at the two brown tabbies with similar markings with a bit of jealousy as Studio was bounding back to them.

That was Radio's defense, at least, until the three ladies exchanged late night conversations.

"We're related!?" Video and Radio both echoed in shock.

"Scandal's been a part of your father and mother's bloodlines for generations, dear. Especially the toms," Studio purred as she winked at Pictures, then smiled half-heartedly when the silver tabby gave no response. "Mind my terrible words, dear." She looked at Radio now. "You just don't know who might be related to you!" Studio laughed softly, then continued when Radio pressed her paws down and looked up at her auntie, eager to hear more. "Most of it is kept secret, but your great-grandmother, the Cinema Star, couldn't hide a litter of kits from the rest of the family. It was hidden amidst the nobles for many ages, but Video's grandmother, Mobile, a daughter of Cinema's estranged litter, came to our door one day with two kits. The little clowder of hers would visit from time to time. Sometimes our mother, the Relay Star, brought Resolution and me along to meet Cinema's secret descendent, Replica, who was the spitting image of her and Relay's mother. We visited before I began training to be a guardian of my fellow nobles. Resolution and I both went on different paths after that, and Relay ceased contact with the family."

Radio's eyes rounded at the idea, but even more so at all the names. She followed that her great-grandma Cinema had two separate litters, the royal being Relay, and the estranged, yet verified, being Replica, but then it branched into Video's family. They barely seemed related if Mobile, Replica's daughter, who was already not of official noble blood, was Video's *grandma*. That was generations ago!

Studio sighed, then turned to Video as the large feline stared at her with wide eyes, and furthered, "My sister and I actually played with your mother, Audio, as a kit, Miss Video." Radio was dazed upon hearing another name and generation before it finally came down to Video, but remained silent as Studio continued, "She had only just opened her eyes, so we mostly slept and stayed inside the playroom as our parents discussed their roles." Studio turned to Radio, then, who could only hold her breath. "Replica had been raised to be a seamstress, adopted by a family when Cinema couldn't care for her. Mobile and her sisters followed that path, while Resolution and I were raised as the next nobles to guard and advise our people."

"Did Replica ever wish to join as a noble, being the Relay Star's younger sister?" Video questioned Studio softly.

Radio tried to listen, but then blinked as she felt Studio's assistant, who had been prowling around the room since they began the conversation, pass her. She had heard, while she and Pictures were waiting in line to be verified, the tom was supposedly blind, for most part, with the exception of a lens he wore when working with monitors, but he just seemed to be *watching* them far too closely. The blindfold covered his eyes, but he still had very fine hearing, and it made Radio wonder about his intent. Video seemed to notice it, too, and it seemed to make the usually brave feline regret her question.

Studio saw their discomfort, and waited until Screen was gone until she replied, "No, she didn't want that for herself or her daughters after hearing of the tasks we had to perform. Some may have called it being overwhelmed; others would say it was because of the ethnic differences. I am not the typical noble you find in Media." Studio smiled at Video, and Radio found herself nodding in agreement before making herself stop.

"True, many would define you as being softer, Miss Studio, but I am honored to know you as my blood." Radio heard Video's voice rise as she

195

started to fidget. It made Radio wonder if it was from the tom's movements around the room. That was confirmed when Video finally asked, "So how long have you had this assistant…"

"Screen." Studio smiled, giving Video the silver, blindfolded tom's name.

"Thank you. I don't mean to be presumptuous, or overstep my bounds, but if I may ask…how long has your assistant, Screen, worked for you in your private quarters?"

Studio laughed. "It sounds just terrible when you say it like that! My private quarters! Right after we've just discussed scandal!" She scoffed, shaking her head before answering right away with a grin. "Not long, actually, dear. With the Jester's threats, I needed the extra security. Screen's incredibly gifted at noticing a presence before anyone else I know. He suggested moving his surveillance into the free room I had, and offered to prowl the grounds during the day when most of the guards slept. He's been so good at it, I've barely noticed him."

Radio wondered how, because it's all she *did* notice in the room. She turned to Video as the large feline asked, "Monitors usually don't travel beyond their offices on duty. Do you mean the grounds of the city, or beyond?"

Radio was curious about the question, too, now. She wished Pictures, the youngest monitor and advisor to the Council leaders of Media themselves, was chiming in as well, but he dismissed himself from the conversation as soon as it turned towards the bloodlines of both her and Video. She knew, likely because of his own childhood and hardship, the tom might not even know who his parents were, if he was raised by the amount of species he inferred. It made her feel sympathy for him, but not enough to stop the conversation when she had a chance to learn about her and Video's family. Radio sighed, and looked to Studio for the lean feline's answer.

Studio blinked, and tilted her head. "Whatever he finds fair. I don't really set down firm rules within the city. I've trusted him and my people. I give them the boundaries to let them know what is safe, and let them make the decision to trust my judgment or not. I imagine that has been the reason why we're the only city that hasn't had any fatalities, yet."

Video stared at the city leader in surprise. "So you don't know where he goes then. Have you watched him on the monitors?" Video and Radio both looked over at Pictures now, but he remained stiffly lying on one of the cushions at the windowsill, no movement besides a small ear flick.

Studio's words brought the younger cats' attention back to the conversation. "He's the one in charge of the surveillance, Video. If I felt threatened by him, I would go through what's needed to make sure everything was secure."

"You need to trust her, Video," Radio chimed, and lifted up her chin.

Video sighed and looked away from the two. Studio pressed her paw near Video's to make the younger feline turn to her again as she assured, "I've had many people that have helped me for seasons and solstices, some even since the beginning of this city, and I've learned who I can and cannot trust." She turned to Radio. "I can't say I always have, but sometimes you can see—no, sense, when someone's intent is coming from the right place, and that's the case with Screen."

Video nodded, putting her head down. "Yes, ma'am."

"Good," Studio laughed, folding her paws back underneath herself. "This was a long day. I imagine you three travelled since dawn if you've made it here in this amount of time. You still smell of the meadows." She giggled. Radio blushed, and then gave a small smile back before she turned to look at Pictures again, who was now at least staring at her with the corner of his eye.

Radio's paws flexed, and she nodded. "We did. It was a tiring trip, but far too worth it to have done it any other way." She then smiled and turned back to Studio. "Thank you for offering us your home for us to sleep, Auntie. I'm so happy to be here." She brushed her muzzle along Studio's neck, purring.

"Of course, my dear," Studio said as she rose up, and looked out the balcony window. "I'm going to start setting up the cleaning assignments for tomorrow, but you three should get your rest. It'll be a big day tomorrow." The city leader then blinked with wonder. "It looks like you'll be getting all the help you need. There's surveillance bots everywhere."

Radio blinked, and looked to Video. "Maybe they found the last shard."

"No, they'd be here if they did, but we must be drawing closer if this is them looking for a pinpoint location. We should head out as early as possible, so get some rest, now," Video answered.

Radio was going to object to the fluffy tabby's firmness, but the large cat already rested down on her bed with her chin on her paws, ending the conversation. Radio gave a pout, and then looked over at Studio, but the older noble was already organizing cleaning patrols with Screen. Radio watched the two speak to each other, then sighed and decided to go over to Pictures.

The silver tabby seemed to be expecting her immediately, making Radio smile as she watched his ears follow the direction she was walking. She snuggled up next to him. "May I join you?" she purred.

"Of course, Radio." He smiled, weaving his tail over hers.

Radio grinned with delight, and wrapped her paws around his shoulders, running her rough tongue against his head and the back of his ears. She was pretty sure he was the biggest bonus of this mission besides Clowder City, as he was quite the handsome catch. Radio purred louder at her own thoughts, her smile broadening as she continued to groom and nuzzle the gray tom.

The two slept together at the windowsill in peace until she felt Pictures stir and get up for a moment. She still felt Video's presence in the room, and was too tired to go and find him. She stretched along the plush cushion, and remained sleeping until it was daytime once more. She dreamed of wonderful things: her favorite foods, the festival, and parties, all with her new found friends.

It was a marvelous dream, and felt so real. Radio could almost describe it being as a dream come true when she woke up around the same people in her dream. It was all so wonderful, so exciting to be around people she could be safe around, those who made her feel accomplished.

The possibilities of what she could be able to so soon explore with the group...she couldn't wait to hear what they wanted to do, too. Everything was going to be possible as long as they stuck together. The fact that they all seemed to believe that, too, made the situation even better. It was more than she could have ever wished. She couldn't be happier as she opened her eyes to start the next day.

Until she saw their faces as she looked up at them.

She got up and stepped forward when Video looked away from her, then turned her gaze to see that Pictures looked more upset than she had ever seen him before. Studio looked solemn, and kept her gaze turned to the ground. Nothing was right. Something must have happened when she slept, but what? What could have affected all of them like this? She dreaded the answer, and already had a feeling of what it was, too.

"What's going on!?" Her throat tightened, and she held her breath, waiting for a response from any of them.

There was a hesitation, but Pictures finally answered, his voice constricted as well. "Recorder just contacted us. The shard's signal completely went out, there's nothing left for us to go by for the rest of the heart." Pictures whipped around, and stalked away from Video toward the door. "We're to return to the Capital with the shards we have left, and abandon the rest of the mission."

Why did the dream just turn into a nightmare? How did the signal disappear with just a night of sleep? Radio shook her head, trying to wake up, but this wasn't a dream, this was all very much real. They had failed the mission? What was the land of Media going to do? "What about the King?" she managed to ask, feeling her heart race and beat against her chest as her fear grew.

Video only shook her head.

No. This couldn't be real. Everything was going so perfectly, they had nearly every fragment. There was probably only *one* more left. How could they miss it all by a day? It hadn't been because of their stay at Clowder City; it had to have been unavoidable, right? She looked out, and saw the sun was still rising slowly. She estimated that they wouldn't have been able to find the shard until the afternoon, so there was nothing they could have done. *Right?*

The shards' signals grew closer when they were near, though. Perhaps, if the three had just gone around like they had been told to, they could have gotten close enough for the surveillance crew to pinpoint a location before the signal was gone, and now the shard could be anywhere in central-eastern Media, for all they knew. This might have been avoided, and she could tell by the two's gazes fixed upon her when they thought she wasn't looking, that they knew that was the case, too.

Radio's chest tightened as much as her throat, knowing they blamed her for it. Video wouldn't have run into Stereo and gotten injured if they hadn't entered the city, so Video wouldn't have gotten hurt if Radio hadn't gone with Studio to explore the city in hope for her future there. They had every reason to blame her. She looked up at her auntie to see the tall feline stalk out of the parlor with her head hung. She probably blamed her decision to make them stay overnight just as much as Radio blamed herself, but Studio had no reason. It wasn't her objective like it had been Radio's.

"We had better get going." Video followed Pictures, leaving Radio alone in the room.

Radio let herself cry then. Her shoulders shook and her paws trembled, but she nodded long after they were already to the elevator, and started for it.

"Radio, let me accompany you to the gates." Studio came back into the room and walked up to her, brushing her black feathery tail along Radio's own.

"N-no, that's okay Auntie," Radio whispered, continuing her way to the elevator, but stopped when Studio touched her shoulder with her paw.

"Please," the regal leader murmured. "I insist."

Radio nodded, letting Studio follow as Video waited for them between the door of the elevator to keep it from descending. Radio stepped in and stood beside Pictures, who looked away from her. The four sat in silence as the elevator brought them down the twenty-seven stories to the ground floor. She looked at Pictures again when they reached the last four floors as the elevator sped down, hoping maybe for the slightest bit of assurance, anything promising this all wasn't for nothing with him, but his stare remained cold against the elevator's walls.

Tears once again streamed down her face as they walked out from the elevator, but she was proud she managed to hold herself together enough not to sob or tremble. There would be no way to explain to either of them. She knew what was at stake, what they had lost for Media and for themselves. They shared themselves with her, and Radio didn't know how to choke out the apology for letting them down. Studio blamed herself. Even while Radio kept herself from trembling, she felt the shaking of her aunt. She pressed herself against the leader, wishing she could purr to comfort the incredible feline, to tell her it wasn't her fault. She couldn't bring herself to break the silence, though, and turned to the others.

Pictures knew who was responsible. He looked at anything that wasn't Radio, and turned his gaze further away from her whenever she looked at him. Radio's teeth grit at his responses as she fought back more tears. He was the one she needed the comfort and assurance from the most. He had the least amount to lose from this, he was the one to whom Radio confided in the most, and yet he was the one that blamed her most harshly. She was used to disappointing her family, she had done that her whole life, and wouldn't have been surprised by even her aunt's disappointment. Video was always upset, directing that upset towards Radio was understandable, and Radio accepted it. *For the most part.* Radio was still guilt-ridden knowing that Video was doing this to make up for her brother's errors and to prove herself to the Council, and there was no apology in the world that could make up for that.

Pictures was the one that taught her to hunt, the one who stood between her and the Jester, the one who ran through the meadow with her like they were kits when she needed something to take away the pain; she had thought of him as her true companion. Radio clicked her teeth and unclenched her jaw. Now this happens, and he can't even look at her. All she could hope was that maybe he could forgive her, if Media could still find a way to save themselves from the Jester.

Once they were to the gates, Studio asked, "Do you want a carriage to bring you all to the castle?"

"No." Video looked up now. "We should travel on foot. We might be able to see something we would miss from the carriage."

Studio nodded, and stepped back. Radio dipped her head to her, then pressed her head against the tabby-and-white cat's chest, seeing the feline's eyes were also flooded with guilt. "You did all you could, and it's not your fault...Save your city, and keep it safe, Auntie."

"Oh, Radio." Studio wrapped her neck around Radio's in an embrace, making Radio hold back a sob when the older noble murmured, "Please be safe, it's not over yet, and I'll do all in my power to make it right."

Radio nodded, and bowed to her before following the two out of the city. She looked up at the overcast sky ahead. There was no way Video didn't see this, and yet she still asked to walk on foot. Radio sighed, and she said nothing for that very reason. She silently followed the two out from Clowder City, which seemed nearly silent compared to all of the festivities yesterday.

She let herself trail behind the other two, and sighed as the three of them travelled in the direction of the mountains to the Capital, where she saw dark clouds gathered, promising a rough journey back. At least, even if it was only physically, she wasn't alone.

- CHAPTER 8 -

TERMINATION

Radio would not dare complain about the pain she felt from the travel now. The only time the three stopped to eat was when one spotted prey seeking shelter from the storm. So far Radio had been lucky enough to catch a tiny mouse. She watched the variety of surveillance bots sent out from the Capital and its surrounding consultants, all recording and running their devices to try and detect the strange item. None of them spotted any sign of a fragment or any mysterious incidents, though. It might never be found, for all they knew.

Whether or not it was, the hopeless idea wasn't the mindset Radio wanted to have on the situation. She pressed forward, deciding to fight back any negative thoughts threatening to come back. While there was no sign of the signal right now, the Capital was prepared to lead without the King, and would have to take whatever they made their temporary policy of rulership and make it extend until the heart could be restored. Between the seasons changing, the additional surveillance needed to find it and with Studio proving the Jester could be faced single-pawed, anything was possible. Even more so if they found the shard on the way to the Capital. That would be the best case scenario.

Radio sighed as the wind picked up, her hopes blowing away with it. She knew it wasn't going to be an easy way back. The darkening clouds promised rain, if not a full out summer storm. She remained optimistic it was only going to be rain, which was something she had never gone outside to experience. When hearing the thunder rumble in the clouds, however, she whimpered.

Frightening or not, she had to keep moving forward, and not let the fear stop her from matching the pace of her silent companions as they scanned the terrain. She took in a deep breath, and kept her eyes focused on the path instead.

There had to be a way to fix this, to make up for her mistakes. Radio looked at the sun. It was now above the treetops into the clouds looming over them. It somehow made the darkness a bit brighter, and seemed to promise there could be light beyond the thick, eerie darkness. Radio would just need to be patient, and wait for that opportunity to arrive. She could mend this.

As though her hopes couldn't already diminish more, though, Video didn't break at high noon, either. Instead, she continued to lead them on silently while they climbed the inclines leading to the even steeper mountains. Radio was grateful to the earth when she was able to catch a bird to eat while the two found their prey in burrows. She pulled it to her paws and feasted on the meat, beholden she could stay at her full strength as they carried on their travel. She looked to the two to share the accomplishment of catching her first bird, but neither of them congratulated her, nor looked overly interested, so she finished eating it silently.

Her limbs may have ached from the mountain climb, but the food helped her, and she felt better as they continued to follow the trail leading to the Capital. She stopped when she felt the first raindrop on her nose, giving herself a moment to enjoy being seeing the destinations they had crossed to gather the first four fragments, and she was proud at the success at that. At the beginning of their mission, she looked down upon the cities, village, and meadow with mystery and an inability to conceive what she was seeing and approaching. Now she felt as though she knew each one of the communities, and would be ready to venture back into them at a moment's notice. She would go back, if it meant bringing back the last shard.

The three of them carried on through the starting rain until Video decided to give a formal break before sunset. "We can sleep for a reasonable time tonight. For now, we'll take advantage of the water source. Drink, eat, and rest, if needed, before we travel any further." She pointed her tail in the direction of the water then marked the earth with one sweep of her tail, causing the surface pebbles to fly from the dirt ground. Radio stepped back to make sure none would hit her, and watched as Video headed towards the stream.

Radio looked at Pictures, but he turned away from her before she could speak, and headed in the opposite direction. She gazed at him until he was out of sight, hoping just once he'd turn to look at her, even just over his shoulder, but he made no attempts at doing so, not even from the corner of his eye. His gaze had been something that she always found so alluring, and even comforting, but he didn't offer it to her. It was harder to keep herself from getting emotional after that, but she refused to be ignored by him, and followed him down the incline silently...for now.

She was a bit confused about why he headed towards the fir trees, and looked around at the mass of burrows he passed, with prey scattering about freely in attempts to find shelter from the rain. Why didn't he stop to catch any of them? The longer she followed him, the more afraid she was of being alone with him. It wasn't a feeling she had felt with Pictures before, but with his anger, and the dark fir trees not seeming to promise any wellness by their setting, Radio didn't want to risk his wrath by following him, and decided not to pursue him.

She turned to head back, her fear building up too much to continue. The rain started pouring down harder, and it was at that moment she heard his voice. "Why did you follow me?"

She swallowed nervously, trying not to cry from his cold tone alone. She turned toward him again, approaching him while he kept his back turned to her, and responded, "I wanted to apologize, Pictures. I'm sorry for everything I did to jeopardize this mission, and I'm sorry I affected your reputation. I never wanted this. Not when..." *I love you so much.* How could she fall in love with a cat she barely knew? She couldn't finish her statement when she knew he'd just take her words and motives as trying to manipulate him into feeling guilt. He had started this conversation with no intention of forgiveness.

"My reputation? You don't think I might have had more at stake here, Radio?" Pictures growled, his fur bristling and tail lashing even though he had still not turned to look at her. "Is that all this mission meant to you? That's all you can perceive to think it meant for *us*?"

"What? No! Pictures, it means more than you know for me!" Radio pleaded, shaking her head. "I'm sorry, I don't know what this meant for you, and I'm sorry I never asked. I just don't want us to go back to the Capital like this, please."

Pictures snorted, and Radio's eyes rounded as he dug his claws into the ground. "What, so you can make better on the Capital's impression of your family? That's why you did this. I'm not interested in helping you with your stature, Radio. I don't know why you thought an apology would simply take away the fact everything we were working for has been destroyed! All of our opportunities to be able to make a difference in this forsaken land are gone!" he snapped, snarling at the fir trees ahead.

Radio's eyes rounded, knowing how frustrated he was about the other species' situations. "I'm sorry! I wanted to make a difference. I wanted to help more than you know! I don't care about what my parents think of me, there's no point or purpose to it! All I ever wanted was to help like my aunt does…and I know I failed! I know I can't fix getting the shard, but I still wanted to try fixing everything else!"

Radio cried out in pain when Pictures' ears flattened. She deduced he still refused to forgive her, and his next words confirmed it. "Stop pretending. You're acting like you're somebody you're not, and you can't prove to me otherwise by changing this. You're too weak," the tom growled, barely audible over the sound of the rain. Radio saw his eyes lit with anger when he looked at her over his shoulder. "Get away from me!" he hissed, whipping around to look at her directly and glaring into her shimmering eyes with his burning ones. She turned away, bolting back for the terrain Video had marked as their meeting point with her tail.

Radio's paws grew weak. She broke down to cry over the rain and the storm as it hit in full force, not caring as the rocks of the mountain terrain scraped against her belly and paws as she lowered her head against the ground and let the rain soak her pelt. Everything was over between her and Pictures. There would never be going back after that, no matter how the situation might turn out. How could this have all happened so quickly? She would regret this for the rest of her life.

Once she could finally muster lifting up her head, she saw Video approaching, the giant cat's pelt drenched. The rest of her strength was gone after running all the way back from the fir trees where Pictures had gone, but she forced herself to stand, and looked up into Video's eyes. The two exchanged their losses as they stared into each other's eyes, Video's reflecting disappointment and frustration, while Radio's reflected her apology and sorrow as the rain poured down on them both. Finally, Video turned away from her.

Radio let another stream of tears fall down her face when she said, "For what it's worth, I'm sorry, Video. I didn't want to let you down."

"I'm sorry I never managed to get you to understand the importance of the mission, and put it aside myself. I'm also sorry we never got to be friends," Video whispered, the soft sounds somehow carrying over the sound of the rain. She then began moving forward.

For some reason, the idea Video had the intent of a real friendship after the mission and now didn't feel it was possible nearly hurt as much as what Pictures had said to her. Radio had to plead, tease, and question Pictures if it was the case, but Video only shared her thoughts and feelings once a friendship no longer felt possible between them. How much had been lost only continued to sink in as Radio followed the larger feline without disturbing her.

Radio didn't bother to look back when she heard Pictures catch up to them again. She felt his glaring eyes still burn into her pelt now that she finally got him to look at her. At least she knew where she stood with him, and felt her chest tighten again with pain and anger as she thought again of his words. *How could he say what he did?* Whatever they had shared, and whatever she did, there had been no reason for him to speak to her like that. Not after everything they had been through together. He had to know his own words weren't true.

She grew frustrated when she realized she only had thought of his anger as a betrayal now that he'd made it clear he only thought of her as a pompous noble trying to boost her reputation. *Create a reputation, that is.* He knew she hadn't even existed in the database until Film found her manually. There had not been a reputation to boost in the first place. His assumption was the only mistake he'd made yet, but a mistake it was! *Right?*

The more she thought about it, the angrier she felt at Pictures only saying those words to chase her away, because he *did* know it wasn't the case. Everything he did was intentional. Why couldn't he just be honest?

He was still refusing to be open with her, even now. She *still* didn't know where she stood with him, just when she thought his glaring finally confirmed it. Who knew what the honesty and what the lies were, anyway? She looked up at Video, the young feline who could take on an army with her tail tied to her ears. Even with how strong Video was, the feline's youth had become more evident during their travels. Radio wondered if she had even lived long enough to see four solstices. Whatever the case was, Video didn't deserve to go through a mission like this only to fail.

Of course, all the loss and all the risk were only evident once they were gone. Radio had failed Media, its followers, and her friends. Now she had to pay the price. She continued forward with the two until the storm cleared. They were halfway to the castle already. None of them saw the fragment, nor was an update given telling them to head back to the valley. She looked up into the cloudy night sky, and closed her eyes. It had been four days since they started their mission, and yet somehow those days, not even a week, had changed her life forever. If only it had been for the better.

The closer the three drew to the castle, the more the knowledge sank into her thoughts that her parents would never trust her with another mission from the Council, that there might not even be a Council much longer unless the Jester was stopped, and that Video might not be trusted for any more courier work. Although she might have the easiest time of the three proving herself once again, she didn't deserve having to restart so early in her career. That's when Radio realized Pictures would lose connections from the failed mission and would have to work for seasons to rekindle them. If Radio had just done what she was supposed to, go around Aureate City, this wouldn't have happened.

She messed up.

The group stopped to sleep for the night once they reached grassy terrain in the mountains, and settled on a ledge where they could see all of central Media. Radio stared down at the land once more before she curled up on the ledge, seeing Pictures once again leave for the lower terrain while Video stayed nearby. Radio took in the sight of the marbled tabby, the feline's damaged harness with its bag of shards having never left her side for the entire mission.

Video and Pictures did all that they could to make this mission possible, Video even doing above and beyond her expectations. Radio had only held them behind. Radio let out a sigh, and closed her eyes as she let herself sink into the ground to sleep. She let the darkness of slumber envelop her to keep her from the troubles of reality.

She thought perhaps she could just stay in the darkness until the sun's light woke her, but the voice of the mage disturbed her, saying many things, sounding like it was directed towards itself, until one sentence was finally clear: "Well, if it isn't the Radio Star..."

Radio quickly looked up from the shadows which surrounded her, shadows that swirled, grew, shrank, and twisted into a form, slowly pulling away from her until she was surrounded in every direction by mist. She shuddered at the chill that shot down her spine as she saw the shadows form and mold themselves into the strange, spindly silhouette of the Jester, until the shadows grew faint, pulling away from the figure like they were the lapping flames of a black fire. The primate stepped out from the mist, sighing.

"The privileged Radio Star, I don't think we have ever formally spoken." The primate tilted its head in a gentle smile, the bells ringing on its hat.

Radio looked at the shadowy monkey, feeling like she should scream, yell, anything to wake herself up. She didn't want to die, she wanted to live, she wanted to know what was going to happen, but even with the awareness of all of that, she couldn't help but be sad to see the monkey instead. She wasn't terrified as she supposed she should have been, just melancholy, feeling both hopeless and pitiful. She rose up to stand on her paws before they locked eyes. She walked away from the Jester, stopping once her back was turned. "I assume this vision is your doing. However, I am sure you already know I am insignificant to your plans. You're going to have to find Video or Pictures if you want something, or someone, who could actually make a difference."

"On the contrary, I very deliberately chose to speak with you, Radio Star. You're the only one that can help me with this."

Radio's brow furrowed, knowing this was a bit far-fetched even for the mage, and she continued walking away.

The primate hung in front of her suddenly, making her take a step back. "Now, now. Don't ignore me. I just can't tolerate it, dear." The mage grinned and then laughed, even as its eyes reflected taking offense at her rebuff.

Radio was sick of laughter, and coming from the Jester made it even more detestable. She blinked, then stood still. "What do you want, then?" Her words came out like a breath of exhaustion, and she sighed after saying them.

She watched the Jester drop down onto its feet. It adjusted one of the bells on the dark hat it wore with its long fingertips, then chuckled. "It seems you have been wronged, Miss Radio. You believe you're nothing compared to your companions because they know how to toss their paws around and use their heads. The brawn and the brains. What does that leave you?"

Radio flattened her ears. "Nothing." She turned back around again.

"Wrong." The mage walked around her, and stopped in front of her, touching a fingertip to her chest, trailing it up her collar to the heart-shaped center gem. "You're the heart, Miss Radio."

Radio blinked at the hand resting on her collar, raising her brow in both surprise and curiosity. "Like the crystal...?" Her voice trailed off as she thought of the possibility, but then she shook her head, realizing all was lost with a broken heart. "Stop. It's as good as being nothing." She raised her chin. "What do you want?" Her tail lashed. As her bravado wavered, she turned her muzzle away from the primate.

"I want you to realize you're the one who can fix this. I need your help, Miss Radio. I need someone who acts with their heart; logic and strength make one prideful."

She stepped away, and started walking through the mist. The mockery was just the final touch for her to continue realizing her mistakes. Her being the heart only confirmed it was her fault the mission failed, and the idea made her eyes water.

"Don't you see? I regret what I've done. *Radio!*" The mage's voice echoed out, the regret so well-rehearsed that Radio almost believed it at first.

"What *you've* done?" Like it knew what regret was! Radio was startled as the monkey suddenly appeared in front of her again, but there was no subtlety or reserve in its actions anymore. The beast matched her pace as she backed up. The mage spoke eagerly, dangerously, and it frightened Radio as she struggled to back away as fast as the monkey walked towards her. "I *need* those shards, Radio. I used to be the guardian of these people, the guide, but my recent action did not teach nor serve. It has only made the situation worse. The King was an unjust, terrible beast, but I see now the Council is even more selfish, even crueler than he. I've found where I need to focus now. I need to fix this, Radio, but they don't understand." Radio stumbled back as the beast took another step forward, but halted as she fell on her side.

The magician loomed over her. "They will never understand." The cold primate eyes gleamed blue as the mage looked down on her.

"Who!?" Radio's outburst came out no more than a squeak in her fear.

"The ones who have wronged *you*," the mage answered as the crystal cube hovered beside it. The cube showed her images of her companions, Video and Pictures, still sleeping, but then it switched from them to her parents, her sister, her servants. "They left you, Radio. Your family, these friends of yours...but you have a chance." The cube then showed Video sleeping, and her bag glowed red.

Radio backed up, steadying on her feet and turning away. "No, there's nothing to gain from helping you, beast. You're mistaken."

"You don't feel they wronged you?" the creature asked, tilting its head as shadows flickered across its face.

"I never said anything of the sort." *I wronged them, you fool.* The sharp retort to mention the Jester being a fool was so tempting Radio almost tasted it, but she kept her jaw shut. "I say there's no chance."

"You don't think they should be put in their place?" the monster pressed further now, easing closer to her with a wide grin.

Maybe Pictures. "They're all where they belong." Radio clenched her jaw now.

"Do you feel you belong at your current rank? Only a shadow of someone else, when *you* were the noble chosen?" The mage didn't move, but with each question, Radio felt as though it drew closer to her. "You don't feel you're greater than what you're seen as by this so-called family of yours?"

"How I feel doesn't make a difference, Jester!" Radio snarled. Her ears flattened against her skull as she furthered, "Nothing will change when we're done with this!"

"Wrong, Radio!" The cube spun, and Radio's vision went white, making her unable to see her surroundings. She closed and opened her eyes to no avail, but still heard perfectly as the Jester exclaimed, "I can't touch those shards, I *need* you. You agree to bring those shards to me, and I will bestow the power and influence you need to escape that wretched class where you're established." Radio gasped as an image of her sitting above the citizens in the Capital, addressing them from the sky balcony, appeared in her head. She shook her head and cleared her thoughts as the Jester persisted, "You will be a hero if you restore this heart with me. I need no credit. You will have, and make, your own choices, dear. You will have control of your life."

"Why can't you touch the spell you cast, Jester? Hmm? Why do you have to get someone else to do your work?" Radio blinked back into focus

217

now, back into the mist, and flattened her ears. She didn't even know where those words came from, but she knew the question was valid.

"I have nothing to gain from answering you, but the original intent of creating this object was different from what occurred. The King's aura naturally repelled the one who created the heart." The mage shrugged. He looked to the side, grinning. "I was upset at that, and so I smashed it and made it a light-hearted game." The primate snickered.

Radio looked at mage blankly. "Really? There's not some deeper meaning to..."

"Those are the reasons that will be said." Radio rolled her eyes at the Jester's quick and curt response. However, he continued and said, "Come now, Radio. You can't overthink an opportunity when it's right in front of you in all its beautiful clarity. You will be as great as those you feel are better—you will rise above them, and it will all be righteous. The best part of it all is that you will deserve every bit of it once you go through this."

"What's the point of this, Jester?" Radio's head sank.

The spider monkey stretched around her, holding her paw in hand as they looked each other in the eye. She blinked at the primate and tried not to flinch as she felt the cube's warmth from behind her head. "The Kingdom will need to fill in the slots of the Council quickly once they start disappearing, and I know you will be a quick choice after you restore this artifact. I know your heart is in the right place, and if you allow my power access, you will not only have the freedoms and impact the Council does, but also will be protected without disturbance. What I have to gain doesn't affect you."

"Or those I care about?" Radio asked. Her eyelids fall from her exhaustion of listening to this nonsense, trying to decipher what might be real amidst the manipulation and games. She wasn't sure how long she'd be able to stay awake for the mage's spiel, until she remembered she was asleep for all of it.

"Who do you care about? Surely not the ones who oppressed you, Radio." The mage's brow furrowed.

"Jester."

The beast rolled its eyes just as Radio had before and chuckled, "Surely not those that ignored you all those seasons…"

"Jester!"

The monkey took in a breath. "Your parents and darling servants will be oblivious and unaware of the situation and I won't touch a hair on their heads when I first root out the Council." It rose up its hands and grinned. "If you succeed."

Great, already setting me up to fail. Radio sighed and looked at the cube as the images formed Pictures and Video. "And what of them?"

"You don't have to worry for Pictures' wellbeing, but Miss Video has to pay for her crimes of murder. Don't be unfair with me, Radio."

Radio looked at the image for a moment, but then her brow furrowed. She thought of the rats, the wolf, and who knew who else the monkey had controlled. Her claws attempted to grip the cube's mist futilely, and she whipped her head back to Jester. "How much control do I have after we agree to this?"

"You will receive my thoughts, power, emotions, knowledge, and reasons, but the decisions are still yours, Miss Radio. You are led by your heart, and strong hearts are mandatory for what you need to accomplish."

The Jester beamed, grinning down at her.

Radio blinked, and looked down as the Jester circled around her, continuing, "I have watched this situation since the beginning. You will see a whole new dimension to your travels. What I describe is an ability with which I live. I am seldom bothered by it." The mage smiled kindly, and looked over at the collared feline. "Won't it be fun?"

Radio lifted her chin, looking at the fool's outfit on the strange form, and said curtly, "I'm done with fun, Jester. With an outfit like that, you don't reassure me."

The primate snorted, but began to defend itself. "It wasn't even…"

Radio sighed audibly, unsure if this was the same animal that actually managed to ruin all of their lives, and quickly continued, "But you know what? Perhaps I need some light to this. You are the one in control of this land right now, aren't you?" There was nothing left for her to do. They were going to arrive at the castle tomorrow, and their fates were sealed unless she did something now. Radio extended her paw. "Give me your power."

"Hmm…" The Jester lifted its brow, almost as though it was surprised, but then held her paw softly. "Yes, Radio Star. I bestow upon you the gift of my influence." The primate smiled, and now gripped her paw.

Radio opened her eyes in the night. Her irides gleamed blue as she gave a small smile. She rose up from where she slept, and scanned the area. It was unbelievable. Everything seemed so much sharper with the power of magic flowing through her eyes. She imagined the world around her would have been foggier with the mist coming from her eyes, but she supposed that was how magic always was, unpredictable. She closed her eyes and cleared the mist from them, letting the magic constrict into a thin cyan rim around her pupils.

Everything made so much sense now. All of the Jester's actions, all of the warmth and power she felt from the fragments as the team had retrieved them, and all the magic she had seen the Jester cast against them. Her tail lashed as she turned away from the ledge, and walked toward Video. She wondered about how she would complete the task once she got the shards, realizing the Jester hadn't shared that information with her, but that was a question for after the time she laid claim to them. Video slept so peacefully as Radio peered down at her. She blinked, questioning if this was the right thing to do.

But it *was*. Radio knew it.

Snap! Radio snipped the tender, damaged thread of the belt of Video's bag with ease, and pulled it off of the umber tabby's waist. She was surprised at the weight of it, the shards and bag's material being much heavier as a unit, but kept a firm grasp on the strap with her jaws so she could carry it. If she could just get this to the Jester, away from the two, she would only have to worry about finding the last shard. She lifted up her chin, and started to back away with the strap firmly in her jaws.

Slash!

Video stood up in an instant, with the white fur of Radio's cheek stuck between her claws, while Radio stood back with the bag in her teeth. She watched her eyes glow eerily through the reflection of Video's, and blinked in surprise to see how vibrant the cyan was. The giant cat's eyes narrowed as Radio pressed her paw to her face, having smelled the blood that began to mat up the fur on the side of her muzzle, and felt the scratch was just below her eye. Video had just struck her, without any hesitation.

"What are you doing?" Video questioned softly but firmly, taking a step closer to Radio, and growled when Radio took a pace back. Radio didn't answer, not that she could if she wanted to, with her jaw clamped so tightly against the bag straps. The gash on her cheek stung a lot more, now, and she took another step away from the looming tabby. She had to think fast if she was to succeed in getting this to the mage. She could sense he was just below the hill, waiting.

"Miss Radio!" Video snapped now.

Radio's eyes widened, seeing Video's claws dig into the earth, and she bolted down the incline. There was no telling what Video was capable of now that she found Radio responsible for failing the mission, not after she saw what she had already done to the foes they faced on their travels. She ran faster than she ever had travelling, feeling so light-footed with the magic flowing through her veins. Even with the boost of power, however, Video caught up with her, halting Radio by leaping in front of her and reaching forward. "Give those back!"

Slice!

Video gasped as Radio's claws shot across her face, and shook her head as the blood welled up on her nose and muzzle. Radio stared in horror at her own actions, even more when she realized how easy it had been, the skin ripping through her nails as though it were nothing more than bread, and she bolted down for the bottom of the hill. The power of magic was too much for her liking but it wouldn't matter if she could make this right. She was so close! If she could get to the Jester, everything would be right again and he could take his power back!

"Ra..." Video caught her breath before whipping around and chasing the smaller feline. "Radio!" Video launched her claws into the bag, tugging with Radio until the strap ripped from her jaws and spilled the bag onto the ground.

Radio gasped with her mouth now free, and backed up under the glare of Video. Their gazes simultaneously shot towards the bag, seeing the corners of the shards inside. Their objective was too important for Radio to give up now. She looked at Video once more and then ran for them, but Video leapt at her and pinned her down.

Radio cried out at the weight of Video's paws, feeling like her breath was squeezed right out of her by the giant tabby. "Let me go! I'm fixing this!" Radio yelled as she began kicking at Video's chest.

"No!" Video shouted, pressing down her paws more firmly. "You're making a mess of things again! Knock it off and stop this!"

Radio sliced her back claws across Video's stomach, and fled, grabbing the shards.

Making a mess again. Radio would prove her wrong!

Video swatted the bag from her jaws again and leapt for her, but the smaller cat's face grew warm. Her eyes glowed brightly enough that she could see the cyan light reflecting off the ground, and she jumped back. With that action, she dodged Video's attack with sudden speed, and nearly stumbled at her own movement. The two both gasped, but Radio regained her footing in enough time to glare at Video when the tabby began to approach her again.

"What's going on!?" Video snarled, lowering her neck to Radio's height. "*What* did you do!?" she hissed, her eyes widening with fear.

You just don't understand. "It seems I gained some of the Jester's power." Radio lifted up her paw, and then slammed it down to cause a burst of plasma to come out from her claws, narrowing her eyes at the giant tabby still towering above her. "I'm fixing this. The primate can't hold the shards, so he is taking me to get the last shard myself. I will bring them back so he can put the heart together."

"He!? Radio!" Video snapped, her tone as though she was chastising a foolish kitten, growling, "The mage doesn't want to put it together, the beast *wants* it to stay broken! You fool!" Video launched at her again, batting at her with her paws, her claws out.

Radio ducked away from each blow, circling around Video as quickly as she could. "You haven't seen what I've seen, Video! I can see the monkey's memories of the situation! I feel his regret." She pressed her paw against her chest, her claws gripping her own fur with sudden frustration, and looked down at the ground before she glared up at Video as the massive cat snorted.

"What!?" Video's eye squinted, and her jaw clenched. "Radio, are you serious!? That monkey is a magician! A fake! Completely false! Nothing you've been shown by that monster is true, why would you even consider anything a part of that beast's magic was accurate?" Video whipped back around the other way and went to grab her.

"No! You don't understand…" Radio slid underneath Video, the top of her ears brushing against the larger cat's belly until she leapt out from under her, and took a step toward the shards again.

"Stop!" Video bolted for her, and Radio quickly pulled back, narrowly dodging the larger feline and ran her claws along the cat's side as she swept past her.

Video fell on her paws, and quickly whipped around and went for Radio again. That's when Radio saw the other feline's thoughts, the tabby's mind as clear as though she said her intent out loud. It horrified Radio to know what she was thinking, not knowing whether the content of the thoughts was more disturbing than having the ability to see them. A cold chill shot down her spine. The words of the stoat leader were strong in both of their minds: *"This spiteful magician has turned them into a beast without any memory of what they once were."* Video had deemed her insentient, and saw her as no more than the rats in the cavern.

"You're beyond saving, Radio," she snarled, and shot out her paw quick enough to catch Radio's collar.

"No!" Radio pulled back. Video dug her claws into the collar of nobility, pulling back until it snapped off Radio's neck. Video sliced her claws across the side of Radio's neck as the silver and sapphire choker fell apart into brittle pieces across the ground.

Radio quickly jumped back, her eyes wide as she gasped, "Video! Stop!" It was a mistake, she couldn't stop Video now, not even if she gave up the shards at this point. Those claws were reaching for a death strike.

"Die, beast!" Video launched at her, and Radio ran away from her, staying within range of the shards.

"Let me have this! Let me fix this! It's me, Radio! I am Radio! Please! It's not what you think! I'm still me!" Radio kicked Video away and threw a blast with a whip of her head that tossed the giant cat back, striking her ear and causing blood to splash across the clearing. Radio knew that didn't help the situation as she grabbed the shards again, but it had been too late to stop the magic, and she had to keep going.

"Anyone could say that! You think I'm so easily fooled?" Video said with rage, chasing after her. Radio began to cry, holding the bag as tightly as she could as her vision blurred with tears in fear for her life and for what she had done. Another mess up. She had to figure out how to make this right again, and only realized now doing anything with the Jester was not the right way of going about doing it.

Radio's paw struck against a rock. All the pain of the journey, the travel and harm that tore up her pads was too much once the stone pierced her raw, torn skin, shooting pain all the way up her arm and causing her to buckle down and fall against the earth. There was probably no hope of saving the shards or getting them back to the mage. Video was right, and it was over.

Video pinned her down, sending the shards across the clearing, and sank her teeth into Radio's neck.

Radio screamed before she began choking, her companion's fangs clamping against her throat and tearing into her skin and flesh. She struggled and whimpered with her last puff of air, begging and pleading silently that Video would stop and realize it was her.

Once she felt the fangs pierce through her pelt, Video pulled away with sudden strength, ripping the skin apart as she did so. Radio failed to cry out in pain now, nothing coming out of her mouth as blood welled from her neck. She looked up at the glaring cat who stared down on her, saying nothing more than, "Die."

Without another moment of hesitation, Video stabbed her claws into the smaller cat's wounded neck. She pulled down the open flesh, opening it deeply for the blood pumping from Radio's heart to pour out freely, and that it did.

The blood immediately spewed from Radio's throat from the intense wound, and the cat's head tossed back as she started shaking and spasming. The blue glow eased into the rest of her eyes like water as she struggled under Video's claws, and cyan tears poured down her face. None of her own magic could save her from this wound. Now she knew she either was going to be left to bleed out or die from the pain. *What is there left?*

"What a pity."

Video looked over at the Jester upon hearing its voice, seeing it stare at the two felines apathetically as it stood on a higher level of the hillside, its brow arched. Video couldn't dare cough out the smaller feline's blood now, and instead stared at the spidery primate coldly with all the loathing she could bring into her gaze, knowing the monster had caused this.

She was lost for words when the monkey began chuckling, giving a shake of its covered head and grinning at her. "Radio wasn't beyond saving, Miss Video. You were looking at this inaccurately the whole time." The mage sighed, resting its cheek on the palm of its hand.

Video tried not to give a reaction back, but she couldn't control the shudder and sudden chill upon hearing the monkey's words and now spat out the blood of the young noble. She heard another noise, then, and turned. She saw Pictures on the other side of the valley, his eyes wide.

"What have you done, Video?" Pictures looked at her in anger, his wide eyes lit with rage as he stepped toward the scene. His brow slowly furrowed upon seeing Radio.

Video stood defensively at Radio's body, looking down at the cat, blood bubbling out from her throat in her fruitless struggles to breathe, still fighting for her life even though it was far beyond saving now. She looked back up at the tom. "I..." *What was there to say?* Radio had been taken control of by the Jester, had been trying to take the shards, she had to stop it...

Pictures didn't head towards the two of them, though, and didn't give Radio another glance. Video wanted to stop him, but found herself unable to move with the blood of the noble soaking into the earth under her paws, and was left to helplessly watch as Pictures approached the bag containing the crystal fragments. "You're so foolish, Video. You accuse me of skewed ethics, but you're the one that's *repulsive.*" He spat the words as he swept the fallen shards back into the bag, then grabbed the strap and looked back up at Video, his one blue eye glowing.

Video's eyes shot open, but the Jester spoke before she could even move. "Don't waste time talking to her," the Jester barked, giving a small head shake as Pictures extended his claws, ready to attack Video. "The last one will be brought to you when you're at the castle if you get there now." The monkey raised up its chin when Pictures hesitated. "Go!"

Pictures nodded, placing his paw down, and shot away.

"No!" Video leapt for him, but smacked into a wall of energy, sending her back onto the ground beside Radio. She looked up at the clear surface of magic, and then glanced over at the approaching primate.

"You're staying here, cat." The mage's eyes gleamed with anger as Video scrambled to her feet. The beast walked up to her, gazing down at Radio. "She was so foolish to listen to me. This situation was entirely avoidable. After you took your detour into the Clowder City, a new order of monitors was hired to find the last shard, and you would have been sent back out to retrieve it without any issue." The mage now looked at Video. "None of this had to happen." Its glance went back down to the fallen feline. "Radio was herself this whole time, but you didn't take the time to learn that, either." The Jester's eyes narrowed as Video turned her head away from it, but continued, "You're just like the rest of your family, aggressive and hateful without thought. You do nothing good for this world! You don't even have the intelligence or charisma to make yourself anything more than being as much of a burden as this noble was!"

That was enough for Video to move her paws again. Video sliced her bloody claws across the monkey's neck, ignoring the mage's scream as she leapt forward and sank her teeth into the beast's muzzle. She dug her fangs as deep into the monster's hairless flesh as she could until she was shoved back, and the mage vanished into the shadows.

Video looked at the blood that had dripped from the primate's face until she turned back to Radio, and curled up beside the tiny form. "I am so sorry…" She looked at the small, feathery-furred cat, unable to move again upon watching the noble's blue eyes dull. Video closed her eyes as well. "What have I done?"

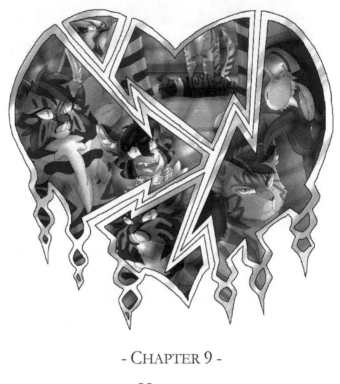

- CHAPTER 9 -

YONDER

Video remained curled up, holding the still feline in her paws. She had killed an innocent noble, nothing more than a cat being manipulated by a mage beyond her power. There was nothing to justify the death in Video's heart, knowing Radio still truly had been there, and Video had killed the poor cat in cold blood. She sobbed as she held the feline close. Radio's warmth was still there even with all the blood which came out of the small feathery cat. Throughout the entire journey, the thought of anything happening to the naive and innocent noble repulsed Video, yet she herself had caused the poor feline's death.

The giant tabby kept still until she opened her eyes at the sound and vibration of a carriage moving on the road, and was unsure what to do from there. If the party was untitled, unverified by Social Media, she could simply scare them into silence, but a verified individual, especially a courier being driven by a rickshaw, would have to be silenced by other means. Video flexed her blood-stained paws in anticipation, and brushed her tongue against the tears which had come down her face. She would have to go rogue like her brother after committing a crime like this.

"Video?"

Video startled at the quizzical question from none other than the Studio Star herself. There was no other cat who could have pulled up just now? She quickly hid her bloodstained paws in front of her again, knowing from where Studio was she wouldn't see the sight before her right away. She heard Studio jump from the carriage cart being driven by a tall serval, and knew there would be no hiding she had killed the Studio Star's younger niece.

She rose, letting the blood drip from her chest and paws as Studio approached her. "Oh, Studio Star, there's nothing I can say that could express the condolences I have to offer...I'm so sorry." Her claws dug into the earth, hoping with all her heart that she wouldn't have to possibly end Studio after seeing the powerful leader's willingness and ability to fight the Jester, let alone the giant serval. She could attack Video and make the situation even worse.

She turned around to look at Studio, still hiding the body of Radio behind her tail. Studio only looked mildly startled by the sight of the blood, and Video realized she probably had already smelled it from the carriage.

"Studio Star...the Jester..."

"What has happened, Video?"

Video's voice shook as she had to explain it. She couldn't explain it as the mage had told her, she had to explain it as she had perceived it, as to what she thought she was doing. There was no other way to remain alive otherwise. "The...The Jester possessed the Radio Star, My Lady—much like it had with the foes we faced before we reached your city. The primate succeeded with her." Video had to pause, seeing Studio's expression. She already knew, but Video had to continue. "I-I didn't know what to do when she tried to grab the shards. I was afraid she'd take them away...that Pictures might be possessed, too. I had to act quickly if I didn't want to..." Didn't want to what? Why couldn't Video finish her own sentences? She felt a sob wrack her body, and pressed forward with her words, mumbling, "She used the Jester's magic against me, and I...I—"

"Ended the threat sent by the mage," Studio answered monotonically as she looked past Video's shoulder to see the crumpled feline lying on the bloodstained earth, her body seeming to glow with a lavender aura from the dawning sun.

"I'm so sorry, Studio Star." Video dropped her head in shame, a noise of anguish escaping her at causing this, at doing this, and having to face her traveling companion's family so soon.

Studio stared down at her in silence, leaving Video in fear of what her verdict was. She tried to assess her own injuries, wondering if Studio was scanning for an instant end to the giant tabby, but she only stared. Video looked back up at her. "I did all I could."

"I know, Video, I do," Studio whispered, and looked up at Video's wounds left by the smaller feline. "You had to."

Video's eyes watered again, but she didn't let the tears that threatened stream down her face. "She was too weak after we got the news from the Capital, but she didn't die in vain, if we hurry." The younger tabby's tone hardened.

Studio looked up at her questioningly. "What do you propose, Video?"

The anger against the monkey and Pictures settled back into her. "That we bring justice. If we get to the Capital, and get back the shards taken, this doesn't need to be in vain. Pictures works for the mage. He's the one who likely helped orchestrate this entire scenario. We need to stop him from getting to the castle and the Council as soon as possible." Video rushed past Studio, and ran up to the carriage cart that was driven by the serval, unfazed as the older cat pulled back a little at seeing the sight of Radio fully. "It's too late, My Lady! We have to get to the Capital now!" Video shouted as she bounded up to the carriage, and turned to see Studio following her, leaping up into the cart.

"I-I was just heading there." Studio blinked at Video as she stood beside her. "Film's extra surveillance spotted the last shard, and being a noble, formerly a courier, and a monitor advisor, I am able to hold it." The noble glanced to her left. "I retrieved it for the Council, and was going to bring it directly to the Capital myself." Studio looked back at Video and reached into her collar. When Video looked at the noble with confusion, Studio extended her paw, revealing the gray crystal piece.

Video stared at it in shock. It was the last fragment. The objective could still be completed if they retrieved the rest of the shards Pictures had taken. She looked up at Studio as she replayed the feline's words in her head, seeing the different effect Studio had on the object as she held it in her paw. "You're lying, though. That isn't the reason why you're able to hold the shard." Her eyes widened as she stared face to face with the distinguished tabby feline. "*You're* the youngest member of the Council!"

Studio startled as she placed the shard back into her collar, but Video didn't wait for a reply, turning around inside the carriage cart. "Don't even try to tell me otherwise. There was nothing I could do to save the Radio Star, but we still have the chance of saving the Kingdom if we beat Pictures and get there right now!" Video slammed her bloody paw down on the lever that disengaged the carriage's brake, and looked ahead at their new task.

"Video, *no!*" Studio squeaked as they were suddenly pulled forward, struggling to balance herself.

The rickshaw took them to the Capital City, double the speed she imagined Pictures would have made. *Unless he has magic, too.* Video didn't put it past the tom any longer. His capability to orchestrate this left her to expect anything, and she swore that she saw that blue eye of his glow before. She had been travelling with one of their enemies this whole time. Her claws dug into the boards of the cart at the thought. She would enjoy ending the two-color-eyed, two-faced beast once and for all, positive that one of the last mages would be removed from the land for good.

And then the Jester, as well. Video's claws dug into the floor of the carriage just thinking about the primate, and her fangs bared in anger and satisfaction that she had succeeded ripping her claws into the monkey already.

234

Once they drew closer to the castle, Video saw smoke and flames surrounding the buildings and area around it. Pictures and the Jester had gone as far as starting fires to strike fear into the citizens. Video couldn't keep count of how many critters were fleeing the crumbling structures, and was horrified to see how many were carrying kits and travelling in units. She leapt out from the carriage, her tail bristling as with each step towards the castle as she grew angrier. She'd fought far too many battles in the past five days to be tired of them now, and she would continue fighting them until both the mages were in the ground.

Her thoughts stopped short when she felt claws slice through her fur and deep into her pelt, and she whipped away from her opponent with one paw before rounding on them. She stopped when she came face to face with her brother, Stereo, and screamed when he drove his fangs into her throat and whipped her down onto the paving stones.

"No! Any time but now, you dumb cat!" she snarled, getting onto her back and propelling her back legs in the air to smash the tom in the chest, flinging him back just enough to get back onto her paws before he attacked her again.

She whipped him back by sidestepping and projecting her claws out. They raked across his flank as he missed her. Video locked herself in battle with him when they both attacked at once, driving her claws and digging her fangs in wherever she could grip him. Finally her back paws hit him again, and she repeatedly kicked him until he pulled away from her.

"Do you think I want this!?" Video snarled, pounding her paw against the earth and hissing, "Don't you think I wish things could be the way they once were, too?"

"Don't," Stereo hissed at her, lifting up his claws as he leapt forward to attack her. They both fell back, rolling in the clearing as they stripped clumps of fur off of each other's pelts in their combat. She yowled in pain as he raked his needle sharp claws through her mane and into the skin of her neck, but she still rounded on him again. She clawed down his abdomen before slicing against his belly, hissing at his face with all her might.

He snarled and knocked her back, not expecting her to keep her grip on him. She pushed him back first, and when he went to attack again, she crouched down to avoid his sharp claws and leapt for his throat. She dug in with as much strength as she could, piercing her fangs through his skin until his blood leaked down her jaws.

Stereo choked at the grip, and ripped his claws into her face, holding onto her with the hooks of his claw tips as he whipped her off of him, and then pulled his claws back and dragged her into the earth, gripping her firmly as she tumbled to find her balance.

She heard his paws thump against the ground as she got back onto her paws, and tensed in anticipation of his attack before she instead witnessed the giant tom cat be tackled down to the ground, and struck by Studio. The lithe brown tabby sliced her claws against his muzzle and hissed, "I've faced you once and I will win again! Get out of here!"

He staggered upwards, and looked to challenge her, but with the blood dripping from his muzzle and throat, he instead ran towards the village away from them. Studio turned to Video, helped the feline to her paws, and swept the dust off of her with her feathery tail. "We have to keep moving! Let's go!"

Video stared in shock for a short moment, but then nodded and followed the smaller feline into the burning castle.

It was astonishing to have seen the powerful structure of just a few days ago now become a burning inferno, engulfed with fire. Here she and her companions had ventured into the castle for the first time only five days ago, but after today, nothing was going to be the same. Video coughed as she moved further into the structure, and had to look through the smoke to find Studio again. Once she saw the glimmer of the tabby's golden collar, Video followed her through the giant halls of the castle which led towards the throne room, remaining as silent as she could to keep her breath.

The two tabbies raced through the castle to the staircase. That's when they saw Pictures.

It wasn't just him, though, much to Video's dismay. He loomed over a still figure, and Video's eyes widened when she recognized the dark pelt of Tape, the bulky tom they had spoken to throughout the whole journey. That tom had welcomed them and congratulated them on their quest, and Pictures had killed him without mercy. "No!" she cried out, running forward and skidding to a halt before Pictures, who looked far too confident for her not to have surveyed the situation first.

"You killed him…" She looked at the lifeless form of the tom.

"You say that like it's such a terrible thing, Video. We all have done our fair share. Really, when you think about it, who are you to judge?" He arched his brow at her bloodstained paws, Radio's blood having dried the same color as the dark border around her pads, while Stereo's blood still stuck above her claws. "That's just fresher than Radio, dear. Your heart really is frozen to the core if you still managed to come here after ending that innocent, naive little kit."

Video had to pause at the audacity of the tom before she snarled at him. She chomped her teeth as he shrank back, looking at her in fear and horror. She could barely believe it when the next words came out of his spiteful mouth. "Video...w-what have you d-done?" he stammered, staring up at her with rounded eyes.

She hissed again, stepping over the tom's body so she could attack the silver cat. He flinched, taking another step back. "N-no, Video, stop! I'm your friend!"

"You're only a friend to me dead." Video growled, unsheathing her claws.

"But how could you do *this?*" He gestured to the tom's body, and looked up at Video in complete and utter horror.

"What?" Video asked, and eyes narrowed.

"Video, no, look!" Studio shouted out, and Video turned back to follow her gaze seeing the black and red surveillance bot that belonged to her father, and knew there was no stopping it as it hovered away after Studio's words of warning.

"Smile for the camera, Video." Pictures laughed, rising back up and leaping past Video towards Studio. The lithe tabby hissed and leapt for him, but her shout of anger was cut off into a scream as the Jester dropped down on her. The shard held in her collar flew through the air, and Pictures tossed up the four other shards once he was in reach. Video cried out in fear, leaping for the two mages, but the primate evaporated into shadows before the shards connected and mingled, gleaming red as they wrapped around each other and connected to restore themselves into the red crystal heart.

Pictures pulled the crystal heart away from Video before she could grab it, and the object hovered beside the silver tabby as the primate reappeared behind him in a burst of shadows.

Video steadied herself as Studio rose back to her paws. Pictures smirked at them both before turning to the clothed mage. "I'll take care of these two in due time. Remove Frequency for me. I'll be in the throne room."

"So be it. I'll see you soon to handle the rest of the matter." The primate's tail lashed as Pictures bolted away with the crystal heart, and disappeared as he turned the corner for the stairs.

"No!" Video leapt for the silver tom, but the primate threw her back and hissed, grinning down at her with a strange, twisted glee. Video landed on her paws and glared at the creature as it laughed, shadows flickering across its face as though it couldn't control its form in the excitement.

She didn't know the first thing about attacking a mage, and also knew her father likely only won against the former foe, Phantascope, because he had the element of surprise. Even with how much damage Phantascope caused to the folk of Media, this mage was a completely different animal, and a much more twisted opponent. She watched as the Jester's expression of delight turned into one of loathing, and her eyes rounded when the primate suddenly attacked her.

The two of them tumbled down and then quickly bounded back onto their feet when Video managed to slice her claws against the mage's outfit. She felt the shadows flick and wiggle under her claws, and dug them into the carpet as she stared at the mage with shock and what anger she tried to muster into her gaze through her fear. She felt Studio's presence beside her, and the nimble tabby pressed her paws down and glared at the mage, ready to fight.

"You both really think you're something, hmm?" The creature chuckled as the shadows continued flickering across its face, eventually even taking over its entire form for an instant before it was back to being the darkly-clothed jester monkey. "Try me."

Video felt her mouth grow dry as she stared at the mage, and could only ready herself to defend against its next attack.

The Jester smiled, and took a step forward, giving the two felines a small head tilt. "Thinking about it, I shouldn't bother with either of you, but you'd be so much better off to me dead, and that *cat* is far too sparing." The monster's eyes gleamed their strange cyan as it advanced upon the two felines, beginning to bear its fangs. Video took a step back and narrowed her eyes at the beast.

"What are you, if you can call him merciful?" she managed to ask, and startled as the beast launched itself at her, quickly weaving away in time to only get the top of her ear tuft cut by its strange shadows.

She inhaled, and hissed at the monkey, her fur standing completely on end. Studio stood in front of her then. The primate laughed, its brow furrowed as it leaned down to attack again.

That was when a flash of white and gold shot out from the surveillance room. Video recognized the form of Sensor as he attacked the monkey and raked his talons across the creature's face. *"Go!"* The word was barely recognizable through the bird's long trill, but Video knew it'd be their only chance to catch up to Pictures, and bolted ahead with Studio.

The primate snarled and swiped at the fast flying bird, but when Sensor dodged its third swipe, the crystal cube appeared behind the bird, trapping him for the instant it took for the mage to leap at him and crunch his ribcage in its jaws.

After two bites, the monkey dropped the mangled bird on the ground, and looked in the direction Studio and Video had run. "I wasted enough time with them as it is." The primate mage scoffed before shadows washed over its form, and it vanished from the halls.

Video and Studio raced up the stairs to the throne room. Video heard the hoarse breath of Studio beside her. She looked over to see the dark tabby's expression was haunted, and asked, "What?" They had faced so many horrors today, but there seemed to be something beyond what Video knew about that Studio did.

"They're going to make themselves the new leaders! That mage is going to kill my Frequency," Studio whispered. "As if losing Radio wasn't enough...they have to take away her sister." Her eyes rounded. "They'll kill my sister, too."

The Resolution Star. Video didn't know what to say upon hearing Studio speak of the mute noble again. The felines had bonded over knowing they were family, and now Video would likely never have a chance to meet the Frequency or Resolution Star, let alone assure Studio that she would see them again. "We're going to stop what we can, Studio," she growled, and leapt into the hall once they reached the last step of the staircase. They ran together towards the throne room.

There was so much to this now which was beyond Video's knowledge, beyond her power. She was only to retrieve fallen shards, not fight against this Jester, not to have to clean out mage-afflicted individuals. Now she was fighting face to face with the worst of them, and had to kill...had believed she had to kill, a noble of Media to protect and fulfill the objective she had to accomplish for the Council. All of it made her eyes turn cold as they approached the room that would lead them to one of their two foes.

They burst through the double doors and saw Pictures on the steps leading to the throne of the King. The solid crystal heart hovered beside him, gleaming a deep, powerful red. He glared down at the two, his eyes glittering in the faint light of the hall. Video growled, seeing his golden eye glow orange as the red lit his face within the dark room, and she extended her claws. His blue eye was barely a flicker, but Video now saw the two different types of magic the feline had, which was more than enough evidence to remove him from under the Council's direction.

He eased back, but bolted away when he saw her claws dig into the flooring. Video chased after him, ignoring Studio's shouts to stop as they raced out of the throne room. The two raced through the castle in their chase, Pictures often throwing a burst of fire or cyan plasma when the red heart was far enough away from him. "Why don't you just give up, Video? There's no chance for you to win!" he shouted back at her.

She leapt over a cyan blast, unfazed by the magic after facing Radio, and resumed the chase. "I won't stop until you're dead, beast!" Video figured once she was able to get the artifact far enough away from him, she'd likely have to fight the plasma once again, but it didn't stop her from dodging each blow and bolting down the halls as quickly as she could to catch up to him.

"You can't expect to live through a battle against two mages, Video!

You won't die so slowly if you just give up!" he hissed, and seemed to strengthen his legs to run faster. His corners became sharper turns, making Video have to keep focused to follow him closely. He seemed to begin playing the game of trying to tire her out or knock her off balance so he could attack her after she faltered. It almost seemed likely with all the injuries she carried, but Video had no intention of being thwarted, and kept pace with him at every corner. What she hadn't expected, though, was him vanishing completely when Video launched herself forward to attack him. She knocked herself right into the stone wall instead.

She shook her dazed head and prepared for an attack, but one never came, and she realized she was alone in the hallway now. She cursed the earth. She knew she had to find the two mages quickly if she and Studio were to have a chance against them. Without a moment's hesitation, she immediately started back to find the throne room again. Pictures may have successfully evaded her chase, but he was about to face the retribution for managing to make her even more infuriated. She wasn't going to stop until he was lying dead at her paws.

Video heard speaking once she crossed the visiting quarters, and recognized both mages' voices within one of the rooms. Her tail lashed, and she approached the doors slowly to the drawing room.

"I knew you wouldn't kill them! You actually developed affection for these detestable *cats*." The Jester's voice was the louder of the two. Video's claws scraped against the wooden flooring as she drew closer to the doors. She had to force herself to relax enough to let her nails slide back into her paws.

"I said in due time. I imagine you took care of the rest of the nobility, then?" Pictures sneered, his tone suggesting to Video that he doubted the Jester's ability to actually do so.

"Of...Of course." The monkey sounded offended.

"You sound so *convincing,* Jester, but if so, then you can direct your time into helping me find the other artifact."

There was another artifact? Video scowled at the idea of there being more mage items, and didn't even want to consider what this next one might be with all the trouble this heart and cube had caused Media.

"You're too weak for it, Pictures, still to this day." The Jester sounded dismissive, and Video realized it might leave if Pictures frustrated it too much.

"No! Don't stall any longer with me! Where is it!? You can't take this opportunity away from me!" Pictures seemed genuinely upset. Video took it as the advantage she needed to attack him, and slid open the doors to see the two mages face to face before a fireplace. She was pleased when the door opened silently, as she could draw closer to them and use the furniture to her benefit.

She was surprised by Pictures' next words, though. "You can't hold that against me when you know the situation is different now! You're the one who almost blew your cover by coming as Enterprise in the first place! It's not like you wanted them dead, either; you were the one who chose Studio and Video! Radio was just a strange mistake. No one knew of her."

"Film did," the Jester spat. "And of course we didn't! Resolution wasn't going to *say anything* about it, and Flash speaks of more kits than I can keep count, nobility or not."

Pictures growled, and the crystal heart began to gleam brightly. "You should have made *sure,* Jester." The primate flinched and backed away from the silver tabby as he continued to approach his supposed partner in crime. Video wondered why the monkey had them retrieve the shards for it, and had to ponder if it really had been unable to touch the object itself as Radio implied.

Not that it mattered now, though. Video was going to kill them both.

The primate looked up at her in surprise as she stepped within its sight behind Pictures, sneaking up on the tom. The moment of hesitation the mage took to question Pictures' possible betrayal was all Video needed to launch herself at the gray cat. The tom whipped around, shocked at her attack, but he wasn't quick enough to jump away. She sent him into the ground, hitting his skull against the wooden flooring and knocking the heart from his possession. He gasped and went to retrieve it, kicking Video away so he could get back to his feet, but she attacked him again, watching as the artifact pulled back to him. His claws gleamed red before Video could reel back. He whipped them across the bridge of her nose.

Video staggered back and hissed at him as her blood flecked across the wooden floor, surprised at the burning sensation that the scratch gave. It had to have been magic, as it was the same feeling she had from Radio's scratch when her eyes glowed blue. She leapt for Pictures as soon as she recovered, not letting him escape. The two sliced their claws against each other's pelts before Video knocked him back with a good hit, then launched herself from the ground to smash him down into the hard flooring again. She heard Studio enter the room, and then could hear the city leader was facing off with the other mage, which had been slowly moving towards the battle until that point. Video's concentration was on Pictures, though. The cat she knew Radio had trusted implicitly, perhaps more so than anyone else besides Studio. "You broke her *heart*, and you let us take the blame."

Pictures' eyes widened, looking up at her in anger and shock. With sudden strength, he managed to kick her back, but she leapt at him again and ripped into him like prey, raking her claws repeatedly down his pelt until he screamed out, and then she slammed her paw down on his throat.

Both the primate and Studio whipped around at the sound, their pelts bristled from nose to tail tip.

Pictures gasped up at her, and her eyes narrowed. There could be no mercy for the likes of an individual who could betray one of the most well intentioned individuals of Media, one who hadn't even known she had been a part of the darkness surrounding her. She sliced her claws across the tom's throat, watching as the blue eye faded into the same burnt yellow of his left. He stared at her with sudden recognition and knowledge, like something had been lifted from his shoulders, as though he had gained some sort of insight, but it was far too late to turn back. Video drove her claws in, and then dug her fangs into the raw flesh that she had exposed.

"Pictures!" the Jester cried out, shoving Studio back when seeing the blue eye vanish, then it startled at Video's bite. "No!"

The silver tom glowed orange for an instant. There was a sudden burst of plasma magic from under the cat, amber threads spreading out like powerful wings in efforts to escape, but Video dug her jaws in more and kept her grip firm as the tom struggled to pull away. She heard Studio only a few paces in front of her now, and looked up to see the smaller feline running over to whip down a giant lever, opening a panel behind the fireplace. The opening connected the fireplace to the furnace in the core of the castle, and the blast of warm air made Video's fur bristle as she turned her gaze towards it, knowing its purpose. *Used for folk that disagreed or displeased the Council.* Video found the apparatus a very fitting instrument for the demise of the cat, and drove her fangs even deeper into his neck until she knew she had a good grip, digging in even as she felt the burning threads of his magic lash against her pelt.

He choked out his last breath. Video whipped around to get a momentum, and flung him, and all his magic with him, into the pit. Both she and Studio leapt back as fire and plasma orange magic exploded from the fireplace upon impact, but then regained their footing. Video stared down into it with all of the cold loathing she could muster before she turned to the primate, her bristling tail whipping up as she looked the mage directly in the eyes.

She hadn't expected to see the horror on its face. There was something far beyond what Video comprehended behind the cyan eyes of the mage, as some calamity had occurred far beyond the death of a magic-tinkering tyrant that would affect lives far beyond her own. Her eyes rounded, fear flooding into her core by whatever she had caused by doing this. The primate smashed Signal's drone as the device flew into the room, and glared at her with pure loathing. What was it!? What had she done!? Video screeched as the Jester leapt at her with full force, knocking them both down. It began smashing her against the floor, snarling at her. She screamed as she felt fangs bite down into her neck, and slammed her back legs into the monkey's stomach.

She pulled herself out of the grasp of the mage and gasped at the attack, backing up and trying to attack it in retaliation, but all she could grip was one of the spikes of its jester collar in her jaws. It sliced her mouth as it pulled back into shadows. The taste of her own blood and the pain in the wall of her mouth burned and made her dazed. She focused just in time to hear the Jester snarl, "Die."

It was the same tone that Video had said to Radio before taking the small cat's life. Video grew fully alert at that, and leapt for the mage's throat as it jumped for hers, causing the two to spin around inside the now darkened, over-heated room, both trying to strike for the killing shot. She could only let out a gasp of what breath she had left when she felt the air knocked out from her, as the Jester slammed its head into her chest. She sliced her claws across the creature's hairless cheek before she backed away, and let out another hiss.

Video and the Jester's gazes locked, and Video knew this was her test to back away. She hardened her eyes and snarled at the primate, digging her claws into the wooden floors to strike again. Out of the corner of her eye, she saw Studio was nearly finished with whatever she was doing with the crystal heart, having grabbed it once Pictures was eliminated by Video. Hopefully it was something that would end the mage, if the creature was really unable to use the artifact. Video's gaze was brought back to the Jester when it moved its tail subtly, and she snarled. She wasn't going to stop until she knew she successfully tore this monkey limb from limb, and with that thought, she leapt for the beast.

That's when the battle suddenly was over.

Video was struck by the corner of the burning crystal cube just above her temple with sudden force. She staggered to the side as the blood began to flow from her head. She gazed down at her bloodstained paws, her own blood dripping down before her, and she felt the world go black for a moment. She inhaled sharply in fear, and looked back up, completely stunned, to see the mage disappear. She wailed in horror that she let the monster escape, and then felt the world spin around her again.

All at once, the pain began to set in. Video felt her heartbeat pounding in her ears, her paws, her chest, and her head. She fell to the wooden flooring, panting as she tried to stay alive as long as she could. It was too early for her to die now, not when she hadn't killed the mage, not when the King was still gone. She struggled to get back up, seeing Studio's rapid movements around her in a blur, and looked toward the crystal heart instead.

She watched as the beautiful item gleamed its rich and deep red color. She wondered as she saw it spinning, if it was her sight or the object itself. In her last conscious moments, she saw the artifact evaporate from a burst of red light, and a crowned, golden-pelted, striped cheetah Video could only imagine was the King stepped out from the glaring light to look down at her.

She had completed her objective, and her eyes closed.

- EPILOGUE -

Studio stared outside her window in her penthouse tower, the only window that allowed her to see the castle from where she was. She admired the bright sky, letting her see every inch of Media down to the very coast of the land. It had been a very long time since she had travelled beyond the central sector of the land, and she pondered when she'd take the time to go adventuring again. She gazed down at the stairwell leading to her main flat, and sighed before she padded down the steps.

There would be none of that any time soon, she was being held under house arrest for the time being, accused of association with the mage. Studio's tail waved back and forth as she approached the surveillance room, looking toward the dark doorway. She stared at the open entrance, seeing her worker Screen busy at the monitors which covered the walls. All that was visible was his eyeless socket, his colorless eye being hidden by the angle she was at. Studio gazed at him for a while before she decided to carry on, not wanting to bother him. Even if she was convicted and taken away from her city, at least she knew Screen and his assistant, Speaker, could protect her citizens.

She had attended over six funerals within the past few weeks before she was put into her confinement. First, for the Capital, was the funeral for the surveillance team and Enterprise. Tape and Sensor had been found in the main hall, where they had been leading followers to the upper level of the castle for safety. The two were honored as heroes who went above and beyond their line of work to help save Media, but just as Pictures had wanted, Video was bound to be unjustly convicted for the death of Tape, and the monitors refused to listen to Studio's pleas saying otherwise. The recordings altered by Pictures were all they needed as evidence.

Recorder and Widget were missing in action. The two were presumed dead once the castle fires were cleared. Studio frowned, having liked Widget. She felt the boy had a lot of potential to grow into a fine director when he grew older. and wasn't sure what the Council might try to pin on the team when it came to the information leak now that no one was there to defend themselves. Enterprise had been found in the library, with years of archives and documentation destroyed by the mage. No one had realized until the mission for the chosen three already started that he died by the hands of the mage. He was buried along with the surveillance crew.

Faith, the stoat leader of the critter village, had invited Studio to attend the funeral for the guardians who protected her village before the mage had taken hold of them, as well as for every villager who passed away prior to their death. Studio was happy Faith decided to honor the guardians as the rats they once were, instead of the monster the primate had made of them, but wished there had been a way to save the unit. Studio couldn't turn down the honor to attend, and had travelled down to participate in the village-wide mourning. It was a village that continued to witness pain, time after time, caused by the mere experiment of a cruel mage. Studio hoped it would be the last.

It was a miracle that there were no casualties in Clowder City or the Ruined City, for how much the Jester had attacked with his magic, as even Transmitter, the raccoon teammate of the feline scavenger, Receiver, had recovered from his wounds from the mage's plasma blasts and wolf attack, but then again, the magic of Life could never kill directly.

Out of everything Studio had attended, the worst was the funeral of her family. Studio's fur rose just at the thought of remembering it all over again: the death of her sister, Resolution, her brother-in-law, Flash, their faithful stoat servant, Stella, and her two darling nieces, Frequency and Radio. The amount of death still astounded Studio, and having to think of it made her struggle to walk. The two weasels, Leil and Hana, had been spared, and had been sent to the Capital to help with the repairs, but first they had to recover from the shock of the attack.

Studio's jaw clenched upon thinking what it all came down to. She was now the sole noble blood-carrier of the courier, Ampersand, from all those generations ago. As though being the descendant of a traitor against his people was an honor. The Council had certainly found no fault with it until now. Studio detested the secret her bloodline had to carry. What kind of family would be satisfied, knowing they had overthrown a government wrongly? All her life she loathed the lives her family led because they had long ago accepted the idea of being traitors to the mages, but now that they were gone, she wasn't sure what to think.

One had been killed for her own magic. Studio knew that while the Jester claimed he was lending his power to her niece, Radio, he had really given her the knowledge of how to use her own. Studio knew that was the majority of the issue, anyway, from what the primate told her in the drawing room of the castle. She and the monkey had battled when the two remaining chosen felines had been fighting for the crystal heart, and had discussed her niece then. Studio wouldn't have been able to save Radio either way, if magic was what Video used to justify slaying the young noble.

She sighed, stopping in her tracks as she approached a lacquered, black-framed mirror in the inner room of the lower level of her penthouse. It was the true colors of her city, the real darkness the Jester had revealed to her citizens. She looked into the object, her eyes dull until she saw her reflection in the mirror. The Council wouldn't dare admit they had made a mage a part of the governing body, whether or not it was known by the rest of Social Media. Now they were trying to be rid of her by other means; claiming her to be an accomplice to the traitorous mage.

What point was holding back her power now? Studio's eyes gleamed golden. An aura of magic flowed from her irides, and the mirror flooded with a golden mist within the crystal surface, waiting for her command.

"Show me Curiosity."

- END –

ABOUT THE AUTHOR

Teelia Pelletier is the eighteen-year-old author of Heart of Glass and five upcoming books in the series, Strong Hearts Are Mandatory. She is working toward a nursing degree and also has interests in criminal justice and library science. This novel was a NaNoWriMo winner in 2016, and was approximately 52,000 words in its first draft. Look her up as Teelia to find out the statuses of books 2 and 3 after Camp NaNoWriMo in April and July of 2017!

Search "LadyTeelia" on Redbubble to see the chapter headers and cover in full color, ready to be printed on all types of clothing and other products!

Thank you for reading!

CPSIA information can be obtained
at www.ICGtesting.com
Printed in the USA
LVHW03s1553150818
587067LV00016B/1692/P